Roger Smith is a new voice from South Africa. Serpent's Tail also publishes his first two novels, *Mixed Blood* and *Wake Up Dead*. Previously a screenwriter, Smith combines extreme violence with politically inspired stories. Several films are in development, with Samuel L Jackson attached to the script of his first book, *Wake Up Dead*.

DUST *DEVILS*

ROGER SMITH

A complete catalogue record for this book can
be obtained from the British Library on request

First published in 2011 by Serpent's Tail,
an imprint of Profile Books Ltd
3A Exmouth House
Pine Street
London EC1R 0JH
website: www.serpentstail.com

ISBN 978 1 84668 795 2
eISBN 978 1 84765 774 9

Printed and bound by CPI Group
(UK) Ltd, Croydon, CR0 4YY

10 9 8 7 6 5 4 3 2

ROSIE DELL HAD COME TO END IT. FOR KEEPS, THIS TIME. SHE LET HERSELF in the back way, like she always did. Walked up to his ground-level apartment from Clifton beach, the sun fizzling out in the Atlantic like a cigarette in a gutter. Glimpsed her reflection – a blur of brown skin and tangled black curls – as she unlocked and rolled open the concertina steel gates that covered the glass doors to the bedroom. That's how they lived in Cape Town, these rich whities. Behind bars.

He was waiting for her. Lying on the bed, in his suit pants and Italian shoes, silk shirt unbuttoned at the collar. Face featureless in the gloom. Rosie threw his keys onto the sheet beside him.

'I can't do this, Baker,' she said. 'Not any more.' When they were alone he was always Baker. Never Ben.

He said nothing, stood and came toward her. Used his bulk to press her up against the wall, the kiss sucking away her words of protest and her resolve. Baker's hands were under her skirt, lifting the cloth above her waist, sliding her panties down her legs. He shed his shirt and she could feel the hot weight of his flesh. She thought of Kobe beef fattened on beer.

When they were done it was night. Rosie sat down on the bed, still dressed. Baker stood over her, silhouetted against the light from the corridor. She heard the teeth of his zipper meshing.

'Pick up the keys,' he said. She felt the cool brass beneath her fingers. 'Put them in your pocket.'

Did as he said. Her wedding band clinking on the metal. Thought she caught the flash of his smile in the dark.

Rosie watched him walk down the corridor into the brightly

lit sitting room, shirtless, the pale skin of his back streaked red from her fingernails. His naked torso was hard with fat, like a seal. *Not even my fucken type*, she thought, as she always did. Whatever that meant. But when he was near, some kind of fever took her. Something beyond reason. It wasn't his money. That she would have understood. Worst thing was, she knew she'd be back for more.

Baker was standing beside the Picasso sketch of a bull, pouring Scotch from a decanter, when the two men came in from the direction of the front door. Black men, dressed in blue overalls. There had been no sound, so they must have had a key. One man was big, young and nervous looking. The other small and older. Calm. Both held guns.

Baker set the decanter down on the polished chiffonier and raised his hands level with his shoulders. Spoke in the assured tones she'd heard him use many times at boardroom tables. 'Okay. Let's keep this cool. Whatever you want. No problem.'

The small man shot Baker in the chest, the gun coughing through a silencer. Baker dropped his hands and went down on one knee. He was turning to look at her when the next bullet entered his right eye and sent part of his skull onto the wall behind him. The man shot Baker once more as he lay on the carpet and his body jerked.

All this took maybe five seconds. Rosie sat in the dark. Frozen. Then the older man looked into the bedroom and saw her. She pushed herself up from the bed and slammed the door, turned the key in the lock. Heard a pop and the wood splintered beside her hand as a bullet bored through and buried itself in the mattress.

She jabbed the panic button on the wall. No sound in the apartment but it would be ringing in a control room somewhere, bringing men with guns. Bringing paramedics. Too late for Baker. She ran out onto the patio, into the night. The security gates were locked in the sitting room, holding the men.

She heard them kicking down the bedroom door as she crossed the tiles. Heard the thin wood tearing. Hurdled a flower bed and hit the pathway to the beach at a sprint. Leaving her sandals behind as she ran, the paving rough on her bare feet. Feeling for the keys in her jacket.

Heard that coughing sound and something spat next to her foot. The pathway twisted round shrubbery and she was at the gate. High wall. Humming strands of an electric fence. A motion-sensitive spotlight kicked in, pinning her. Battled to get the key into the lock, fingers shaking like a Friday night boozer's. Heard the drumming of footsteps.

Fok, fok, fok. Her tongue finding the Afrikaans of her childhood. Fingers finding the slot.

Opened the gate and she was through. Slammed it locked as the men came into view. The older one lifted his pistol and a bullet sang past her head. She chased her shadow into the darkness of the beach, felt the sand gripping her feet. Fought on toward the water's edge where she could run more freely, her breath coming in rasps, louder than the surf. Sprinted from Second Beach to First.

Rosie saw a group of teenagers in baggies and hoodies, on their way up to Victoria Road, bodyboards under their arms. She fell in with them as they climbed the stairs, zigzagging between beach bungalows that sold for millions in dollars and euros. The boys were sharing a joint, a firefly dancing from one face to another. She was older than them by fifteen years, but they looked at her with interest.

One of them said, 'Hey.'

She said 'Hey' back and he held the joint out to her.

Rosie took it, sucked on it, felt the familiar heat in her lungs. She released the smoke and handed the joint on. They were up at the road now and she scanned the area. Dog walkers and night joggers. No men with guns.

She left the kids at a rusted minivan and crossed to where the silver Volvo was parked under a street light. A car guard in a cap and a day-glo green bib gave her a wave. He was an engineer, a refugee from somewhere in Africa. She always tipped him. Not tonight.

Rosie sat behind the wheel of the car. Numb. No shoes. No panties. Felt the stickiness between her legs as she started the engine and drove home to her husband and her children.

chapter 2

' **I** BUSTED NELSON MANDELA'S BLACK ASS. YOU'RE LOOKING AT THE REASON he got sent to prison. I changed the course of history, and that is no word of a goddam lie.'

Robert Dell, head thick with lunch wine, slumped in the passenger seat of the Volvo – not asleep but not fully awake either – haunted by the memory of his father's voice from deep in his childhood: loud, overbearing, marinated in Jack and Coke and unfiltered cigarettes. Defiantly West Texas, like Tommy Lee Jones in a lesser role. He hadn't seen his father in twenty-five years, but his voice was right there in the car, unwanted fragments of Dell's past circling him like bats.

He sat up. Glanced at his wife, concentrating on the road as she steered into a sharp bend, heard his children laughing in the rear. Dell looked out at the sun. Let the bright light burn the bad shit away.

They were driving over a narrow mountain pass, road switchbacking its way down to a far valley, a sheer drop falling away to Dell's left, the small town where they'd eaten lunch lost behind them. Franschhoek, an hour out of Cape Town, always reminded Dell of a movie set: vineyards encircled by mountains, gabled white houses built by Huguenot settlers God knew when, gift shops and pretentious restaurants with French names. Over lunch Dell had flattened a bottle of red wine, trying to blur the edges of a fucked-up couple of days. Not surprising that his father had spoken to him, after yesterday's news.

'You okay?' Rosie asked, eyes on the road.

'Ja. Too much vino.'

'Hell, you were really hammering that bottle.' Shot him a

smile. Smart schools and college had smoothed out the guttural accent of Rosie's childhood, but he could still pick it up on the roll of the 'r' – the slight bray of the Cape Flats that was almost Spanish. *Rrreeely. Hammerrring.*

'Sorry,' he said.

'Don't be. It's your birthday. Relax.'

His birthday. Jesus, how the hell had he ended up being forty-eight anyway? Dell ran his fingers through his long sandy hair, streaked with gray. Two weeks' beard itching on his face. Mostly silver. Time to thin it out. His wife said his stubble was sexy. Or she used to.

Dell turned to look at the twins in the rear, strapped into kids' car seats, side by side. Mary and Thomas, five years old, sucking fruit juice through bent straws. Tommy saying that *Ben 10* was way cooler than *Pokemon*. Mary disagreeing. Tommy emphatic.

Mary said, 'Tommy, you're a complete and total idiot.' Sounding middle aged.

The sun haloed their wild hair, halfway down their backs in dark corkscrews. Their mother's hair. They had her skin, too. Exactly the color of caramel.

Dell put a hand on his wife's leg, feeling her warmth through the denim. 'And you, Rosebud? How're you holding up?'

Rosie worked on another smile but it didn't take. She was doing her best to give him a treat on his birthday but her heart wasn't in it. She'd been in a dark, interior place since he'd walked in on her two days ago, huddled on the sofa, hugging her knees, watching the early morning news on TV.

Saying, 'Ben Baker's dead,' as Dell saw images of cops around a luxury apartment on Clifton and heard the TV anchor announce that Baker had been killed in a home invasion the night before. A robbery gone bad. All too common in Cape Town. Only reason it made the news was because Ben Baker had been one of the richest men in the country. His loot had endowed the arts foundation Rosie headed. He was the reason they were driving in this shiny new Volvo.

'I found myself looking in my pocket for a smoke just now,' Rosie said. She'd quit when she fell pregnant with the twins. 'What does that mean?'

'Means you're stressing.'

Ben Baker dying meant that she'd be out of a job soon. Leaving them both unemployed. 'It'll all work out,' he said. His words hollow.

He touched her hand on the wheel. Elegant, beautiful fingers ending in long nails. Manicured, these days. When he'd first met her, the nails had been kept short, her fingers stained by the oil pigments she'd used to make her giant abstracts. But she'd stopped painting when she became a bureaucrat. He missed the smell around the house. Turpentine and linseed oil.

Dell looked away from his beautiful wife. Today he was feeling the age difference more sharply than he ever had. He watched the road. The cultivated land had fallen away. Gone were the fruit farms and the vineyards. In the last week a fire had attacked the mountains and torched the fringe of indigenous bush, leaving a post-apocalyptic landscape of rock and gray ash, some of it still smoking. Dell stared over the edge, down to where a dry river bed lay in a narrow gash of a valley. He felt a rush of vertigo and closed his eyes. Too much wine.

Dell opened his eyes and spoke before he could stop himself. 'He's out, Rosie.'

'Who?'

'My father. He's been released.'

His wife's hands tightened on the wheel. She looked away from the road long enough for him to see distress in those big dark eyes. 'You're kidding me, right?'

He shook his head. 'I got a call from a talk radio station up in

Jo'burg yesterday. Bloody ambushed me. Wanted a comment.'

'Why didn't you tell me?'

'Jesus, Rosie. You've had the whole Ben Baker thing to deal with.'

Her eyes flicked across to him, then back onto the road. 'When did they release him?'

'A few weeks ago, apparently. Let him out the back door, which is why we didn't hear.'

'I thought life meant life?'

He shrugged. 'In this case it meant sixteen years.'

'Think he'll contact you?'

'No way, Rosie. Don't worry.'

'He's their grandfather.' She glanced at the twins in the rearview, still caught up in their TV debate.

'He knows better than to come near me. And even if he did, you think I'd let him within a fucking mile of them?'

Mary's radar ears caught this. 'Daddy said a bad word.'

Dell turned in his seat. 'Yes, Daddy said a very bad word. And Daddy's sorry. Okay?'

'Where is he?' Rosie's voice edgy.

'Dunno. I imagine his right wing buddies have taken him in.'

'Jesus, Rob...'

'I know, I know. It was rough when he did what he did, being his son. Now, it's all going to start up again, isn't it?'

'You're not your father, Rob.' Rosie's eyes were on the road, but she reached out a hand and touched his face.

'No. I'm not.'

He'd taken his mother's surname. Spoke with her South African accent. Practiced a leftist brand of politics that had made him his father's enemy. Sired mixed-race children. But sometimes, when a mirror caught him unawares, he glimpsed the older man staring back at him.

There was a commotion in the rear. Tommy trying to get

Mary's drink, spilling juice over her. Mary shouting, Tommy shouting back.

Dell turned, yelling. 'For Chrissakes, you two, can't you bloody behave!'

His outburst left a vacuum that was quickly filled by Mary's bawling.

'Okay, okay, okay. Take it easy,' Dell said, fumbling in the glovebox for a container of wet wipes. He unclipped his seatbelt and turned around to face his daughter, kneeling on his seat, reaching into the rear to dab at her damp T-shirt. 'Relax, Mary, it's only juice.'

'Daddy shouted.'

'I'm sorry, baby. I didn't mean to.'

The girl clung to Dell and he buried his nose in her hair. She smelled of coconut shampoo. He could feel her ribs beneath his hands, small bones shaking as she sobbed. Heart pumping. There was little physical sign of Dell in the twins, but he believed Mary had his nature. Pensive. Sometimes sad. Tom was more volatile, like his mother.

The boy was sniffling now too, so Dell freed his left hand and embraced his son. Holding the two of them. Back when he was working, when he was away from his family, lying alone in a hotel room or sitting in the darkened tube of a passenger jet, Dell had caught himself repeating the names of his wife and children in a silent mantra. As if that would keep them bound together in an unbreakable unit. *Rosie, Mary, Tommy.*

Tom was wriggling and Dell let him go. But Mary held on. 'I love you, Daddy.'

'And I love you too, my angel.'

Finally his daughter's small fingers released him and Dell, still kneeling, lifted his face from her hair and saw the black pickup truck, a four-wheel-drive with smoked windows and bull bars, coming up behind them. Fast. He watched it grow in the rear window, waiting for it to swing out and pass. It didn't.

The bull bars smashed into the trunk of the Volvo. The car yawed, and Rosie fought to keep it on the road. The children screamed and Dell was shouting at the truck, as if that would stop it.

The black fender and fat nubby tire loomed up next to Rosie, who cursed in Afrikaans, fighting the wheel. She lost control when the truck rammed them from the side, edging the Volvo toward the skinny silver guardrail. The truck hit them again and the car leapt at the crash barrier, tearing free the short wooden uprights that tethered it to the edge.

The impact of the collision sent Dell, unrestrained by a seatbelt, through the windshield. He went out backwards, in an explosion of glass, like he'd been ejected. Hanging over empty space for what seemed like hours before he hit the earth, landing on his side, on the narrow strip of coarse grass that grew between the torn and twisted steel and the endless drop.

The last thing he saw before the world went black was the Volvo with everything he loved inside it, turning in the air, tumbling for ever, as it fell toward the jagged rocks below.

chapter 3

INJA MAZIBUKO WAS HUNGRY. HE HADN'T EATEN SINCE HE'D SHOT THE FAT white man. His fast an attempt to starve the dark thing that ate his strength, and a penance to appease the ancestors, a plea to them to lead him to the woman who had escaped. The one who had seen his face. The half-breed. Now, watching her car smash into the rocks, exploding in a ball of dirty orange fire, he felt his appetite stirring.

The Xhosa idiot at his side laughed, pointing down at the car. 'Yoh, yoh, yoh!' A braying donkey who never shut up.

Inja shoved the Toyota truck into gear and started down the pass toward distant Cape Town. He was a Zulu by birth, his home nearly two thousand miles away, up the East Coast, past Durban, where he was an *induna*, a headman, in the service of his chief. He'd flown in to kill the rich white man and he was anxious to leave, now he'd cleaned up the mess. He didn't like this place, full of half-breeds and Xhosa fools. Like the boy yapping at his side.

Inja had recruited the youth in Cape Town, one of the animals running wild in the shack settlements that festered around the city's airport. He didn't know the town and needed a local to guide him. He hadn't let the boy out of his sight for three days and he was growing weary of his empty-headed babbling. Inja tuned him out and thought of food. He was lusting after a sheep's head, the way it was cooked in the ghetto townships, his mouth heavy with saliva.

At the bottom of the pass the empty road flattened and ran straight toward a dam that lay like a mirror in the blackened veld. Inja slowed and turned off the asphalt, drove a little way up the gravel path that led to the dam wall.

'Why are we stopping, *baba*?' The idiot calling him *father* in deference to his greater age. He'd never shared with the boy his clan name. Definitely never shared the nickname that had haunted him since his childhood in Zululand. *Inja*. Dog.

'I need to pass water.' He opened the door and stepped down. 'Get me a Coke from the back.' Inja, skinny and black as a stick of licorice, walked a few paces from the vehicle and stopped beside a tree trunk that lay singed and twisted in the ash.

While he pissed, Inja saw the boy open the flap of the camper shell and climb into the rear of the Toyota, on his hands and knees, rooting in the Coleman cooler. Inja shook himself and zipped. Opened his check sport coat and took the pistol from the holster at his hip. Not the weapon he used to kill the white man. This was the one he'd given the boy to carry. Still unfired. He found the silencer in his pocket and screwed it on while he walked back to the truck. Nobody for miles, but better to be careful.

The Xhosa's fat buttocks bulged out toward him. 'There's no Coke, *baba*. Only Pepsi.'

Inja leaned in and placed the gun barrel against the base of the boy's skull, where the skin furrowed like the rear of a bull. Pulled the trigger twice. The fool slumped forward, his backside still in the air. Inja reached up a gray belted loafer and shoved the ass until the boy sprawled flat. Grabbed the tarp that lay on the metal bed of the truck and covered the body. He slammed the tailgate closed and locked the camper shell.

Then he took the intimate garment from his coat pocket, held it between thumb and forefinger. Regarded it. The panties that he had found in the white man's bedroom. Tiny, immodest. The underwear of a whore. If he caught his wives wearing something like this, he'd take a horsewhip to them.

Some people would say that he had tracked the colored

slut via the e-mail correspondence – of a sexual nature – that he had found on the BlackBerry he'd taken from the fat man's apartment. But Inja knew better. Those panties, soaked with the half-breed's juices, had allowed the ancestors to guide him to her like she was carrying a homing beacon. To the house in the suburbs of Cape Town, where he had been ready to go in and finish her, before she and her family drove away in the silver car and presented him with a neater alternative.

Inja dropped the panties to the ground, and used his loafer to cover them with ash. He didn't like them, coloreds. Impure people. Neither white nor black. But the unfaithful woman had got what she deserved. He slid behind the wheel of the Toyota and bumped out onto the blacktop.

DELL OPENED HIS EYES. A glare burned into his brain and his head hurt. Flashes of memory burst like grenades in his skull. The black truck. The Volvo smashing through the silver rail. His wife and children screaming as the car tumbled.

Jesus.

He looked to his right and saw the drop down to forever. Saw oily black smoke boiling from the tiny crumpled Volvo that lay on its roof, burning against the rocks and the ash.

Dell closed his eyes. Tried to rewind and erase the nightmare. *Rosie, Mary, Tommy.* Wings flapped and he opened his eyes as a bird landed. A Cape vulture with a bald head, hooked beak wobbling on a skinny pink neck, dusty wings like an undertaker's coat. Wrinkled gray talons scuffed through the ash toward Dell.

He sat up, shouted and waved an arm. His skin was patterned with blood and one sleeve of his shirt was torn away at the shoulder. The bird made a sound like an old man coughing and lifted off, suddenly graceful as it fell away into the void and found its wings.

As Dell shouted, blood bubbled from his mouth and fragments of shattered glass glittered like diamonds when he spat onto the sand between his feet. He saw his shoes were gone. And one sock.

Dell stood up and the world spun, nearly sending him over the edge. He heard an engine straining up the rise, in low gear. Staggered out into the road, waving a bloody arm. A small green Japanese car came straight at him. As it braked Dell saw a man driving, sun catching his freckled hands on the wheel. A woman sat beside the driver, her face blank with shock.

Then the car accelerated and veered around Dell, speeding away. Two blond children stared at him through the rear window as the car disappeared behind a shelf of torn rock. He was unsurprised. This was South Africa where good Samaritans were gunpointed at fake accident scenes.

Dell found his cell phone in his jeans. The glass face was cracked and when he tried to dial an emergency number the phone stayed mute. He dropped the useless thing back in his pocket and started to walk along the road that snaked down to the dry river. Down to his family. He didn't get far. The blacktop rose up and smacked him in the head.

INJA DROVE FOR AN HOUR, toward Cape Town. He smoked a fat hand-rolled spliff, heavy with the potent weed of his home. Durban Poison. Famous the world over for its almost hallucinogenic power. Not a drug in his culture. A medicinal herb. The weed that had sent Zulu warriors into battle against the Boers and the British, eyes red with bloodlust.

Durban Poison grew green and profuse on the rocky red hills of Inja's home, and he had made a fortune out of it over the years. Using the locals to tend and harvest his illegal crop. Shipping it down to Durban for export. It was his first smoke of the day and he felt that familiar sense of his own strength. His own power and invincibility. A feeling he thought he had lost.

Inja was on the freeway into Cape Town, the flat-topped mountain in the distance, when he saw an exit leading to a gas station and a diner. His rumbling belly demanded he stop. It would be white man's food, tasteless and without nourishment, but it would hold him until he could get a sheep's head later.

Inja whistled as he left the freeway and parked the Toyota outside the diner. He walked in and took a seat in a booth by the window, with a view over the car park and the gas station. Ordered a double cheeseburger, fries and well-done eggs on the side.

His order came and he fell to. Ignored the looks of the white and half-breed families as he shoveled food into his mouth. He waited for his stomach to rebel, his appetite to turn itself off like a faucet, leaving him sweating and sick, the curses of the ancestors bouncing off the bones of his skull. But the food stayed in his gut and the plate was nearly empty before he started to feel satisfied. Slowed down. Burped. His stomach swelling happily against his belt. The warmth in his belly spreading down to his testicles.

He reached into his pocket and removed his wallet, flipped it open to reveal the snapshot inside. A beautiful virgin from the Zululand hills, her bare breasts like buds. Sixteen years old. Inja would take her as his bride one week from today. His fourth wife. He stared at the photo as he chewed.

Inja heard a dog bark and looked across to the parking lot. A cop car had stopped next to his truck and two uniforms, one white, one half-breed, stepped out. The white cop let a police dog – a big thing on choke chain – out the rear. It led him to a patch of grass and drilled a stream of piss against a dead tree. The half-breed leaned his elbows on the roof of the car and lit a cigarette, watching a woman in tight jeans fight her way down into a convertible.

The white cop walked the dog back after it was done. It stopped at the tailgate of Inja's rental Toyota, its long snout sniffing. The uniform pulled at the dog's chain, but it wasn't to be moved. The white cop ran a hand over the tailgate, inspected his fingers, said something to the half-breed, who flicked his smoke onto the pavement and joined his partner. The two men looked into the back of the truck. Tried the camper shell, found it locked.

The cops spoke to a pump jockey who pointed to where Inja sat, in the window booth. They shut the dog in the car and walked into the diner, sidearms drawn, spooking the other customers, who ducked for cover beneath the tables.

Inja dipped one of the fries in ketchup, chewed on it, watching the cops approach, Z88 service pistols locked on him. 'That your truck?' the half-breed asked. Inja nodded.

'Keep your hands where we can see them,' the white cop said.

Inja looked at them, still chewing. Reached for the wallet, lying open on the table, their guns following him. He held up the wallet, so they could see his ID in the plastic window beside the photograph of his betrothed.

'Agent Moses Mazibuko,' he said. 'Special Investigation Unit.'

TWO BARE-BREASTED ZULU GIRLS APPEARED THROUGH THE WATER GRASS, balancing large clay calabashes on their heads. Naked except for a fringe of colored beads around their waists and their calves, they crossed the rocks to the river, heads perfectly still on their undulating bodies.

The younger girl – the pretty one – lifted the calabash from her head and knelt down at the water to fill it, the sun catching her braided hair. And catching the white headphones that twisted from her ears, disappearing into the shiny iPod slipped into the waist of her pink and yellow beaded skirt.

Cameras clicked and whirred. A Dutch tourist, florid and sweating in shorts and a T-shirt, crouched as he focused his long lens on those pert young breasts. His wife, sunburned red as a wheel of Gouda, looked away in disgust, fanning herself with a guidebook.

A big Zulu man, dressed in a loincloth and leopard skins, proudly bearing his beer-gut before him, addressed the small knot of European tourists wilting under the African sun. The nameplate Richard was pinned to his leopard-skin bib. 'Ladies and gentlemen, *siyabonga*. I thank you. That is the end of our traditional Zulu village tour. Please to make your way back to the souvenir area by the bus.'

The Dutchman walked backwards in his sandals and socks, still shooting the two girls, who gathered up their calabashes and headed to the hump-backed reed huts visible above the grass.

'Girl! Come here!' Richard shouted in Zulu.

The pretty one, Sunday, turned and walked back toward where the guide stood alone now on the riverbank, hands on his fat hips. His birth name was Xolani, which foreign tongues could never wrap themselves around. So he had become Richard for the tourists, and the name had stuck.

Sunday kept her eyes downcast, as befitted a young maiden talking to a man of his years. When she reached him, she knelt in the sand, still not looking at him.

He yanked the headphones from her ears and they trailed in the dust. 'Where do you get this?'

'I found it, *baba*,' she said.

He held out a fleshy hand. The same hand that roamed like a rooting warthog over the bodies of the young girls in his charge. 'Give it to me.'

She slipped the iPod from her waist and handed it to him. He squinted at it, forehead furrowed beneath his crown of feathers, the iPod lying flat on his palm. He closed his fist and it disappeared. 'Go now. I will deal with you later.'

She bobbed her head, and waited until he followed the tourists before she got to her feet and hurried off. The thing was dead anyway, stopped working a few days after she'd found it lying in the dust after a tour bus had left. She hadn't known what it was, this flat little blue rectangle with no buttons, when she'd concealed it in her clothes and taken it to her aunt's hut. It had looked so clean and pretty. Like an artifact from a distant and better world.

She'd kept it hidden until the earnest young AIDS educator from Durban had come to the valley. The boy, Sipho, in his I'M POSITIVE T-shirt, was only a few years older than Sunday but he was from the city and could have come from another planet. He told her it was called an iPod. Had shown her how to use it. Laughed when she put the headphones in her ears and noisy white man's music thumped out.

Sipho told her that the battery inside would die unless it was charged on a computer. Where was she to find a computer?

There was no electricity in her village, never mind a computer. She listened to a wind-up radio, hearing crackling Zulu choral music broadcast from Durban. On a good day, if the weather was kind, she might hear some African pop.

Sipho went away, leaving her with safe-sex pamphlets in the English that she couldn't read and silver foil packages of condoms. Her aunt found the condoms and beat Sunday, even though the girl hadn't properly understood what they were used for.

The blue music player died, as Sipho said it would. But she had still worn it, as a kind of charm. Pretended she could hear music through the white headphones. A reminder of better things.

Sunday walked up to the circle of reed huts, built in the traditional Zulu style. Nobody lived here. These huts were part of a cultural village. Small buses from Durban arrived each day filled with pale-faced tourists who listened to Richard's version of Zulu history. Sunday and the other workers came from miles away, from the shacks that grew on the sides of the rocky hills in the rural ghetto.

Sunday ducked into the hut where she'd left her clothes. Felt her insides turn to liquid when she saw her aunt sitting on the dung floor, eating a packet of chips and waving away flies with her skinny hand. Sunday had prayed she wouldn't come. But here she was.

'You are late, Sonto.' Calling her by her Zulu name, the name on her birth certificate. Her mother had always used the English, Sunday, and she'd held onto it. All she had left of her mother, dead more than ten years.

'I'm sorry, Ma Beauty.' As always, Sunday struggled to find a resemblance between this woman, dried up as a tree root, and her sister, the angelic mother of her memory.

Sunday slipped out of the beaded skirt. Pulled on a white

T-shirt and reached for her no-name-brand jeans hanging on a wire hanger stuck in a hole in the wall of the hut. Her aunt scratched in a bag and came out with the short gray pleated skirt Sunday had once worn to school. Before the flaking asbestos building with broken windows and a leaking roof had stood in the path of a veld fire and been eaten.

'Put this on,' her aunt said. 'It will make it easier for the inspector.'

Sunday obeyed, tugged the skirt up over her narrow hips, smelling the smoke of another fire, long ago. Staring past the ugly woman, the air heavy with memories.

'Hey, girl, stop dreaming. Get a move on.' Her aunt's voice pulling her back. 'What is wrong with you?'

'Nothing, Ma.'

The skinny woman scowled up at her. 'You are broken, you?'

'No, Ma. I swear. I am not broken.'

'You! If the inspector finds you are broken I will kill you, I swear!'

Sunday shook her head, slipped her feet into white tennis shoes without laces. She stood by the door, waiting for her aunt to rise.

'Where are the betrothal beads?'

Sunday forced back words of refusal and found the beaded necklace lying under her clothes: diamond shapes on a dark background. The sign that she belonged to a man. She hated it, hated the ugly old dog who had given it to her. Bought her with cattle. She wanted to break it, see the beads falling to the dung floor like blue and red rain. But she didn't. Hooked it around her neck, feeling like somebody's animal.

Her aunt stood, her one leg withered from an old curse. Complaining about the ache in her back, she ducked out of the low doorway, gasping. Stood panting like a hyena out in the bright sunlight.

Sunday folded her jeans and her work costume into a plastic shopping bag and left the hut. She followed her limping aunt along the footpath, a short cut to the road, where Ma Beauty would flag down a minibus taxi to take them to town for the inspection.

chapter 5

THE WHITE COP STANK OF SOMETHING SWEET. SOME PERFUME, MIXED with his sweat and the smell of stale tobacco. The Boer was in shirtsleeves, necktie loose at his throat. He leaned across his desk and offered Inja a pack of Camels. 'Smoke?'

Inja shook his head. He had no use for tobacco. The white man lit a cigarette, sucked in deep, then exhaled, never taking his eyes off Inja.

He'd clapped Inja on the back when they'd met, saying, 'Captain Hans Theron. Like Charlize, 'cept I got better tits.' Laughing, showing his teeth. Speaking English with that accent like a bone was stuck in his throat.

Inja knew these white men. Boers. He'd killed enough of them back in the apartheid days, up in the bush war. Spent time in dark cells being interrogated by them. They smiled and joked while they tortured you. Inja buttoned his coat. Put his hands in his pockets. The office was as cold as a meat locker.

Theron was watching him. 'So, my friend, tell me how you found this piece of shit who killed Ben Baker.'

Inja thinking, *I'm not your friend, you white pig.* But shrugging, staying relaxed in his chair. 'It's part of an ongoing investigation. I can say no more.'

For a scrawny man, Inja had a deep voice. A beautiful voice, able to summon the poetry of his ancestors when he spoke in Zulu. His English was less florid, but his voice still carried authority.

Theron ran a hand through his thick hair, looked past the beige vertical blinds that caught the breeze from the AC and tapped the glass of the window. Stared out over Cape Town, the city that had a mountain growing out of its middle, as if a giant mole rat had burrowed beneath, leaving high-rises and houses clinging to the lower slopes of the mound.

Theron turned to Inja. 'Look, I'm not bloody stupid. I know your boss, the honorable minister of fucken justice, is also your tribal chief up in Zululand. And he was like this with Ben Baker.' Holding up his hand, index and middle fingers squeezed together. 'Right?'

Inja said nothing. Stayed as impassive as one of those soapstone carvings the tourists bought up in his home town.

The Boer shrugged. 'Good luck to them. Couldn't give a shit. Couldn't care if they were screwing each other up the ass. But I'm hearing, lately, that Baker was under investigation. The opposition having another nerve jerk about corruption. That Baker was maybe going to talk to save that fat backside of his, ready to squeal about all the fucken money he's poured into your boss's pocket. Then he ends up dead. And you, a Zulu warrior far from home, got a dead fucker in your truck with Baker's cell phone in his jeans and the gun that killed him in his jacket. Makes me think, my friend. Makes me think.'

Inja stared him down. Silent. Theron, cigarette dangling from his lip, opened his desk drawer and brought out a bottle of Klipdrift brandy and two glasses. Squinting through the smoke, he splashed three fingers of liquor into each glass and pushed one across to Inja.

Theron lifted his glass. 'Good luck.'

Inja didn't return the toast but he drank, smelling the sharpness of the fermented grape, feeling the burn of the alcohol warming him from inside. He liked brandy. Preferred it mixed with Coke, but he'd drink it neat.

'Look, Mazibuko, I'm not going to be a stupid cunt about this. I'm on my way out, I know that.' He pinched the flesh of his cheek between thumb and forefinger. 'We all know that white isn't this year's color. They put me in charge of the Baker investigation because they needed a fucken stooge. Someone to get his ass kicked by the media and the politicians till his nose bled. So, I'll take this body and this gun and I'll go to the press conference and I'll take the credit for cracking the case.' Staring at Inja with those shrewd blue eyes. 'But I'm gonna ask you just one more question, my friend.'

Inja drank. Said nothing.

'Is this whole fucken thing gonna blow up in my face? Are you gonna make more shit down here or are you gonna get your black ass the hell back to Zululand?'

Inja shrugged. 'My flight to Durban is booked for tonight.'

Theron smiled his easy smile. The one that never reached his eyes. 'Okay, then.' He poured himself another brandy, stretched the bottle across the desk. Inja covered his glass with his hand, pinky ring catching a shaft of sunlight that pierced the blinds.

The phone rang and Theron answered it. Swiveled in his chair, looking out the window. He grunted and said 'Ja' a few times. Inja saw a photograph on his desk: a blonde woman with the face of a horse, smiling at the camera, her arms around two teenagers. The girl blonde, the boy dark haired like his father.

Theron finished the call and stood, shrugging on his suit coat. 'I've got to get to that press conference. Let me walk you out.'

They left the office and headed toward the elevator. Theron pressed the button and almost immediately the doors slid open, revealing two young uniformed female cops inside. Half-breeds. They saluted Theron, who winked at them. One giggled, caught the Boer's eye, then looked away. A blush on her high yellow cheekbones. Theron jangled keys in his pocket, hummed to himself as they rode down. The elevator pinged and the doors opened onto the parking garage.

Inja's rental truck stood near the elevator, the garage nearly empty of cars on this Sunday afternoon. After he'd shown his ID to the cops at the diner they'd spoken to headquarters and one of them had driven into Cape Town with him, the other following in the cop car. The body of the Xhosa idiot had long been removed from the rear of the Toyota.

The Boer was speaking. 'Interesting call I got, upstairs. A car went over the pass outside Franschhoek a few hours back. Silver Volvo. Burned out. Belonged to a woman called Rose Dell. Sound familiar?' Inja shook his head. 'Worked for an organization Baker funded. Her name has come up a few times during our investigation. Heard rumors that Baker was screwing her. Apparently she was one of those hot pieces of colored ass.' Laughing. 'Lot hotter now.'

They had reached the truck. Inja unlocked it, thinking of the sheep's head that he was going to eat on the way to the airport.

'Apparently the woman and her two kids were killed but her husband was thrown clear. He survived.' Theron had Inja's attention. 'Funny thing is, he's saying a black truck forced them off the road.' The cop lifted a shoe and nudged the bullbar, where silver paint had been scraped onto the black. 'You watch yourself now.' Smiled. Turned to walk away.

Inja said, 'Wait.'

The Boer faced him. His smile even wider. 'Something I can do for you, my friend?'

THE STINK OF DEATH ALMOST MADE DELL LOSE HIS NERVE AND FLEE THE police morgue. He sat in the lobby, spaced out from pain-killers and shock, trying not to breathe. Waiting for a young police constable – a dead ringer for Rosie's younger sister – to come and lead him to the bodies of his wife and children.

It was a hot day and this part of the Cape had been affected by rolling power cuts for the last week. So, no matter how much disinfectant they sluiced onto the tiled floor, the smell of death was always going to win. Dell opened the door to the sidewalk and inhaled fresh air. Stood in the sunshine looking over the small town strip mall and taxi stand, up at the mountains where it had happened, not even three hours ago.

The hospital had given him a pair of flip-flops and a striped pajama top. He still wore his jeans. They carried the story of his birthday in bloodstains and rips. Almost fashionable.

He touched a hand to the bandage on his head. Another bandage wrapped his ribcage. He'd suffered lacerations and bruised ribs. The disintegrating windshield had left a filigree of superficial glass cuts on the skin of his back. Otherwise he was unhurt. Shock and grief, not injury, had felled him when he'd tried to walk away from the accident scene.

Really lucky, the paramedics said as they scraped him from the blacktop and brought him back down to Franschhoek, to the clinic where everybody had been so bloody nice he'd nearly cried. *No crying*, he'd sworn to himself. Not yet. Not until he found out who'd killed his family.

'Mr Dell.'

He'd slumped down on the sidewalk like a homeless man,

and looked up to see the cop standing over him. Her name was Constable Goliath, which was hilarious because she was tiny. Skinny brown arms sticking out from her short-sleeved blue uniform. The big black boots and the weapon holstered at her hip made her look like something from the manga cartoons the twins had loved.

'Mr Dell, are you okay?'

Gripping the buff brick wall, he hauled himself to his feet. 'I'm fine. Thank you, Constable.'

She put a hand on his arm. 'You really don't have to do this, you know.' *Rrreeely.*

Her accent made him think of Rosie's parents. He'd have to break the news to them. It would destroy her father, the man who had spent years driving a garbage truck to save up the money to get his exceptional daughter an education. To this day he battled not to call Dell *Mr Rob.*

'We could get dental records sent from Cape Town tomorrow to make the identification,' the constable said. 'You shouldn't do this to yourself.'

Dell shook his head. He had to do it. Otherwise none of this would be real. He'd put them in the ground and still not believe it had happened. 'I want to. Take me to them. Please.'

She nodded. Led the way through the lobby to a pair of scuffed swinging doors, painted a pale yellow. Two small frosted windows stared at him like blind eyes. She stopped with one of the doors half open and the smell of decaying flesh rushed out and hit Dell. He worked hard to hold down his puke. The cop looked like she was going to speak again, then she shook her head and let him enter.

A man in a stained white coat lurked near the back of the room, beside a wall of metal freezer drawers. He had skin the color of flat beer, four strands of black hair lying like tendrils across his bald skull. He came forward when he saw Dell, passing a fan that fought a losing battle against the heat and the stench. The wind of the fan lifted the hairs on his head, and they stood like antennae for a moment, until he moved out of range and they flopped down again.

There were five chrome tables in the room. Two of them were empty. Three of them were covered by black waterproof plastic. Dell could see shapes under the plastic. The man looked at the constable, who nodded. Then he took the corner of the first cover and drew it back, in one practiced motion. Dell had to grab hold of the table to stop himself from falling.

Later, he remembered only flashes. Like jump cuts from a movie. Remembered the buzzing strip lights in the ceiling, the whirr and rattle of the fan. Remembered the sound the man made, a constant sniffing and swallowing, his Adam's apple a yo-yo beneath his wrinkled skin. Remembered the young constable looking away from the tables. Used all of these images to try to erase what he saw when each cover was lifted.

Tommy's features burned away. His right arm sheared off above the elbow, hanging by a piece of charcoal flesh. His one kid-size Chuck Taylor almost intact around a severed foot.

Mary's brain visible beneath a skull that had been shattered like an egg. A clump of dark hair still twisting from the side of her head. Her legs ending at the knees.

Rosie a torn torso with charred intestines. Beautiful hands gone, blackened stumps in their place. Legs twisted and broken. Eyes empty holes in scorched bone.

Dell turned for the exit, fell through the swinging doors, toward the sunlight. Stood on the sidewalk and sucked air. The world went on outside. Cars drove by. He heard the blare of hip-hop pumping from a sound system. Saw a man and two kids walking out of a KFC, carrying tubs of fried chicken.

The smell of his family's burned flesh was still thick in Dell's nostrils. He spewed. Vomit hot on his bare toes. Crouched with his hands on his knees, gasping, necklaces of drool dangling from his mouth. A woman in bright green hair rollers stared at him from inside a dented car, her face like a closed fist. Dell wiped his mouth on the back of his hand. Stood up. Saw the young constable watching him from the morgue doorway. Looking like she wanted to cry.

A white Volkswagen, with the South Africa Police Services blue and gold insignia on the door, pulled up. A colored man in plain clothes climbed out, observed Dell for a moment, then went across to the constable. They spoke. The constable glanced at Dell, then back at the man. When she looked at Dell again, something in her expression had shifted.

The plainclothes walked over to Dell, flipped open his ID. 'I'm Lieutenant Palm.'

Dell nodded, waiting for the cop to give him information on the madman who had destroyed his life. That bastard in the black truck. Then he realized how strong the painkillers and the shock were, because he could have sworn he heard the cop reading him his rights.

'What?' Dell said. 'What's going on?'

The cop cuffed Dell's hands in front of him. He hardly felt the pain when the metal gripped his torn and bruised flesh. The man grabbed his arm and walked him toward the car. Put a hand on Dell's bandaged head and pushed him down into the rear of the Volkswagen.

The cop was speaking. 'You're under arrest for the murder of your wife and children. Do you understand?'

No. He didn't understand.

The car sagged as the cop sat behind the wheel. He cranked the engine and the Volkswagen took off. Dell looked up at the young constable as they drove by. An expression of loathing on her face.

chapter 7

AS THE TAXI RATTLED DOWN TOWARD THE VILLAGE, SUNDAY'S DEAD mother spoke to her. Told her to open the book. Sunday was used to hearing her mother at night, lying in bed in Ma Beauty's hut, the iron roof cracking like gunshots as it cooled in the sudden chill. But the voice shocked her in the brightness of the packed minibus, Sunday jammed in beside her aunt.

She squirmed forward, scratching in her bag, her nose almost touching the creased neck of the man in front of her, finding the torn spine of the book, easing it out onto her lap.

Ma Beauty's elbow jabbed her in the ribs. 'Sit still, you.' The miserable woman, as sharp edged and spiky as the aloes that blurred by.

Sunday opened the book, careful with the charred pages. It was her most precious possession. Too precious to leave in the hut when she went to work. Ten years ago Sunday, wandering among the bodies of her mother, father and cousin, had rescued the burned book from the smoking ruins of her hut. It had been a spiral-bound photo album, long ago. On what was left of the cover, smiling white people with hair like straw stood in the snow with planks tied to their feet.

Inside, two singed and crumbling photographs remained. One was taken on her parents' wedding day, her father just a shoulder in a striped suit. Half of her mother's beautiful, smiling face burned to ash. The other a blurred snapshot of Sunday as a fat baby, sitting on a woman's knee. The woman's head was gone but Sunday knew it was her mother. The mother who spoke to her. Told her fingers to go to the rear of the book.

On the inside of the back cover, trapped beneath warped

and discolored plastic, Sunday felt the fragment of blackened cardboard. Like the printed cards Richard handed out to the tourists, advertising his services as a guide. This card was burned away except for a telephone number. Sunday had stared at it all these years, never knowing whose number it was. Or why her mother had kept it.

The taxi skidded to a stop in a cloud of red dust and Sunday smacked her forehead on the seat in front of her. She looked up to see they were in the village, the passengers fighting their way out of the minibus.

Ma Beauty scowled down at her. 'Come on, you. We are already late.'

Sunday returned the book to her bag and followed her aunt out of the taxi.

Bhambatha's Rock was one short street, ending at an iron bridge that spanned the dry river. Low cinderblock buildings flanked the road in two uneven rows, some untreated gray, others painted in blues and pinks faded by the sun.

Sunday and her aunt dodged the cows and the goats and the drunks clotting the doorway of the liquor store, picked their way between vendors squatting in the dirt selling cigarettes and the cheap sweets that made your piss go pink. They arrived at a store, dwarfed by signs advertising Omo washing powder and Sunlight soap. A group of women and girls sat on the sand behind the store, in the shade of flat-topped thorn trees.

A big woman waited for Sunday and Ma Beauty, casting glances at the watch that cut into her fat wrist. She wore a floral blouse, a gray skirt hanging to her thick ankles, elephant feet overflowing sandals that had been made for a more delicate body. A blue beret was pulled low on her head and she had a big imitation-leather purse slung over her shoulder. Auntie Mavis. The sister of the ugly dog who had bought Sunday. Come to see the inspection was carried out in the traditional manner. And that the results were beyond dispute.

The two women greeted one another. Sunday was ignored. Auntie Mavis spoke down her flat nose at Ma Beauty as she led the way to where around twenty teenage girls stood in line, chattering and giggling nervously. A young woman in too-tight jeans and evening shoes with rounded heels perched on a rock, writing the names of the girls in a notebook.

Sunday's aunt dug in her pocket and produced a coin. 'Here. Go pay.'

Sunday stood in line. Gave her name. The woman laboriously wrote it down, and pocketed the payment. Sunday joined the girls who waited, but she didn't make conversation.

A girl was called forward and disappeared behind a tree where an auntie in black and white beaded ceremonial headdress sat on a grass mat. A group of older women formed a cordon around the auntie, protecting the girl from prying eyes.

A shout went up, and the women cheered and ululated. Calling out '*Imomozi*!' Vagina in Zulu. The girl stepped from behind the tree, proudly wearing a circle of white paste on her forehead that announced to the world that she was a Zulu virgin.

One by one the girls went forward. And the cheers and shouts followed. Then a girl disappeared behind the tree and emerged to silence. No white marking. No cheers. Just shakes of the heads and clucking from the older women. Tears on the girl's face, her disgraced mother scuttling off after her.

Sunday prayed that it would happen to her when her turn came. But she knew it wouldn't. Knew that the skin was still inside her, stretched tight as a little drum. Alone in the hut the night before, she had squatted over a piece of broken mirror, holding one of Ma Beauty's knitting needles, ready to shove it into herself and pierce that precious skin. Ready to make herself worthless. So the ugly old man would take his cattle back and go and find another victim.

But as the point of the needle brushed her thighs she'd heard her mother's voice: *no, my child. No.* Sunday had dropped the needle and sobbed herself to sleep on the dung floor of the hut.

Sunday was called forward. Ma Beauty and Auntie Mavis joined the group of watchers. Sunday approached the mat, set her bag down. Stayed standing. The inspector looked up at her and flapped her hand. 'Come, girl, lie down. I don't have all day.'

Sunday kneeled, lifted her skirt, and slipped her panties down her legs, tears welling in her eyes.

Ma Beauty shouted, 'What is wrong with you, girl? Lie down!'

Auntie Mavis hissed like a puff adder, 'You see, I'm telling you, this girl is a rubbish. She has been laying with men!'

Sunday rolled off her panties, sitting her backside down on the mat. She lifted her skirt and spread her thighs. The inspector opened her up and peered inside her, like she was checking bread in an oven.

'Nice. Perfect,' the inspector said.

Sunday pulled on her panties and stood, staring at Auntie Mavis, who half-heartedly joined in the cheering. Ma Beauty, as shrill as a shrike, screamed out, '*Imomozi.*' Sunday felt one of the women dab the white paste on her forehead. Another gave her the rubberstamped certificate that was like a death sentence.

Auntie Mavis snatched the paper from her hand, examined it. Then she folded it and hid it in the hills of her cleavage. 'I will give this to my brother.'

Auntie Mavis and Ma Beauty walked back toward the road, her scrawny aunt flapping alongside the fat woman like a tickbird after a cow. Sunday lagged behind. Heard Ma Beauty's wheedling voice. 'So, Sis Mavis, when can I expect the rest of the *lobola*?' The dowry. The cattle and the money.

'So much money for such a skinny girl.' Auntie Mavis shook

her head at Sunday, who had joined them. 'He has spent too much money already, my brother. Look at this.'

She pulled a stack of printed pages from her purse and flapped the Western-style wedding invites in their faces. A photograph of Sunday in the traditional outfit she wore to work, standing miserably next to the ugly old dog, dressed in a suit that was too big for him.

'Now that she has been pronounced worthy of my brother, I must post them out.' She separated two invitations from the stack and handed them to Ma Beauty. 'You better have these.'

The skinny woman grabbed the pages, clutching them to her body. Auntie Mavis shoved the rest of the invites back in her purse, and walked off toward the post office, her buttocks rolling like a cement mixer beneath her skirt.

Sunday followed her aunt to the taxi stand. She wished her mother would speak to her now, explain why the man who had killed her family was going to be allowed to kill her too.

chapter 8

THE TOYOTA WAS A BLACK SHADOW AGAINST THE WHITE SAND. INJA
stepped down from the cab and walked to the rear of the
truck. A railroad track lay between him and a cluster of shacks,
silver roofs liquid in the afternoon heat. Beyond the squatter
settlement, sand and scrub sprawled flat and empty to the
distant dunes and the Atlantic.

He heard the scream of jet engines and looked up as a plane
lifted off from nearby Cape Town airport, low enough to see the
bright colors of one of South Africa's low-cost airlines, gaudy
as a township taxi. The earth vibrated beneath his loafers as
the aircraft banked and headed north. Inja thought of his own
delayed departure. Stuck here until he had cleaned up this new
mess.

As the rumble of the engines faded, Inja heard two sharp
bleats from the phone in his back pocket. He thumbed the
Motorola to retrieve a text message from his sister. Four words
that lifted his mood: *the girl is intact.*

Inja felt a surge of optimism. The coming union between
him and his new bride would placate the ancestors, restore the
natural order of things. End this run of poor fortune. And purge
the demon from his blood.

Inja breathed. Exhaled. Rolled his shoulders beneath his
sport coat. Tried to relax. Focused his mind. Then he came back
to the present, opened the flap of the truck's gas tank, unscrewed
the cap and threw it to the sand. He inserted a length of white
mutton cloth into the dark mouth. Shook the Toyota, hearing
the gasoline washing the sides of the full tank. The sharp smell
of fuel reached his nostrils.

He found the yellow box of Lion matches in his coat pocket and lit one, shielding the flame from the hot wind that blew sand over his shoes. He set fire to the soaked cloth, heard a suck as the gasoline ignited, purple flame chewing its way toward the tank.

Inja turned and walked to the Mercedes Benz idling beside the road, the AC ticking over the low murmur of the engine. The white cop was at the wheel, leaning forward as if he was searching for something on the dashboard. He looked up at Inja and the chrome frame of his dark glasses flared in the sun. As Inja opened the car door the truck blew and he felt a draft of heat on his back.

He slid in beside Theron, closing the door. The Boer had spread a narrow trail of white powder, like a silkworm, on the black dash, and he inhaled it though a rolled banknote, snorting like a pig. Theron sniffed a couple of times, ran a tongue over his gums. 'Want some?'

'No.'

'Pure as a nun's pussy, my friend.'

Inja shook his head, watched the Boer stow a twist of paper in his coat pocket. He felt a moment of rage so intense that he had to will his hand away from his pistol, so ready was he to send this white shit to hell. This weak fool who had no self-control.

Theron clicked the automatic into drive and made a U-turn, heading back toward the freeway, driving too fast. Inja shivered. The Benz was as frigid as the Boer's office had been. They were cold-blooded creatures, these whites. 'Can you turn off this ice?'

Theron flicked a switch on the dash console. 'Whatever you say, Shaka.' Laughing.

Shaka, the Zulu king of legend. The Boer's idea of a joke. Inja bottled his rage. *Soon, white man, soon. Soon I'll have no more use for you.*

Inja looked back over his shoulder, watching the Toyota blaze until the flames were lost behind a dune. It had been a day of burning cars.

chapter 9

DELL FELT THAT THE BROWN COP WAS STARTING TO BELIEVE HIM. STARTING to allow that he might not have been driving when the Volvo went off the cliff. That a black truck had pushed them over. A black truck that was still out there somewhere.

They were in an interrogation room at Franschhoek police station. The AC rattled and coughed but did little to disturb the air in the windowless room. He could smell wood smoke and cooked meat on Lieutenant Palm, as if the man had been called away from his Sunday barbecue. The smell took Dell back to the morgue. He gripped the edge of the table to keep himself inside his skull.

Palm was speaking, accent as thick as a barrel of tar. 'So you say your wife took the wheel of the car, when exactly?'

Dell told Palm what he'd told the skinny constable at the hospital. When they'd left the restaurant after lunch he'd walked out with Mary and Tommy, while Rosie went to the bathroom. He held the twins' hands as they strolled around the Cape Dutch house to where the Volvo was parked under a chestnut tree in full pink bloom.

When Dell released their hands to unlock the car, the twins ran onto the lawn that sloped down to a vineyard, chasing after an Egyptian goose that blared out a complaint. Mary yelped and sprinted back to where Dell stood. Hiding behind her father's legs as the heavy bird heaved itself into the air, barely scraping over a fence, flying off toward the Drakenstein mountains. Tommy laughed, imitating the bird's honk as he ran back.

Dell saw their waitress from lunch standing by the cars, sneaking a cigarette. A middle-aged colored woman in a gingham pinafore, with coarse hair pulled back into a bun. She caught Dell's eye, smiled shyly as she cupped the cigarette in her hand, like she was in a prison yard.

Dell strapped the kids into their car seats and started the Volvo, drove round the side of the restaurant in time to catch Rosie as she emerged. They had swapped seats and driven away into the nightmare that waited to ambush them in the bright sunshine.

'And nobody saw you, when you changed seats?' Palm asked.

Dell shrugged. 'I don't know. I didn't notice anyone.'

'So the last person was the waitress, who saw you driving?'

'Yes.'

'You know you were well over the legal limit, when they tested your blood at the clinic?'

'I know I was. I drank nearly a bottle of wine. That's why my wife was driving. She'd only had one glass.'

'And this truck… Black, you say?'

'Yes. Black. Could have been a Toyota, but I'm not positive.'

'Didn't see a license plate?'

'No. It happened too fast. It just came from nowhere and then it was ramming us.' Dell stopped. Reliving the moment of impact.

The cop looked at Dell, something softer, more sympathetic creeping into his features. 'I'll go back to the restaurant. Go talk to the people. Must be somebody saw your wife take the wheel.'

Dell nodded. There was a knock at the door and the young constable stuck her head in. Ignored Dell, gestured toward the corridor and Palm stood up, pushed his chair back and followed her out. Closed the door after himself.

Dell sat and stared at the scarred wood of the table. The numbers 26 and 28 had been carved into the wood. Rival Cape Flats gangs. Rosie's cousin had belonged to one of them.

Dell couldn't remember which. The cousin had died last year, gunned down outside his house. They hadn't gone to the funeral. Dell saw coffins. One large. Two tiny. Saw red earth waiting to swallow his family. Felt his throat squeeze closed. Tried to breathe through it.

The door opened and two men he'd never seen before stepped in. The black man was scrawny and looked like a pimp, in a loud check sport coat, blue shirt, beige slacks and gray loafers with gold chains. At first Dell assumed the white man was a lawyer, or a prosecutor. He was around fifty, but in good shape, tanned, wearing an expensive suit, his thick hair carefully styled. Then Dell saw something crude beneath the suntan and knew he was looking at a cop.

'Mr Dell, I'm Captain Theron.' The cop hooked the plastic chair with his shoe, dragged it back to the table and sat down. 'Like to have a chat with you.'

He didn't introduce the black man, who leaned against the wall and fixed Dell with a stare as blank as a lizard on a rock.

'Where's Lieutenant Palm?' Dell asked.

'Gone back to Mrs Palm and her five daughters.' Theron cupped his right hand and moved it up and down in a jerking-off gesture, laughing. Nothing but coldness in his blue eyes. 'I'm heading up the Ben Baker investigation, so this is my case now.'

'Why? What's this got to do with Baker?'

'Maybe nothing directly. But your wife was a person of interest, shall we say.'

'What do you mean?'

Instead of answering, Theron turned to the pimp. 'Hey, chief, do me a favor. Go check if those printouts are done.'

The black man looked as if he was going to protest, then he shrugged and left the room. Theron put a pack of Camels to his mouth and drew a cigarette out with his lips. Held the pack out to Dell. 'Smoke?' Dell shook his head. Theron fired up, watching

Dell through the fumes. 'I knew your father, you know?'

Dell said nothing. Things coming at him from too many angles.

'You're Bobby Goodbread's son, right?'

Dell nodded. No point in denying it.

Theron laughed as he puffed. 'Crazy bloody Yank. Ja, knew him thirty years back. I was just a kid, hardly any hair on my balls. Straight out of school into the army, ready to go kill fucken commies in Angola. Ended up in some volunteer unit didn't even have a name. Me and one or two other whities and a bunch of crazy fucken bushmen and local tribesmen. Your old man was our commanding officer. First time I heard him speak I thought he was taking the piss out of us. *Dallas* was on TV then. Remember *Dallas*? Jesus, I had the hots for Victoria Principal.' Theron's hands described a pair of heavy breasts in the air in front of his chest. He tried out a bad Texan accent. 'Who shot J.R.?' Laughing. Then he switched off the laugh. 'But he was for real, your dad. Cowboy accent and all. Was just after the bloody Yanks pulled out of Angola, just like they done in Vietnam. He came and fought for us. I've never met a tougher motherfucker, I got to tell you.'

Dell had heard it all before. The legend of Big Bobby Goodbread. Had heard the other side too. The rapes. The body-part trophies. The dead babies.

Theron shook his head. 'Fucken unfair what happened to him. All because he wouldn't name names. Finger his buddies, like so many of those other useless bastards did. There's people running around done far worse things than him. Never sat a day in jail. Ask me, I should know.' Running a hand through his layered hair. 'He was a man, your dad. He had honor. Glad to hear he's out.'

The door opened and the pimp returned carrying a sheaf of papers. Theron took them from him and the black man went back to leaning against the wall.

'You lost your job recently, didn't you?' Theron asked, camaraderie gone.

'Yes. The newspaper I wrote for folded.'

'So what you do now?'

'Freelance.'

Theron snorted. 'Means you're out of work, right?' Dell didn't reply. 'So there were financial tensions, maybe?'

'What are you getting at?'

'What I'm fucken *getting at*, is you got drunk on wine then drove that car through the barrier. Wanted to take your family out and you with them. Family murder-suicide. All too common, you and a whole lot of other losers. Pity it all went fucked up and you're sitting here and your wife and kids are…' He drew a finger across his throat.

Dell battled to find words. 'You're crazy. Why in God's name would I want to do something like that?'

Theron fixed him with his blue eyes. 'Did you know Ben Baker was screwing your wife?'

'What?'

'Ja, had been for some time, apparently.'

Dell shook his head. 'This is obscene. My wife and children are lying dead and you come at me with this…'

Theron slung the printouts onto the table. 'Here. Have a read. From Baker's BlackBerry.'

Dell lifted one of the pages. Recognized Rosie's e-mail address. Saw the mail was from Ben Baker. Read the words: *I want to fuck your brown ass blue*. Read Rosie's reply: *Don't promise things you can't deliver*. Flicked through the pages. Words jumping out at him. Rosie: *Told R I'm going to gym, I can meet you at five*. Baker: *I'm going to be in Jo'burg for a conference on the weekend, can you come?*

Dell pushed the pages away as if they were hot as the flame

that consumed the Volvo. 'I want my lawyer.'

Theron nodded. 'Ja, reckon you need one.'

The cop stood, shoved the printouts back toward Dell. 'You hang onto those. Show them to your lawyer.' Opened the door. 'Come, Shaka. Let's go get us a drink.'

SUNDAY AND HER AUNT SAT ON THE SAND BESIDE THE MAIN ROAD, WAITING for a taxi. A few people waited with them. A young mother whose baby chewed at her breast, as if he wanted meat, not milk. A drunk old man in a threadbare suit, feet bare and calloused. Two girls in jeans, giggling as they shared a soda. A stout woman with a chicken in a wire basket. The chicken sent its red beak through the wire, scratching in the dirt for feed.

Every few minutes Ma Beauty would grunt and shift her withered leg, muttering under her breath, using the wedding invites to wave away the droning flies that circled her head. Sunday watched the shadow of the AIDS billboard inch across the sidewalk and up the wall of the undertaker's.

She heard the bleat of a horn and a dented minibus rattled over the bridge and came to sliding stop, sending up a cloud of dust. The driver stayed at the wheel, smoking a cigarette as the co-driver jumped down and ushered passengers into the rear, collecting fares.

The mother shrugged the baby onto her back, tying it in place with a tartan blanket, clucking as it let out a thin cry. Sunday stood and Ma Beauty levered herself to her feet, gripping Sunday's arm for support. Then she hobbled off toward the taxi. Sunday lifted her bag, about to follow. She stopped. Heard a low growl.

Ma Beauty scowled over her shoulder, lips moving, but Sunday heard only that deep rumble. Getting louder now. She turned to look up the road. A car was coming. A blue car, sun kicking off the chrome wheel rims, the windshield ablaze with glare. When the car slid into the shadow of the under-taker's building, Sunday saw the pink dice swinging from the rearview mirror, as slowly as if they were under water. Saw the blurred shapes of the driver and his passenger. Saw the open side window, the sun flaring on metal as the passenger sent out a sinewy arm, something dark growing from his hand. Heard hard, flat slaps. Like doors banging in the wind.

The mother with the baby opened her mouth and a speech bubble of blood floated out. As she sagged, the blanket on her back loosened and the baby took for ever to fall to the dirt, where it lay face down like a red doll.

The woman carrying the chicken stopped, one foot on the running board of the taxi, the other on the sand. Put a hand to where her jaw had been. The wire basket hit the ground and fell open and the chicken fled, leaving a single white feather floating in dust. Sunday heard screaming and the roar of the blue car as it sped to the bridge, its tires drumming over the metal joins. Then it was gone.

She found herself on her knees, lifting the dead baby. Fingers gripped her arm and she looked up at her aunt. 'Put that down, girl.' Sunday obeyed, laid the baby next to its mother's body. Her aunt was tugging at her. 'Come, you. Let somebody else clean up this mess.'

As she stood, Sunday felt something stuck to her shoe. One of the wedding invites. She pulled it free and put it in her bag. Saw there was blood on her hand. Wiped it on her skirt.

Ma Beauty grabbed Sunday's wrist and walked her away. They passed the taxi, the dead driver slumped over the steering wheel, arm dangling through the open window, cigarette still smoking between his fingers. The drunk man and the girls in jeans sat in the sand, bleeding, faces blank with shock.

As Sunday let her aunt lead her through the crowd that swarmed around the minibus, she heard fragments of sentences, words strung together like beads on a wire: *Taxi war. Hit men from Durban.*

Her aunt limped toward a tree encircled by whitewashed rocks, where the African Zionist Church held its open-air services every Saturday. Ma Beauty sat down on a rock, dabbing at her forehead with a Kleenex. 'Uh-uh, my nerves they are finished.' She drew a banknote from her purse and handed it to Sunday. 'You, go buy me a Coke and a Grandpa. Make quick now.'

Her aunt's recipe in any kind of crisis: a headache powder as bitter as bile, chased down with a Coca-Cola. Sunday took the money and crossed the street like she was sleepwalking, still carrying her bag. She skirted the ambushed taxi. Heard the moans and sobs of the wounded, the excited chatter of the crowd.

As she headed toward the store she passed the bright red metal container stenciled with white silhouettes of people talking on telephones. Thought of the number in the burned book. Sunday looked back, saw her aunt talking to a woman who had come to sit on a rock beside her, hands flapping toward the taxi. Sunday ducked into the container.

A man in his early twenties stood in the doorway, watching the activity in the street. He grunted at her as she passed. A woman thin as death was crying into one of the phones. Sunday stood looking at the telephones. Unlike any she had seen before. These were small, shiny, modern. Like cell phones. The man turned from the doorway. Sunday showed him the number on the burned card.

He squinted at it. 'Pretoria. Long distance. Ten rand.'

The value of the note Ma Mavis had given her. Sunday handed over the money and the man dialed for her. She had no idea what she was going to say to whoever answered in that city in another world.

The man shook his head. 'It is a fax number.' Sunday stared at him. 'A fax. You know, you can send a letter or a picture?' He pointed to a machine that sat on the counter, black and full of buttons.

Sunday nodded. She had seen something like that in the office at the cultural village. But it was no help to her. Then she heard her mother's voice again and she scratched in her bag and found the wedding invite. She held it out. 'Please, brother. Send this.'

He fed the invite into the machine. Sunday wondered whether it had been eaten, but after some clicking and whirring it slid out the other end and the man handed it back to her. He also gave her a slip of paper. 'That tells you it was received,' he said.

Sunday thinking, *Received, yes. In Pretoria. But who received it?*

She left the container and threw the paper onto the mound of garbage that lay in the gutter. Sunday crossed the road toward her aunt, trying to decide on a lie to explain why she was returning with no Coke, no Grandpa and no money.

chapter 11

DISASTER ZONDI SAT AT HIS DESK, STARING OUT ACROSS THE EMPTY expanse of soiled carpet, seeing a head on a stick. The head of one of his ancestors, a Zulu chief named Bhambatha who'd led an uprising against the British colonial powers a century before, protesting against a poll tax his people were too poor to pay. The British had used machine guns and cannon against the spears of Bhambatha's men. Cut off his head, impaled it, and toured it around Zululand as a warning.

The British were long gone and so were their successors, the apartheid butchers. But in the last weeks Zondi had watched as another head, that of his boss and mentor, had been taken and paraded. Also as a warning. Don't fuck with the minister of justice, the man widely tipped to be the country's next president.

The beheading had been virtual, of course. Done with smear campaigns and innuendo and commissions of inquiry held in camera. But Archibald Mathebula, once the fiercely principled chief of a special investigative unit tasked with combating corruption, had been left broken, banished from the ruling party he'd given his life to. Zondi had been one of the handful of mourners at Mathebula's funeral a week ago. Dead of a heart attack, the media said.

Bullshit. He'd died of disgust. Plain and fucking simple.

Mathebula's downfall was caused by his unit's probe into the crooked relationship between the minister of justice and Ben Baker, an entrepreneur who had thrived in post-apartheid South Africa. Fat but agile, Baker had quickly learned to dance to the new drum, enjoying endless photo-ops with sleek black men in

Italian suits. When Mathebula's crusade drew unwelcome media attention, the minister had the unit dismembered like a stolen car in a chop-shop. And now Baker had danced his last dance and the minister was smiling his way toward the highest office in the land.

Some of Zondi's colleagues had been absorbed by the police. Some by academia. Others were setting out their stalls as consultants on crime and corruption. Making a killing talking to businessmen over breakfast, giving them statistics and indigestion.

Zondi had refused all offers. So here he was – a dark man, in a dark suit and a white shirt, no necktie – sitting at his desk on a Sunday afternoon in the vast, empty room that, until two days ago, had been a warren of partitioned cubicles.

In the morning men in overalls would carry the desk down to another office in the gray building in downtown Pretoria – South Africa's administrative capital – joined by a sprawl of bedroom suburbs to Johannesburg, its greedy Siamese twin. If Jo'burg, built on a honeycomb of dead gold mines, was all about money, Pretoria was all about political power. It had once been the showcase of apartheid. Now the statues commemorating Boer generals had been felled and lay gathering dust in warehouses on streets named after Marxist heroes.

Zondi sat with a small cardboard box on the desk in front of him. It contained a dictionary, a stapler, three pens and a dog-eared copy of Trotsky's *The Revolution Betrayed*. The book had lain forgotten in a drawer for years. He was tempted to open it and wallow in the irony. Instead he dropped the box into the trash basket beside his chair and stood, ready to start his last walk to the elevator, toward his uncertain future.

When he heard a warbling from beneath his desk it took him a moment to realize it was his fax machine ringing. The machine – an ancient thing held together by duct tape – whirred and groaned as it expressed a page, millimeter by millimeter. A high-contrast black and white image emerged, like a Rorschach blot on paper discolored by age. The machine beeped and Zondi reached down and tore the page free.

He saw a man and a girl, posing stiffly for the camera. At first Zondi was convinced that he was looking at a youthful photograph of a woman he had once loved, dead more than ten years. But the girl in the picture only resembled her. This photograph was recent. The man was familiar, too, and when Zondi placed him, he felt another part of his carefully managed life slip out of alignment. He was holding a wedding invite. But Zondi knew he wasn't being invited to a wedding. This was an invitation to something altogether different.

He crumpled the page, still warm from its journey out of the belly of the machine, ready to toss it into the trash. But some impulse stayed his hand, and instead he put the fax in the pocket of his suit pants and left the room for ever.

chapter 12

INJA STOOD AT THE STAINLESS-STEEL URINAL, PISSING DOWN ONTO THE LITTLE white balls that lay in the trough, smelling his urine mixing with the fake pine. He held his cell phone in his free hand, speaking Zulu, saying, 'Yes, yes. When? And who is dead?' Voice booming off the tiles, loud as if he was using a public address system.

An old white man in short pants, knee-length socks and polished shoes came into the men's room, took one look at Inja, and chose the privacy of a stall. Inja ended the call and pocketed his phone. Shook and zipped. Left the bathroom.

One of his taxis had been hit in Bhambatha's Rock. Driver dead. Part of the ongoing war he and the other operators waged against one another for control of the rich taxi routes. There would have to be reprisals. Even more reason for him to get out of this place.

Inja walked across the steakhouse in the town of Stellenbosch, forty minutes outside Cape Town. Dodging waiters in cowboy hats and white and half-breed children shouting, running wild. If a child of his behaved this way he would feel the whip till he bled.

Theron sat eating in a booth in the smoking section, behind airtight glass, a haze thick as a veld fire hanging over the tables. Inja sat down opposite the Boer. A steak and chips waited for him, the meat well cooked the way he liked it.

'I want it cremated,' he'd told the colored waitress with the tits Theron couldn't keep his eyes off.

Breasts meant nothing to a Zulu man like Inja, growing up with girls walking around topless in the traditional way. But the flesh of a woman's calf – just below the hollow of the knee – now that aroused him. And that was the area the Zulu girls always kept covered, with skins and beads. The waitress wore a short skirt, and when she'd walked away his eyes were drawn to that area just south of her knee. Inja had a flash of his fingers untying the beads around his new young wife's calf on the night of their coming nuptials. He had to send a hand down to adjust the fit of his trousers.

The Boer was speaking. 'Okay, time to tell you what I want. For all the help I've given you.' Theron gulped at his brandy and Coke.

Inja sliced into his steak and took a mouthful, chewed, eyes fixed on this arrogant white pig. 'There is still the bail hearing tomorrow.'

'Relax. Dell isn't going to get bail. I've got the prosecutor and the magistrate by the balls. They'll do as I say.'

'So,' Inja said. 'What do you want?'

Theron laid his knife aside, lighting up a cigarette, blowing smoke into Inja's face. 'There are only two things a man wants: sex or money. And since I don't want to fuck you, chief, it's gotta be money.' Laughing.

The Boer looked up as the waitress arrived with an Irish coffee. Theron flirted with her, winking. Watching her ass as she moved through the tables. 'How much you wanna bet me she'll write her phone number down on the check?'

Inja said nothing, chewed, working his way methodically through the steak. Covered in the sweet sauce the whites loved, hoping it didn't trigger the sickness that lurked out in the shadows.

Theron switched off his smile. 'I want half a million. Cash.'

Inja stared at him, speaking around his food. 'You are mad. And where must I get such money?'

'Come, Shaka. Don't play coy with me. Talk to the minister.'

Inja chewed, saying nothing. 'I know you and him go way, way back. You guys were in exile together, running around in the bush with your AKs.' Filled his mouth with steak, pointing his fork at Inja. 'Down here in the Cape he can't throw his weight around like in the rest of the country. You fucken need me.'

Inja knew the white bastard was right. In this province run by whites and half-breeds, they scorned his chief. Mocked his many wives and Zulu customs. Thought of him as a savage. Inja's appetite was gone. He pushed his plate away.

Theron puffed on his cigarette, leaking smoke through his nostrils like a donkey on a cold morning. 'This is a nice meal and I don't want to ruin it with threats. But you know what I know. Tell your minister he's getting a bloody bargain.' Washed the meat down with his Irish coffee.

Inja watched as the dead man wiped cream from his lip.

chapter 13

DELL LAY ON A BARE MATTRESS IN THE DARK. THE TWO DRUNK FARM laborers who'd shared the holding cell with him had been kicked loose. One of them'd had diarrhea and the stench of the blocked toilet hung in the air, acrid and dense.

A lawyer had come up from Cape Town a few hours back. The son of a friend of Dell's from the old days. The father, a political activist who'd morphed into senior partner at a massive legal firm, hadn't bothered to come himself. The boy – Jeremy? Jerome? – told Dell to chill until the bail hearing in the morning. Like he was talking about catching a wave at Clifton. Assured Dell he'd be kicked loose after the hearing. *A no-brainer*, the kid had said.

Dell was exhausted, but when he closed his eyes he saw the black truck. Saw the Volvo tumbling into space. Heard the screams from inside. He sat up, holding his bandaged head.

A car sped by outside, pumping Bob Marley's 'Redemption Song', and Dell was back in 1994, at a party the night of the elections, South Africa caught up in the fever of freedom. Apartheid was officially dead. Nelson Mandela was in power. Dell was joyous and optimistic for his country, but felt sorry for himself.

His marriage had ended. A love affair that had been fueled by student politics and rebellion had run out of gas in sight of the finishing line. So, standing among a crowd of revelers on the lawn of a house in a Cape Town suburb, he felt sour and a little old, at thirty-three, to be single again.

Dell went into the house to help himself to a glass of nasty boxed wine from a table lit by melting kitchen candles. He found himself staring at a big oil painting. Presumed it was oil, the meaningless swirls applied to the canvas in thick gouts.

'Like it?'

He turned to see a girl of maybe twenty, breathtakingly beautiful, her skin the exact color of caramel, he remembered thinking. Wild hair halfway down her back in black curls.

'No, I don't actually,' he said. 'I think it looks like fecal matter.' Trying to impress her, knowing he sounded like a dick-head as he said it.

'That means shit, right?' *Rrrright.* The accent neutral, except for the roll of the 'r'.

'Yes. And you? Do you like it?'

'Oh, I hate it.' She sipped her wine. 'But it paid my student loan for a couple of months.'

'Jesus. Sorry.'

Laughing, the candle flames repeated in miniature in her almond eyes. 'Don't be.' She was leaving him, and he didn't want her to go. She cast a last look over her shoulder. 'I like your critique. I'll use it.' *Crrritique.*

He saw her at an exhibition the following summer. Took her for a drink. They moved in together three months later. Married the next year. Dell had thought of himself as a happy man. Had thought his wife was happy, too.

He lay back on the mattress and felt the sheaf of e-mails still folded in his pocket. He stood and walked over to the filthy, lidless toilet, filled to overflowing. Fought back his nausea and tore up the pages, dropped them into the bowl. Was taken by a wave of dizziness and had to put a hand to the wall to steady himself. Saw the bodies of his family in the morgue. The memory of the charred flesh hit him and made the stink of the shit seem sweet.

chapter 14

DISASTER ZONDI FOUND HIMSELF IN A COMMUNITY CENTER IN ONE OF those suburbs in the north of Johannesburg that looked exactly like twenty others. Desperate people moping around a coffee urn on a Sunday night. He'd tracked down the address online. Googled sex addiction.

The moderator called the meeting to order and the group scraped plastic chairs into a circle. Zondi's the only dark face in the room. People started talking. Stories of lost marriages and lost fortunes. Familiar stories.

It had always been easy for Zondi, finding casual sex. It had a way of finding him, truth be told. He'd walk into one of those fancy Jo'burg bars – a place pretending that it was in New York or Berlin – not even thinking about getting laid. Order a drink, ignoring the desperate men around him, who tore off women's clothing with their eyes. Then Zondi would look up and there she'd be. The blonde. His female opposite. The yin to his yang. A smile. A few words, and then off to her place for the transaction. Zondi had two rules: no one came to his apartment, and he never stayed the night with his pick-ups.

Lately, he'd leave the sleeping woman, get into his BMW. Still restless. Find himself driving through the night toward the inner city. A place that had imploded in on itself from poverty and crime and decay. He'd see the feral black whores who lurked outside buildings that looked as if they'd been shelled, the women locking on to his smart car like heat-seeking missiles.

He'd call one over and sit staring out over the apocalypse while the woman went down on him. Hearing the smack of her mouth on the condom, catching the bushfire stink of meth or crack in her hair. When he didn't come, she'd bitch, want more money and he'd lay a banknote on her and let her go.

Last week one of them had pulled a knife on him. A long blade with an ornate bone handle. The kind of thing white women had once used to carve Sunday roasts. The whore was so blown on crack she could hardly see and he could have taken the knife from her, but he gave her money and pushed her out of the car. Drove away knowing that he had to stop this before it stopped him.

Zondi came back to the room, unconsciously making eye contact with a wholesome-looking blonde sitting opposite him. He'd never seen her before, but he'd met her a hundred times. Another one curious to merge her whiteness with his blackness. Doing a TopDeck, they called it in South Africa, after the white and dark chocolate combo sold in local stores. He looked away. She didn't. Zondi shifted in his chair, but still felt her eyes on him.

The moderator got to a gaunt man, called him Horst, and asked him if he was ready to share. The man shook his head and the moderator moved on. Zondi had the feeling that this wasn't the first time it had happened.

A desiccated woman in her forties spoke about how her serial adultery had caused her husband to commit suicide. She wept. The blonde kept on forcing eye contact. Zondi got up and walked outside. He stood out in the dark, breathing in bougain-villea and eucalyptus in the garden, wishing that he smoked. The man named Horst appeared at his side.

'You would maybe like a drink?' he asked in a German accent.

'Yes,' Zondi said, suddenly realizing that he would like nothing more.

He expected the German to suggest a bar in a nearby strip mall, but the man led him to an aging Mercedes parked not far from his own car. Horst slid in behind the wheel and Zondi took the passenger seat. The German produced a bottle of Scotch and a couple of foam cups from the glovebox.

He poured two drinks, handed one to Zondi. '*Prost.*'

'Cheers.'

Horst flattened his drink and poured another. Held the bottle up to Zondi, who shook his head. 'May I tell you something I have never before told anyone?' Horst asked, in his fussy, over-precise English.

'Go ahead.' Zondi knew how to listen. It was talking he had a problem with.

Horst told him that a few years back he had been on holiday in Thailand, Phuket, with his wife Lotte and two children – Dieter, an eight-year-old boy, and Dorothea, a fifteen-year-old girl. One morning he left them on the beach, saying he had to return to the hotel to make a business call. Instead, he walked to a brothel, a ten-story building a couple of blocks back from the beachfront.

On the ground floor of the brothel around twenty Thai girls were displayed behind glass, like merchandise, with price tags hanging from their necks. The cheaper ones dressed in jeans and T-shirts, the more expensive in cocktail dresses and high heels.

'So I end up on the tenth floor with a girl maybe younger than my daughter. On the bed she can put her legs behind her head, very supple. While I am fucking her she makes funny noises. Reminds me of the sounds my first Volkswagen made on a cold morning, when I could not start it.' Horst laughed, throwing back his drink.

Zondi balanced the cup on the dash and cracked his door, wanting to get away from this man and his pornographic ramblings. The dome light flicked on and he saw the haunted look on the German's bloodless face.

Horst put a hand on his arm. 'Wait, please. This is where it gets good.'

Zondi paused, the car door still open.

'So we are fucking and I hear another noise. A loud, unbelievable, smash of water.' He laughed. '*Ja*. The tsunami.'

Zondi stayed in the car. Closed the car door. Gave the man back his shadow.

The German saying he ran to the window, a red condom still hanging from his wilting dick, and pulled away the heavy drapes that blacked out the room. Had a narrow view between buildings up to the beach where his family was. Saw the water and the cars and the trees and the bodies. Saw the sea suck back and the second wave hit.

Zondi lifted his cup and emptied it. The German telling him how he had wandered through the devastation. Cars washed into hotel lobbies. Naked dead people in trees. Days later he identified the bodies of his wife and son, rotting in a makeshift morgue. His daughter was never found.

'So,' Horst said. 'You are my confessor.'

'Why me?'

'You looked like a perfect stranger.'

Horst laughed and so did Zondi. He opened the door again, stood up out of the car. 'Thanks for the drink.'

'You won't come back here, will you?' Horst asked.

Zondi shook his head and closed the door. As he walked away from the Mercedes, his fingers found the folded fax in his pocket. He thought about the girl in the photograph. Thought about the place he hadn't been back to in years. Home. He used the remote to unlock his BMW, turn signals blinking. Alarm chirping like an urban birdcall.

chapter 15

I T WAS STILL DARK WHEN SUNDAY LEFT HER AUNT'S HUT, CREEPING OUT SO she didn't wake Ma Beauty who snored in the single room where they ate and washed and slept. Sunday had a blanket around her shoulders, to keep out the chill of the mist that clung to the hills like smoke.

The hut was halfway down a rocky slope, looking as if it had slid down from the top, then lost interest. Sunday passed neighboring huts, walked past the chimney of the communal pit latrine poking up out of the fog, the stink of human dung heavy on the morning air. The sun tore an orange hole in the sky and she saw goats and a few thin cows, legless in the mist.

She walked for two hours, her feet finding the paths that took her across a valley thick with a marijuana crop, over a dry stream and up another hill. It was fully light by the time she reached the top, and the fog had burned away, leaving a view over the valley.

The mud floor of her parents' hut lay like a tombstone on the crest of the hill. Part of one crumbling, fire-blackened wall remained, leaning like an old man in the hard light. It had been many months since Sunday had last been here. She sat down on the cracked floor of the hut where she had spent the first years of her life. Pulled the blanket around herself as she remembered.

It was nightfall, and her mother was cooking in the hut. Beans and maize meal on a paraffin stove. Sunday, five years old, sat with her, on the floor, paging through the photograph album with the beautiful white people on the cover. Her father was outside chopping firewood. Sunday could hear his axe splitting the timber.

Then she heard loud voices. She went to the door and looked out. Saw men shouting at her father. Saw a man lift a machine gun from under the blanket he wore around his shoulders. Saw her father lift his axe. Before her father could bring the axe down the man shot him. Sunday's mother ran out of the hut, screaming, trying to reach her husband. The man shot her and she fell, something wet and twisted spilling from her abdomen.

Sunday hid in the shadows. Watched the men kill her cousin, who came running from where he tended the goats. Watched them set fire to the hut. The flames leaping like dancing devils in the black night.

Then the men were gone. Sunday sat next to her mother, crying, looking on as the hut burned to nothing. Holding her mother's hand. A hand that was cold when the morning sun washed away the haze of smoke.

She saw the burned scrap of the photo album lying on the blackened floor of the hut. Held it to her chest as she walked down to town. She lost her way and it took her hours before she arrived at the police station. A giant man in a blue uniform scooped her up and sat her on the counter in the charge office. Listened to her story. Called other men.

They put Sunday in a white truck, sitting between two policemen. Two others in the rear, crouching under the low roof. She showed them where to go, and they drove to the foot of the hill, until they could drive no farther. She was told to wait with the fat policeman, who was happy not to be climbing. The other men walked up the hill.

It was very hot, and the shadows of the aloes drew long black lines across the rocks and the sand by the time Sunday saw them return. The three sweating men each carried a body on his back. They dumped the corpses of her mother and her father and her cousin on the sand. The bodies were stiff as boards, arms and legs spread wide like those of scarecrows.

The fat policeman took Sunday by the hand, walked her away, and held her face to his soft belly. But she peeped out, under his arm, smelling his sweat like old meat. And she watched as the men broke the legs and arms of the stiff bodies with rocks, so they could get them into the rear of the truck.

Now, as she sat in the ruins of the hut, Sunday saw the face of the man with the gun, hot in the flames of the fire. The face of the man she was to marry in five days' time.

chapter 16

'**B**AIL DENIED.'

Dell didn't understand what he was hearing. The words not penetrating the fog of grief and pain that he wore like a coat. Didn't realize things had gone badly wrong until he heard the kid lawyer's shrill voice. 'Your honor, this is absurd! Mr Dell isn't a flight risk, and he's an upstanding member of the community.'

The magistrate, a khaki-colored man with a snowfall of dandruff on the shoulders of his black robe, peered over his glasses. 'That is my ruling. The State has requested that this case be transferred to the jurisdiction of the Cape Town High Court. Take it up with them, if you want to appeal. Until then the accused will be held in custody at Pollsmoor Prison.' The magistrate shuffled papers. 'Next matter.'

Pollsmoor. A prison where a hundred men shared a cell. Where gang rape and murder were commonplace. Dell turned to his lawyer, waiting for him to make this all disappear.

'I'm on this, Mr Dell. Don't worry,' the boy said, looking shocked. 'Hang in there.'

Dell felt a hand on his shoulder and a uniformed policeman pulled him toward the stairs leading down to the holding cells. As he was hauled away Dell saw the plainclothes cop and the man who looked like a pimp standing at the rear of the courtroom. Theron said something to the black man and laughed.

INJA AND THE BOER were in the Mercedes, driving back toward Cape Town, the mountain and its cloth of cloud already looming on the horizon. Theron drove fast, weaving through the traffic on the freeway, forcing cars out of his way like a train with a cowcatcher.

'You spoken to your minister?' Theron asked. ''Bout my money?'

'This thing is not done yet.'

'Jesus, you're like an old woman with a sore tit, you know that?'

Theron flew past a small Japanese car, the woman at the wheel a frightened blur behind glass. The Boer was using the car lighter on a Camel, speaking with smoke trickling from his mouth.

'I've organized that when Dell gets to Pollsmoor he gets thrown in with the 28s who're awaiting trial. You know the 28s?' Not waiting for an answer. 'Cape Flats gangsters. The hardest motherfuckers you'd ever wish to meet. Few weeks back they killed a guy in a cell one night. Cut his body into pieces and fed it down the shithouse. Problem was, his fucken head got stuck and the toilet overflowed, sending crap and body parts down the corridor.' Theron laughed smoke. 'Talk to the minister. Tell him your Mr Dell is dead meat, my friend. No loose ends.'

DELL SAT ON THE FLOOR of the holding cell beneath the courtroom, jammed in with maybe twenty colored men. The older men huddling together, in fear of the young ones who stalked the cell, demanding money and cigarettes.

Dell had been the only white face in cells full of dark men many times before. But that was back in the eighties, when he'd been arrested for being part of illegal protest marches, and he was held with the other politicos. The general prison population had considered the political prisoners as part of an elite. And Dell had received major cred, as a white man who fought apartheid shoulder to shoulder with his black comrades.

But those days were long gone, and now a white skin made

you a target. The boy standing over him hadn't even been born when Nelson Mandela was released. A yellow-brown boy with a broken nose and missing teeth, crude tattoos coiling like snakes from under his clothes. 'Hey, whitey, that's a nice watch.'

The black and chrome Swatch visible on Dell's wrist under the sleeve of his pajama top. His birthday gift from Rosie. The glass was cracked, but the second hand ticked on.

'Gimme it.' The kid held out a palm stained by years of meth pipes.

Dell looked at him, slow to react. Earned him a kick in the teeth with a dirty Nike. Dell's head smacked the wall and he tasted blood on his tongue. Something snapped inside him. The kid was lining up another kick. Dell grabbed the boy's shoe, tipping him backward so he sprawled into a group of men looking on.

There were shouts and cheers. 'Yaaaw, the white man only wants to die!'

The kid was up and cursing, coming back at Dell, bringing three friends with him. Coming to get them some white meat. Dell with his back to the wall. Felt hands grabbing at him, then he heard the rattle as the cell door opened.

A white cop in uniform came in, shouting, 'Stand still, you fucken rubbish.' The men obeyed. 'And who is Dell?' Dell raised his hand. 'Come, then. You going to Pollsmoor.'

Laughter and jeers at that. 'Hey, you better stop by the drugstore and get him some Vaseline. His white ass gonna be working overtime.'

The cop had Dell by the arm, shoved him out into the corridor. Cuffed him. Pushed him toward the door that led out into the car park. Dell expected to be put into a truck with other men, but he was led to a white Ford sedan, dented and without hubcaps. A man at the wheel and another sitting in the rear.

Something was thrown over Dell's head. A coarse jailhouse

blanket. Stinking. He struggled, heard the car door open. He was propelled forward and landed on the floor of the car, wedged between the front and rear seats. The engine cranked. He fought to lift himself.

Felt a hand push his face down onto the floor, heard the man in the rear speak. 'You just be still now, boy, or we'll be obliged to lock you in the trunk.'

The voice that had been in his head just before the nightmare began. The voice of his father. Earl Robert Goodbread.

chapter 17

FIRST HIS CELL PHONE SIGNAL WENT MISSING IN THE HILLS. THEN THE PINE forests were strangled by dry veld, and the wide road – white lines vivid on the smooth black asphalt – gave way to a narrow track of cracked tar and potholes. Finally the blacktop dwindled to nothing and the tires of Zondi's BMW drummed on sand corrugated from drought, a cloud of dust pursuing him.

He pulled off the road, left the air-conditioned cabin and stepped out into heat so dry that when he inhaled it, it seemed to microwave him from within. Looked out over the valley spread below him. Once he had called it home.

This place, with its red hills and craters of erosion like axe wounds in the flesh-colored soil, reminded him of a corpse. The corpse of the boy Zondi and Inja Mazibuko and the others had killed, in sight of where he stood now.

Zondi had left the valley not long after the boy's death. Made his way up to Johannesburg, where he had found himself in other mobs that had dispensed street justice to suspected informers and collaborators. But he'd always stayed at the rear, an observer, feeding on the rush, but never striking the killing blows. And he'd been back here only once, to bury his mother. Sixteen years ago.

And what the fuck are you doing here now? he asked. Got no reply.

Zondi saw a man pushing a bicycle up the hill. Part of a car fender, mangled and twisted, lay across the saddle and handle-bars. A boy of maybe ten walked behind the bike, supporting the weight of the metal, stopping it from dragging on the ground.

The man, in a torn brown shirt and old suit trousers, was sweating, urging the boy on. The child was shoeless and Zondi remembered when his own feet had been immune to the heat of the sand and the sharpness of the rocks. He saw the boy's hands were bleeding from the sharp metal slicing into his flesh. The child kept his head down, following his father without complaint.

The man pushed the bicycle up to where Zondi stood. Stopped, sweat patterning the dust on his face. He leaned the bike against a thorn tree and approached Zondi with his hands cupped.

'A cigarette, please, brother.'

Zondi told him he didn't smoke. The boy looked at him, taking in the BMW that pinged as it cooled. Taking in Zondi's city clothes and Diesel sunglasses. Zondi reached into the car and came out with a plastic bag containing fruit and two cans of Coke. He didn't normally drink the stuff, but he'd felt tired on the road, and had used the caffeine rush to stay awake.

He held the bag out to the boy, who looked at his father. The man nodded. The child wiped his bloody hands on his shorts, and approached Zondi with his head bowed, not looking him in the eye. The boy extended his right hand, gripping his elbow with his left hand in the African way, and took the bag. He muttered his thanks and retreated, never showing his back to Zondi.

'When last did it rain?' Zondi asked the man.

The Zulu laughed. 'Can a dry old woman remember her wedding night?'

These fucking people, Zondi thought. *Everyone a poet.*

The man said, 'Are you going through to Greytown, brother?'

Zondi shook his head. 'Bhambatha's Rock.'

'You are with the government?'

Zondi opened his car door. 'No. It is my home.'

The man said nothing, but Zondi could see the disbelief in his eyes.

Zondi started the car, thought about throwing a U-turn and getting the hell out of there while he still could. But he released the brake and drove down toward the jumble of small buildings and sprawling huts, iron roofs sending back the sun like signal mirrors.

chapter 18

Sunday was late. Running across the veld toward the cultural village, her tennis shoes slapping the hard pathway, the betrothal beads rattling in her bag like a curse. She ducked into the gate, under a pair of crossed elephant tusks and a sun-bleached sign written in English. Passed a small bus, red with dust, the driver sitting behind the wheel reading a newspaper. A handful of sweating white people flicked through postcards in the shade of a reed gazebo. She saw Richard, in his skins and plumage, his fat belly leading him toward her.

Sunday sank to her knees. 'I'm sorry, father. The taxi was late.'

'Stand, daughter, stand.' She got to her feet and risked a glance up at him. He had never called her that before, used the term of respect. 'Is it true that you are to marry *Induna* Mazibuko this weekend?' Respect and something else in his voice. Fear.

She nodded. 'Yes, father.'

'Then it is not fitting for you to do the maiden's dance. You will demonstrate the loom weaving and help with the beer ceremony. And make sure you wear your betrothal beads, do you hear me?'

'Yes, father.' She bobbed and turned and hurried away to change.

How the word *induna* had flowed off Richard's tongue. Headman. Advisor to the chief. A man feared in these parts. She knew the old man by another name. Inja. Dog. That suited him far better. Like one of those scavenging mongrels down in Bhambatha's Rock, blue tongues panting, skinny ribs poking through mangy fur. The thought of his hands on her body made her want to vomit.

Then she saw something that cheered her. The small car belonging to Sipho, the AIDS educator from Durban. Parked in the shadow of the bus. There was no sign of Sipho, but she knew he would be in the vicinity, handing out the English papers nobody here could read.

Sunday sleepwalked her way through the next hour. Sat on a grass mat, her breasts covered by a bib of skin, as befitted a betrothed woman. The beads clutching at her throat. She weaved cloth on a wooden loom as the whites took their photos, her fingers moving automatically, braiding the colored strands, her mind far away.

Later she helped to serve traditional gourds of beer to the tourists. The men and women sitting in separate groups, according to custom. The women pretended to sip, grimacing. The men drank the beer and smacked their lips as if they were enjoying it, but looked as if they wanted to spit it out. Richard, as always, threw back a full gourd of the mud-colored liquid, patted his belly and burped, flashbulbs exploding as the tourists captured him to take home with them to whatever country made these pink people.

Sunday changed into her day clothes, stuffed the beads in the bag and hurried out to the car park. Sipho sat beside his car, beneath a tree, writing in a book. It was hard to believe he had the sickness. He seemed so young and healthy and his eyes shone when he looked up at her, smiling.

'How are you, Sunday?' He stood, pocketing the notebook.

She gave him a shy smile. 'I am well, thank you.'

'Are you going to the road?'

She nodded and he opened the car door for her. 'Let me give you a ride.'

Sunday hesitated. Knew it wasn't proper for a betrothed woman to be with a man unchaperoned, but when she saw nobody was watching she ducked into the car. Sipho closed the door and came around and got behind the wheel.

When he tried to start the car it made a sound like a sick animal. Then the engine caught and he laughed. 'One day I'll have something better.'

They bumped out onto the sand track that led to the main road where she would find her taxi. This was the third time Sunday had driven in a car. She knew minibus taxis, of course, but only twice before, on church trips, had she been squeezed into the rear seats of old cars, the flesh of the aunties at her side overflowing onto her like brown jelly. To sit up front, alone with a man, was a new experience for her.

'I hear you are to be married this weekend?' Sipho glanced across at her.

She nodded. He saw her expression and said nothing more.

'When are you going home?' she asked.

'In two days. I'm just here to finish my project. I don't think I will be coming back. I'm needed in the city.'

Sunday's heart sank. She hardly knew this boy, but the idea of not seeing him again was too much to bear. As if all hope would leave with him. Before she could stop herself she spoke. 'Take me with you to Durban. Please.'

He was staring at her. 'Are you serious?'

'Yes. If I marry this man, my life will be over. Please, Sipho.'

'But what will you do in Durban? It's not like here.'

'I'll do whatever I need to do. Please. I beg of you.'

He put his hand on hers for a second. 'I will be here in two days' time. If you still want to go, you can come with me. If you change your mind, that's okay.'

'I won't change my mind.'

They were at the main road. Sunday wished they could turn right and drive out of the valley now. Drive to Durban and a new life. But he stopped the car and she climbed out.

'You're sure of this?' Sipho asked.

'I'm sure.'

He waved and pulled away, and she watched as the red road swallowed the little car.

chapter 19

DRIVING. NO IDEA WHERE. OR FOR HOW LONG. DELL LAY UNDER THE blanket, hearing the tires on the blacktop. They had left the town behind. No more bleating horns and yelling taxi drivers. The car was out on the open road, moving at a constant speed.

The man in the rear didn't speak again, but it was his father. For sure. Dell could smell him. The same smell that had come from the clothes that hung in the bedroom closet of the house he grew up in, heavy with nicotine and booze and something indefinable. The smell of his father. He and his mother left behind in Durban while Goodbread was away killing people. First in Vietnam, and then in a bush war that had brought the superpowers to the ass-end of Africa, lured by Angolan oil.

Goodbread had been part of the CIA's covert 'black ops' in Angola until Jimmy Carter had pulled them out. Then he'd joined up with the South Africans, who had their own reasons for trying to bring Marxist Angola down.

Dell lay feeling the vibration of the car, but hearing the chatter of a helicopter, back in 1988. In the rear of a South African Air Force Puma, fighting nausea, watching the chopper's shadow skim the yellow dunes of the Namib desert. The seats had been removed and Dell sat on the floor, his head throbbing with stale booze and avgas.

Two South African crewmen upfront and five men in the rear with Dell. An Angolan with one empty eye-socket. A feral-looking Afrikaner. A child-sized bushman as wrinkled as a tortoise. A Cuban prisoner of war. And Earl Robert Goodbread.

Since midnight, when Dell – up in South West Africa

reporting on the last days of the bush war – had run into his father in a beer hall in Windhoek, he'd heard Bobby Goodbread holding forth in Portuguese, German and Afrikaans.

'Languages are like goddam viruses, boy. I just pick them up,' Goodbread had told him on one of the rare occasions he'd been home when Dell was a kid.

And now he was speaking Spanish to the Cuban Mig pilot who had been shot down and paraded before the media in Windhoek. The Cuban sat with his back to the chopper door, staring into his lap, his hands cuffed before him. Goodbread, wearing faded brown fatigues, crouched beside him. At fifty he was tanned and muscular, good looking in a craggy, Clint Eastwood way. White teeth exposed in a *fuck you* grin.

Dell caught the word '*niños*' above the smack of the rotors. This got the Cuban looking up and he nodded, mumbled in Spanish. Dell thought he heard '*dos*'. The prisoner held his cuffed hands level with his head, then a little higher. Maybe showing the height of his two kids. Trying out an uncertain smile. He was dark haired, with an almost pretty face. Bruised around the left eye.

Goodbread said something and pointed at Dell. The Cuban said in English, 'This is your son?'

'*Sí,*' Goodbread said.

'Okay. I can see it.'

Goodbread laughed. Dell shut his eyes. The night before he'd been out drinking with a guy from the *New York Times*, knew it was time to leave when the beerhall started spinning and the correspondent lost his tongue down the throat of hooker who looked like Grace Jones. As Dell pushed through the crowd, he felt somebody grip his arm. Turned and looked into his father's face.

'You not even going to greet your daddy?' That voice. Big and loud as Texas.

Dell shook his arm free. He hadn't seen his father in ten years, wanted to keep on walking. But he knew if he didn't sit, he'd fall. So he slumped into a chair. Bobby Goodbread poured him a Jack and Coke and pressed the glass into his hands.

The night passed in a blur of booze. At dawn Goodbread had told Dell that he and his men were escorting the Cuban back up to the Angolan border. Offered to take Dell along for the ride, let him see a commie war hero up close. Dell too wasted to disagree. An hour later, head vibrating and stomach heaving, he regretted his decision.

Goodbread, squatting beside the prisoner, lit a smoke and handed it to him. The man said, '*Gracias*.'

'So you like to fly?' Goodbread asked in English.

'*Sí*, I love it,' the Cuban aviator said.

'You wanna fly again?'

'*Sí*, I hope I shall.'

'Then you may just be in luck, *señor*.'

Goodbread nodded at the bushman, who rolled open the chopper door behind the Cuban. Dell felt the tug of the wind, his hair flying across his eyes. Gripped the bulkhead behind him. Saw the South African pilot, in his Ray-Ban aviators, look back over his shoulder, sun catching a gold tooth as he grinned beneath his Magnum P. I. mustache.

The prisoner turned and stared out over the endless expanse of desert. The pilot banked the chopper and the Cuban started sliding backward out the open door, his cuffed hands scrambling for purchase. Goodbread stood, surefooted as surfer, and swung a boot, catching the Cuban in the head. Kicked him again. The man hovered for a moment in the doorway, eyes wide, clothes flapping, then he was gone, screaming, a black dot falling toward the yellow sand.

'*Adios*,' Goodbread said, and the bushman slammed the door shut. His father shouted to the pilot, 'What just happened here?'

'Commie fucker jumped, Major.'

Goodbread smiled down at Dell. Challenging him to say different. Dell said nothing and his father ignored him for the rest of the flight and left him standing on an airstrip just south of the Angolan border. Dell never wrote a word of what he'd witnessed in the helicopter. Never spoke of it.

After the bush war ended the South Africans had found a use for Goodbread's talents in their security police. The last time Dell had seen him had been on television, in 1994. On trial for massacring a black family in a ghetto township east of Johannesburg.

Dell heard doors slam. The car engine idled under the mutter of men's voices. He lifted himself up from the floor and was about to pull the blanket from his head when he felt the weight of a hand on his back.

'Do that, boy, and you're likely to be shot,' his father said. 'There's men out there skittish as deer.'

Dell allowed himself to be led from the car, flip-flops slapping cement. Pushed into another vehicle. Higher off the ground. A pickup truck or SUV. The smell of his father followed him in. He caught something else mixed in with the booze and cigarettes. Something sour, almost medicinal. Heard the low rumble of a big engine and they were moving again.

chapter 20

THE HALF-BREED WHORE LIFTED THE ORANGE DRESS OVER HER HEAD IN one motion, standing naked in front of Inja. She hadn't bothered with underwear. Inja looked at her breasts. Small, stretched and used up. A scar like raw liver ran across her belly, above the thick scrub of hair. Where a child had been pulled from her.

She kept on her red high heels. Toenails painted with chipped black varnish. 'What's your name?' Speaking fast like she was spitting the words, the way these people did.

'Moses.' Inja sat on the bed, fully dressed, hands dangling between his knees. Despite himself, he felt aroused.

'You going to part the waters, Moses?' Touching herself between her legs. Laughing the laugh of a street woman. He let the whore push him back on the bed, and felt her hands loosening his belt. 'Where you from?'

'I'm a Zulu.'

'Jesus,' she said, unzipping him. 'That's one hell of a cultural weapon you got on you.' Laughing again. An axle in need of grease. 'I better get danger pay.'

He watched as she tore a condom open with her teeth and forced it down onto him, using both hands. It pinched his flesh. He never used these things. He was an African man, he believed in meat on meat. No room for plastic. But today was different. He wanted to leave no trace of his presence.

Inja stood, still in his shirt, trousers bunched around his ankles. He grabbed the half-breed by the arm and pushed her onto the bed, kneeling, ass facing him.

'Hey, be nice, man,' she said.

He shoved himself into her, heard her grunt. Rode her like a mountain pony.

They were in a bedroom in some fancy apartment in Cape Town. Not as smart as the one belonging to the fat white man, but still nice. With a view out over the city and the harbor. Theron's idea. Saying they should have a little fun before Inja left. Saying a brothel keeper owed him, gave him use of her apartment and would throw in a couple of girls. On the house.

Inja had been tempted to end it in the car park beneath the apartment block. Then he'd thought it through. A dead cop in a car was one thing. A dead cop in bed with dead hookers was another.

Inja heard his flesh slapping against the woman's backside. Looked down and saw her cracked heels hanging over the edge of her shoes. Saw the swelling of flesh beneath her knees. Reached down and pinched her calf between thumb and forefinger, hard enough to leave a bruise.

'Jesus fuck!' she said, twisting, one shoe slipping off and hitting the blond wood floor like a gunshot.

Inja finished, heard his breath, hard and loud. Sagged against her, holding onto her wide hips for support. Withdrew.

The half-breed looked at him over her shoulder. 'You don't waste time, hey?'

'Wait here,' he said, pulling up his trousers, tucking himself in, condom still in place. Forcing his zipper closed. 'I'm not finished.'

She shrugged, rolling over onto her back. He left the room, walked down the corridor. Heard Theron and the other whore busy in the main bedroom. Inja went into the bathroom, tugged off the condom and flushed it. Watched it spin and disappear in the whirlpool of water. Wiped the chrome handle of the toilet with a towel.

Went back to the bedroom, the smell getting him before he'd

crossed the threshold. The whore, still naked, sat on the bed smoking a meth pipe. A thin glass tube held over a lighter flame, the contents bubbling.

She exhaled a lungful of bitter smoke. Offered the pipe. 'You want?'

He shook his head and she brought the pipe to her mouth again. Inja stood behind her, lifted his duffel bag onto the bed. Unzipped it and took out the pistol. Screwed on the silencer. The whore oblivious, lost in her pipe. He slipped the gun into the waistband of his trousers, covered it with his shirt.

'Come,' he said.

'Come where?' she asked, turning to him. Her eyes like burn marks in brown cloth.

'To the others.'

'You mean like a foursome?' He nodded. 'Okay. Cool by me.'

The half-breed sucked the last of the pipe and coughed so hard she almost puked. She blew her nose on the sheet and laid the pipe and lighter beside the bed. She slipped her foot into the shoe that had dropped and stood up, wobbled, dizzy from the tik. Sent a hand to the wall to steady herself.

'Wow. Happy days is here again.' Laughing as she clattered out the room ahead of him, naked flesh wobbling.

Inja nodded at her to open the main bedroom and followed her in. Theron and the other half-breed were screwing on the bed, the Boer on top, his pimply ass white where his tan ended. Theron stopped pumping and looked up at them. 'What's this?'

Inja's whore said, 'He thought you want some company.'

'Hell, I'm up for it,' the Boer said, rolling over to prove he was.

Inja shot him in the forehead. Shot the whore under him next. His whore turned and fell off her heels, trying to get away. He shot her in the back of the head, the entry wound invisible in her kinky hair, but a mess on the bedroom door. The gun coughed three more times as he shot each of them again, just to be sure.

Inja lifted Theron's suit trousers off the back of a chair, found the keys to the Benz. Then he wiped down everything he had touched, got his bag and left the apartment. As he hit the stairs, his stomach rumbled. He was going to get that sheep's head. Then he was going home.

chapter 21

ZONDI PARKED OUTSIDE THE RED TELEPHONE KIOSK ON THE MAIN ROAD of Bhambatha's Rock, waves of heat rising from the corrugated metal container, making the cartoony silhouettes of people talking on phones look as if they were dancing. He stepped out of the BMW and heard the shrill chirp as he locked it. Drawing eyes like meat flies, the tall black man in his fancy car and city threads.

He stood in the lava-colored light of afternoon, smelling the old familiar smells. Dust. Dung. Rotting garbage. The stink of rural poverty. Ignoring the blank stares of the vendors who squatted on the sidewalk, selling sweetmeats and snuff and purgatives, alongside baboon skulls and roots and skins. Deaf to the pleas of the beggars with cupped hands and minds numbed by alcohol and disease. Only five hours' drive from Johannesburg, but another world, this.

The minister of justice watched Zondi from an election poster tied to a pole. The familiar bullet head, hooded eyes peering out from behind wire-framed glasses. The small mouth that looked as if it had bitten into something sour. The man who had put Zondi's mentor into the ground. Zondi breathed through his anger, letting it drain away. That was another battle. For another time.

He walked into the phone container. If it was hot outside, the interior of the metal box was like a convection oven. No windows. No AC. Not even a fan. Just a fleshless girl in a cheap nylon dress slumped on a stool, fluffy high-heel slippers lying beside her like a pair of dead parrots. She wafted at the air with a gossip magazine, jaws working on a stick of gum. Her cheap perfume smelled like urine.

Zondi unfolded the wedding invite and showed it to her. 'Was this faxed from here?' She looked at the phone number and date printed on the bottom of the page and nodded. 'Do you know who sent it?' he asked.

'It wasn't my shift. You must come back later and see Vusi.'

'What time?'

'After last dish.' After supper.

Zondi went out to his car, unlocked it. Heard somebody call his name. An enormous man, as tall as he was fat, lumbered toward him, carrying a plastic bag in one hand and a liter bottle of Coke in the other. Despite the heat the man wore a dark suit, vest, white shirt and black necktie. Zondi could hear the stranger's massive thighs whisper to one another as he approached.

The man said, 'It's me. Giraffe.'

Zondi tried to find any trace of the lanky, skinny kid he had once known. He couldn't. 'Giraffe?'

The fat man wheezed a laugh. 'Ja, don't tell me. More like a hippo these days.'

He stuck out a hand and Zondi shook it. Like shaking a damp dishtowel. Zondi freed his hand and wiped it dry on his trousers.

'Come, open this car, put on the fridge,' Giraffe said. 'It's too bloody hot out here.'

Zondi was about to make an excuse and drive away, then he shrugged and slid behind the wheel. Turned the key in the ignition and felt the AC blast out.

The fat man heaved himself in beside Zondi, and the car sagged. 'So, my friend, are you back for long?' Mopping his face with a blue handkerchief.

'No, just a day or two.'

'I hear you're up in Jo'burg?'

'Yes.'

'Good for you. This is no place for a man, I'm telling you.'

Giraffe unpacked his meal onto his lap, and the car was filled with the stink of rural junk food. Chicken feet and beaks, known as *walkie-talkies* down here. A full loaf of white bread, the top sliced off, the center hollowed out and filled with curried meat. A *bunnychow*.

'And what do you do these days?' asked Zondi, watching as the man lifted a yellow chicken foot, wrinkled and gelatinous, to his mouth. Crunched his way through cartilage, skin and claws. Reached for a beak cooked in batter.

'I'm an undertaker. That's my place over there.' Pointed an oily finger toward the cinderblock building across the road, picture window filled with coffins.

'Business must be good.'

'Too good, Zondi. Too good. Lots of TB, and of course the taxi wars are keeping me busy right now. But mostly AIDS.'

The undertaker tore loose a chunk of bread and dunked it in the curry. Zondi remembered that this full loaf was known as a *coffin bunny*. Giraffe crammed in the food, the white bread bulging out. He belched and leaned toward Zondi, who caught the ripe mix of curried meat and embalming fluid.

'This AIDS. It is worse than anybody says, my friend. Especially the women and the girls – they are dying like flies. And you know what these people are like,' waving a beringed hand at the passersby, 'they must have the very best coffin even though they don't have two cents to wipe their asses with. I tried, Zondi, to offer them cheap pine boxes. But no. Top of the range, my friend. Top of the range or nothing.' Shaking his head. As the light caught his face, the features of the delicate youth Zondi remembered surfaced for a moment in the sea of fat, then sank again. The undertaker belched and shoveled in more curry. 'Have you stayed in touch with Inja?'

Zondi shook his head, staring down the street, watching a minibus taxi take on passengers. 'No. Maybe I'll bump into him while I'm down here.'

'He's away, I hear. Out of town.' Chewing. 'You know, we three are the last from those old days. I buried Mussolini, Dudu and Solly myself. Gunshot. AIDS. AIDS.' Swallowing and fighting for breath. Chasing the food with Coke from the liter bottle. Gas escaped from him, like from a punctured blimp. 'Inja has done well for himself. The chief has rewarded him, made him an *induna*.' Waving a greasy hand toward the man on the election poster. Feeding again. 'And you know Inja's got a badge, now?' Zondi turned to look at the undertaker, playing dumb. 'Ja, the chief has appointed him a special agent in that police unit of his. A powerful man now, is Inja.'

Of course Inja the dog ran with the minister's new pack – a *Tonton Macoute* of licensed killers, ready to do their master's dirty work. Zondi's boss had been vocal in his opposition to the special unit. Left him dead and buried.

'You know he's taking a fourth bride this weekend? Inja?' Zondi lied with a shake of his head. Giraffe sat back and sighed. 'Poor child. She's a replacement, I suppose, for the wife I buried last month.' Zondi stared at him. Said nothing. 'So small and skinny, that one, I could have fitted her into a tomato box.'

The big man had ingested all the food. He shot a cuff and looked at the gold watch recessed into the fat of his wrist. 'I must go. An appointment with the recently bereaved.'

Giraffe reached out a limp hand, sticky now. Reluctantly, Zondi shook it.

'Pop in for a visit before you leave. I'll show you my set-up.'

Zondi nodded and watched the fat man roll out, halting a taxi in its tracks as he held up a hand and crossed the road. The undertaker stopped before the picture window, lifted an arm and wiped at a spot on the glass with the sleeve of his suit coat. Turned, paused for a moment, then walked away, as padded as the insides of the coffins on display behind him.

chapter 22

DELL, STILL WITH THE BLANKET OVER HIS HEAD, WAS LED FROM THE CAR. He heard the sound of chickens, and a sheep's low moan in the distance. No city buzz. The smell of the country in his nostrils. Rich soil and animal shit. He could see part of his one flip-flop, past the drape of the blanket, crunching on dark gravel. Night had fallen. Dell stumbled, sent out his cuffed hands and felt the shape of a doorframe.

'Easy,' his father said. Guiding him up a step.

'Where the fuck am I?' Dell asked.

'Watch your tongue, boy. There are children present.'

And Dell heard the unmistakable patter of kids running on wooden floors. Light drumming, almost animal-like. The sound the twins had made on the floors back home.

The pain of memory sharpened when he was led past a TV warbling out the intro to a program that had been one of Rosie's lowbrow pleasures. An Afrikaans quiz show, where contestants listened to snatches of music and had to identify the tunes. Dell heard the greetings of the show's host, a man with the smile of a pedophile. He saw Rosie curled up on their sofa, eating popcorn, laughing, singing along with the mindless songs of her childhood.

A door closed, muting the music. Dell shuffled on, his father's hand on his arm. He heard a young man's voice, a low mumble. Another door closed. The fingers released him and bedsprings creaked as somebody sat down.

'Okay, you can lose the blanket,' his father said.

Dell lifted his cuffed hands and pulled the blanket from his head, blinking in the sudden light. He saw an old man sitting on the bed, in the glare of a lamp. Looked around for Bobby Goodbread.

'It's me, you dumb bastard.' The old man spoke in his father's voice.

Goodbread was hollowed out. Emaciated. His frame stripped of flesh and muscle. Skin, gray as dishwater, pulled across sunken cheeks. Thick white hair cropped close to his skull. Dark eyes peering out from under heavy lids.

'What the fuck's going on?' Dell asked.

'Good question, boy. One I can't give the answer it rightly deserves. Not until we have more time. Let's just say I saved your skinny white butt, and leave it there for now.' The Texan accent was as Dell remembered it. Strong and loud. Like a ventriloquist's voice emerging from the wasted body.

Dell shook his head. Staring at his father. 'Get these cuffs off. Get me to a phone.'

Goodbread lit a cigarette, sucking on it like it was an iron lung. 'Who you gonna call, boy? The cops?' Coughed. Wiped his mouth on the back of his hand. 'The people who murdered your kin were fixing to send you to Pollsmoor Prison. Throw you in with the half-breed gangsters who'd kill you for the price of a cigarette. And believe me, nobody would ask no fucking questions.'

'And you know this how?'

'Same way I knew what had happened to you. Same way I know who drove the big old truck that killed your family. I'm still connected, boy.' Drawing long and hard on the cigarette, speaking around smoke. 'Lot of seriously disaffected people in this sorry country. Law enforcement. Military. People who look out for one another.'

Dell watched him. Listening for the lies. A knock at the door. Goodbread held up a hand, went to the door, opened it a crack, then stepped out and shut it after him. Dell heard his father's low drawl, and a female voice in reply.

Dell was in a woman's bedroom. A double bed with a floral comforter, hastily pulled straight, two Afrikaans gossip magazines lying beside the single pillow. Dürer's praying hands in copper, hanging above the bed. Thick orange drapes across the window. An old-style wooden vanity table, with chipped legs and a mirror gone smoky. A pine closet loomed over the bed, one door open, clothes bulging out. And a smell: cloying perfume and aging woman flesh. Like Dell's grandmother's room, when he'd visited her as a kid.

The door opened and Goodbread came back in, followed by a blonde woman. At first glance Dell thought she was middle aged, busty, with a cigarette dangling from her lips. Then he saw she was much older, at least sixty, gray hair dyed straw yellow, thick make-up caking the cracks in her face. She wheeled a plastic basin mounted on a metal frame.

'This fine lady, who will remain nameless, has kindly agreed to give you a shave and a haircut.' Goodbread said.

The blonde smiled at Dell, painted lips curling back from the cigarette. The smile of a woman who flirted as a reflex.

Dell didn't smile back. 'What the fuck for?'

Her smile disappeared, and she clucked. 'He's got his daddy's mouth, okay.' Speaking English with an Afrikaans accent. A low voice, that crawled out from under years of booze and cigarettes. His father's kind of woman.

Goodbread had an arm around her thick waist, smiling down at her. 'Now, that's a lie and you know it.' He was screwing her, Dell supposed.

Goodbread crossed to Dell. 'Meet the new you.'

He held up a South African driver's license, a laminated plastic rectangle the size of a credit card. Dell saw the face of a man his age, clean shaven, with short, dark hair. Gazing blankly at the camera. Caught the name David Stander before

Goodbread set the license down on the vanity table and unlocked Dell's handcuffs. Dell flexed his fingers, wrists tingling where the metal had cut into his flesh.

'We'll talk later, okay?' Goodbread left the room, closing the door after him.

The woman wheeled the basin up to the vanity. 'Come, sit.'

Dell did as she said. The blonde, cigarette still hanging from her lip, unwound the bandage from his head, saw him wince.

'Shame,' she said, parting his hair, squinting through the smoke. 'It's okay, just a few cuts. But I'm sorry, this is going to sting you a bit.'

She stubbed out the cigarette in an overflowing ashtray and pulled the basin closer. It was filled with warm water and she had him sit with his head hanging back over the rim as she shampooed his hair. It stung. Then she rolled the basin away and laid a towel across his shoulders, turning him so that he faced the mirror.

'Where am I?' he asked.

'You better wait and ask your dad.' Scratching for a pair of scissors and a comb in the vanity drawer, squinting down at the photograph on the driver's license.

'Just tell me,' he said.

'I don't want no trouble.'

He looked up at her. 'Lady, you've already got trouble. You know who I am?'

She took his head in her hands and turned it to face forward again. 'You his son. That's all I need to know.'

The blonde lit another cigarette, left it pressed between her wrinkled lips, as if it would keep her secrets safe. Then she started cutting Dell's hair. She was good, her hands moving in a practiced blur, his salt-and-pepper curls falling to his shoulders and onto the floor.

He hadn't had short hair in nearly thirty years, since he'd

finished his compulsory stint in South Africa's apartheid army. Went into basic training as a conscientious objector. A pacifist. Marched with a broomstick instead of an R1 rifle. The Afrikaners he was with had called him a faggot. A commie. Beaten the shit out of him for sport. He'd ended up as a medic on a Pretoria infantry base, consuming all the chemicals he could lay his hands on, two years passing in a fucked-up smear.

The woman left him with a fringe and sideburns. Looking like somebody he'd avoid on the street. Then she slipped on rubber gloves and mixed up a thick paste in a plastic bowl. Massaged the paste into his hair, dying it dark. Got busy with a hand dryer that screamed in his ears and burned the cuts in his scalp. She trimmed his beard with the scissors. Lathered his face with foam and shaved him with a straight razor. Did it expertly.

Goodbread was back in the room. 'Well, I'll be dipped in shit,' he said, checking out Dell's reflection.

The woman laughed through phlegm. 'Ja. He's almost as handsome as his dad.'

Dell stared into the mirror. The man looking back at him was a dead-ringer for the one who'd kicked the Cuban out of the chopper twenty-five years ago.

chapter 23

THE BOY LIFTED A SHEEP'S HEAD OUT OF THE BUCKET AND STUCK IT ON the fence pole, under the yellow light of a naked light bulb. Then he fired up the blowtorch that snaked away from a rusted red gas cylinder and applied the blue flame to the head, until the wool burned away and the eyes popped and bubbled.

Inja sat on an old car seat, drinking a brandy and Coke, letting the smell of burning flesh fill his nostrils. He was in the shackland that spread like a disease beside the freeway between Cape Town and the airport. Sitting in the yard of a house thrown together from pieces of rusted corrugated iron and bits of wood. A one-roomed hovel identical to the others that sprawled out into the darkness.

The yard was lit by the cooking fires and the one electric bulb that drew pirate power from a cable patched into the nearby mains pole. A shiny new TV sat on top of a ten-gallon drum, blaring out a soccer match. Drunken men crowded around it, hurling abuse at another bad South African team performance.

Inja watched as a crone slid the sheep's head from the fence pole and threw it onto an open fire. She stabbed another head, already cooked, with a sharpened spike, and lifted it out of the flames. Split it down the middle with an axe. She dumped one half of the head onto a tin plate and brought it across to Inja. He gave her money, which she tucked into her bra, and she went back to the fires.

Now that Inja had the food before him, his appetite evaporated, and he felt nausea grip his innards and squeeze them hard. He put the plate down beside him, and forced back the scalding bile that filled his mouth. Washed it down with a slug of his drink. It was back again. The thing in his blood that wanted to kill him.

It had started when he was shot three months before. One of his rivals had ambushed Inja's car on the winding pass down to Bhambatha's Rock. Thrown a tree trunk across the road, and riddled the car with AK-47 fire when Inja's driver slowed. The driver died, his brains flung onto the windshield, and Inja had been shot in the leg.

The man with the AK-47 had fled. But not before Inja saw his face. After he was discharged from hospital, Inja went to his enemy's house with an axe and took his head, like one of these sheep. Stuck it on a pole in the village and posted armed guards under it. Forced the people in the village to watch as the birds picked out the eyes and tongue and the flesh rotted and blackened over the next week. A message.

When Inja returned to the hospital to have the sutures removed from his leg, a young white doctor came to speak to him. A woman with yellow hair and a foreign voice that he struggled to understand. The doctor told him it was routine to test the blood of people admitted to the hospital for HIV, here where the incidence was the highest in the world. Told Inja that the virus was eating him, that he had what was called *full-blown AIDS*. That he needed to go on medication called antiretrovirals. Inja had refused. Left the hospital.

He didn't believe in this white man's nonsense. And he was in good company. A previous president of South Africa hadn't believed HIV caused AIDS. The health minister had said you could cure it by eating beetroot and garlic. The new president, a Zulu, said you didn't need to wear a plastic when you fucked, all you needed to do was shower afterwards.

And the men in Inja's area said if you got this thing it was easy to cure if you had sex with a virgin girl. The only way to be sure of their maidenhood was to get them very young. Inja had abducted a toddler child playing in the dirt near a hut of one of his enemies. Raped it and killed it and shoved it halfway down a pit latrine. Waited to be cured.

But he had still felt the weakness. So he had gone to his traditional doctor, his *sangoma*, told him what he had done. The witch doctor said he had brought disgrace upon his ancestors by raping and murdering a child. That the only way he could properly purge himself of this curse was to marry a virgin in the traditional way.

Inja had known immediately who to choose to save his life. And now he had the proof that she was intact. Come the weekend, he would be cured. The thought of this relaxed the knot in Inja's stomach, and he lifted the jawbone of the sheep, the teeth grinning at him, and he gnawed at the flesh, feeling the juices flow down his face and onto his shirt.

Inja's work here was done. He'd dumped the Boer's Benz in the shackland. It would be stripped by morning. In an hour he would fly home and report back to his chief, the minister of justice. Tell him there were no mouths left to speak to his enemies.

Then Inja saw that the soccer game had given way to a news broadcast. Saw a face on the screen that he recognized. Inja stood, still holding the jawbone of the sheep in his hand. He shouted for quiet. Shouted so loud, and with such authority, that the drunken men fell silent.

Inja stared at the photograph of the white man on the TV. The half-breed's cuckold of a husband. The one who had survived the car accident. And had now escaped from prison. Inja dropped the sheep's jaw onto the dirt, grabbed his bag, and walked toward the street. He would find this white man. And kill him himself.

chapter 24

DELL, HEAD AGAIN COVERED BY THE BLANKET, LET HIS FATHER LEAD him from the farmhouse across an expanse of gravel. Heard a door squeal open and shut. Felt concrete beneath his feet. Shrugged off the blanket and found himself in a cramped room that looked as if it had once been a garage. Unpainted plaster walls. Silver sheet iron supported by bare roof beams. A metal door, bolted, still painted primer red. One small window, covered by frayed yellow curtains. A bed. A sofa. The medicinal smell that clung to his father was thick in the air of the room.

Goodbread sat down on the sagging sofa positioned with its back to the door. A bare electric bulb dangled from the roof, hard shadows hiding his eyes and pooling beneath his sunken cheekbones. His hands, a mottled landscape of veins, rested on the knees of his khaki trousers.

A half-empty bottle of Jack Daniel's stood beside his work boots on the cement floor. No sign of a glass. Dell sat on the narrow bed. Pillow and blankets squared away like in the military. Or prison.

He stared at the old stranger. 'Who killed my family?'

Goodbread fired up a cigarette, waving the match dead. 'As I hear it told, the man driving the truck goes by the name of Moses Mazibuko. Better known as Inja. Means dog up in Zululand.' Sucked smoke. Coughed. 'Takes his orders from the minister of justice. Now, if that isn't a fucking joke, kindly tell me when one comes along.'

'Why did he want to kill us?'

'He was after your wife. Rest of you were collateral damage.'

Pulling hard on the cigarette, the end glowing red. Holding the smoke in his lungs, eyes closed. Then exhaling.

Dell shook his head. 'Bullshit. Nobody had reason to murder Rosie.'

'But they had a few million reasons to kill Ben Baker.' Goodbread looked at Dell out of the shadows. 'You know about her and Baker?'

'Yes.'

'I suspect she was with him the night he was hit. Saw who did it. Got away somehow, but this Inja tracked her down and...' Shrugging his bony shoulders. 'Guess I don't need to sing you the rest of that sad song.'

Dell saw Rosie's face the morning after Baker's murder. Her eyes empty. In emotional lockdown. He watched the old man smoke. 'Where are we?'

'An hour and some north of Cape Town. That's all you need to know. For the protection of the people over yonder.' Waving his cigarette toward the farmhouse.

'And what happens now?'

'You sleep. You look like ten thousand miles of bad road.'

'Don't fuck with me. You've got a plan. Talk.'

Goodbread paused with the cigarette halfway to his lips. Held up a hand for silence. Dell heard the low rumble of an engine, the crunch of tires on gravel. Moving fast for an old man, Goodbread dropped the smoke to the floor, crossed to the wall switch and killed the light.

'Hunker yourself down behind the sofa, where you can't be seen from the window. And stay there. Don't move one goddam muscle. Got me?'

Dell obeyed, squatting down on the cement floor. A flare of headlamps lit the drapes, throwing a sick yellow light into the room. Goodbread stood with his back flat to the wall between the door and the window. He took a pistol from under his baggy shirt. Cocked it. The headlamps slid away from the window and Dell heard the moan of brakes as the vehicle stopped, engine idling.

Heard footsteps on the gravel and then a fist hammering at the door, a voice saying in thick English: 'Police. Open up.'

GOODBREAD STOOD HOLDING THE PISTOL. READY. MORE KNOCKING. Somebody tried the handle of the locked door. He heard the woman's voice coming from outside, speaking in Afrikaans. 'That room is empty.'

A man's voice in reply. 'Unlock it and let us see, Mrs Vorster.'

'I can't. My son has the keys. He's in town. At church.'

'Who lives in here?'

'I told you. Nobody. A foreman used to. But he's gone now, to Walvis Bay.'

Heard another voice, a man with a colored accent. 'Lady, if you seen this Goodbread or his son, better you tell us now, otherwise you gonna be in big trouble.'

'I'm telling you, I haven't seen these people. Where do you come on this?'

Goodbread was about to risk a glance out the gap in the drapes when a flashlight beam sliced through the darkness, the cop outside standing so close that Goodbread could hear him breathing as he peered into the room.

DELL WATCHED THE DISC OF LIGHT skim across the wall and the floor and land on the back of the sofa. For a moment he nearly stood up with his hands in the air. Ready to surrender. Get them to call his lawyer – the senior one – and bring him up from Cape Town to straighten out this mess. Then he saw Theron in the courtroom, laughing with the black man who looked like a pimp. Saw the bodies of his family in the morgue.

Dell stayed down.

GOODBREAD FELT THE TRIGGER of the 9mm beneath his fingertips, ready to bring the gun up in an arc and shoot the cop through the glass. Then the beam sucked itself back into blackness and was gone.

The white cop spoke as he walked away from the window. 'I'll leave my card with you, Mrs Vorster. If you hear anything you call me. It would be better for you.'

Doors slapped closed and the vehicle reversed, headlamps raked the drapes again, floating a yellow rectangle of light across the room, then the driver shifted gear and the vehicle crunched across the gravel and the room went dark.

Goodbread heard the truck bump down the track to the main house where it stopped. Heard a snatch of conversation in Afrikaans, Althea Vorster and the cops talking. A car door slammed and the cop truck took off, motor fading into the night.

Goodbread stayed still, waiting. Listening. Till all he heard was the wheeze of his breath and the ticking of the tin roof as it cooled. He engaged the safety on the pistol and laid the gun on the counter beside the sink. Switched on the light bulb.

'Okay, boy. You can stand.'

The man who looked like he once had came slowly to his feet, blinking. Gripping the bottle of Jack Daniel's by the neck, like it was a weapon.

'What the hell were you gonna do, boy? Invite them in for cocktails?'

Goodbread laughed. And then coughed. A spasm that he couldn't control. He turned away from Dell, leaned against the wall and hacked like a sick dog, covering his mouth so that his son didn't see the blood that flowed up crimson from his lungs.

chapter 26

ZONDI SAT ON A NARROW BED THAT STANK OF SWEAT, LISTENING TO THE window glass vibrate in time to music from the tavern next door. Zulu bubblegum. Music from his youth, when he had lived in this hellhole of a town. An unhappy time. All about waiting to escape.

He'd checked himself into a room for the night. A cinder-block square, hidden behind the beauty salon in an alley off the main road of Bhambatha's Rock. A bed, a sink, a wooden chair, and a chipped closet with one door that hung off a broken hinge. Judging by the wrinkled pile of skin magazines that lay beside the bed, it was a room used by truckers and delivery men.

Zondi could have stayed in one of the quaint bed and break-fasts – all fluffy comforters and brass beds – in the white town of Dundee, an hour away. A place that catered to tourists come to visit the battlefields that had absorbed plenty of blood during wars between Zulus and Boers. Zulus and British. British and Boers. This was an area famous for its bloodshed.

But he wanted to be here. In Bhambatha's Rock. As much as he told himself he was here to find the girl, he knew that was only part of this journey. He needed to be back here where it all started, where his source code was written. Where all those zeros and ones had combined to make him what he was. Whatever that might be.

Zondi stood and put his duffel bag in the closet, his nostrils twitching at the smell of sweat and cockroach pellets and the ash of mosquito coils. He wouldn't unpack. Keep his clothes in the bag, protected from the stink.

He opened his wallet and removed a few banknotes, put them

into his pocket. Enough for tonight. Then he knelt and wedged the wallet and the keys to his BMW between the bedsprings and the reeking mattress. Not very secure, but better than keeping them on his body, in this town of bandits. A frontier town ruled by Inja Mazibuko, the nearest cops fifty miles away.

Each leg of the bed stood on a brick. An African superstition. To make the bed too high for a little demon known as a *tokoloshe* to climb up and take you during the night. He remembered being terrified of the *tokoloshe* as a child. Didn't fear that devil any longer.

Zondi locked the room, catching the night soil stench of the communal shithouse. He walked up the alley to the main road, passing the entrance to the tavern. Fluorescent strips threw a sordid green light down on men sitting in plastic chairs, arranged around steel tables, drinking beer from bottles, shouting at each other about girls and money and soccer. Black men of all ages, united in one common purpose: to drink themselves comatose. The few women in the room were wide hipped like skittles, ready to roll onto their backs for the price of a beer or two.

Zondi heard a woman in the doorway shout a comment at him. He was wearing jeans and a T-shirt. Reeboks. But he didn't look like he belonged here. He ignored her. Only rural Africans seemed to find her body type attractive these days: huge ass and thighs. The urban definition of African beauty had changed for ever when Naomi Campbell pranced down the catwalk. These women were of no interest to Zondi. No blondes. No skeletal apocalyptic whores. He was safe.

Zondi passed his car, parked on the sandy sidewalk, and crossed to the red phone container that squatted beneath one of the few streetlights. Zondi stepped into the container. A woman with a baby tied to her back was shouting into one of the phones, speaking to her husband in Durban. Asking him when he was going to send her money. The call ended with the woman cursing. She bumped past Zondi, the baby crying as if it had sucked sour milk from her tit.

A chubby guy in his mid-twenties, wearing small-town bling and designer knock-offs, sat on the stool beside the phones, clipping his toenails. Zondi watched as a crescent of nail spun through the air and landed in the dust on the metal floor. The man gave him a glance, then went on to his next toe.

'You Vusi?' Zondi asked.

'Ja. And?' the man said.

Zondi unfolded the fax of the wedding invite. 'You remember sending this?'

Vusi eyed it, shrugged. 'Ja.'

'Who did you send it for?'

'A girl.'

'What girl?'

'Just a girl.'

Vusi attacked his big toenail with the clippers. It was a thick yellow nail, and the small chrome clippers weren't up to the task. He grimaced as he squeezed, and the clippers broke and one half flew off and clattered to the floor.

'Fucken fong kong shit,' Vusi said.

Zondi held out a fifty-rand note. 'You need to buy yourself a better pair of clippers.'

Vusi reached for the money. Zondi kept it just out of his grasp. He pointed to the photograph of the girl in tribal dress. 'Was it her?'

The man squinted, shrugged. 'Could be. She wasn't dressed like that.'

'You know where I can find this girl?'

'Looks like the Zulu Kingdom.' Saw Zondi's blank look. 'Where they do the tribal shit for the tourists. On the Greytown road.'

Zondi handed over the money and walked out. He'd drive up

there in the morning. To see the girl who looked so much like her mother. Didn't know what he'd do when he found her.

As he stepped off the sidewalk, a white minibus taxi, made yellow by the sodium light, slammed to a halt. Blocking his path. He saw a man at the wheel and another man sliding the side door open, stepping out. Zondi moved to his left, to skirt the taxi. Heard the sound of a weapon being cocked, then felt something cool at the base of his skull.

'Get in, Zondi.' One of those voices that needs an elevator it comes from so deep. A voice he knew from somewhere long ago.

He felt a knee catch him on the thigh and he sprawled forward, onto the floor of the taxi. The gunman was in with him, slamming the door against Zondi's legs until he pulled them in. The taxi took off at speed. He'd come looking for his past. Seemed it had found him.

chapter 27

WHEN ZONDI TRIED TO LIFT HIMSELF FROM THE RATTLING FLOOR, THE man pushed him down. Frisked him. Zondi had no gun. He'd handed it in with his badge.

'Want to tell me what the fuck's going on?' he asked in Zulu.

A lighter flared in the man's left hand and he brought it to his face. Set fire to a fat spliff that dangled from his lips. 'Don't you remember me, Zondi?'

In the flickering light, Zondi saw a bald man in his forties, with a skull so scarred and pitted it looked as if he was wearing his brain on the outside. Zondi matched the face to the voice. 'Lucky,' he said.

The man smiled, exhaling a plume of bitter smoke. Clicked off the lighter. 'You think you can just come back here? Like you owe no debt?'

'Where are we going?' Zondi asked.

'I'm taking you into the hills. I'm going to shoot your knees fucked up. So you can't walk. And your elbows, so you can't crawl. Then I'm going leave you there to feed the hyenas.' Lucky laughed around the spliff.

He was the brother of Jola, the boy Zondi and Inja and the others had killed as teenagers. A man who had sworn a blood oath of vengeance. When Zondi had returned to this town for his mother's funeral, Lucky had been in prison in Durban, doing life for a taxi hit. And now he was out. Ready to make good his promise.

This was a land of Shakespearean feuds. Clans who lived facing one another across narrow valleys fought each other to the death, for reasons that time had obscured. Eighty years ago one man stole another's cow. Fifty years ago a man had insulted another. And generations of men were drawn into the faction fights. Zondi and his friends had killed Jola twenty years ago. No time at all.

Back in the eighties he and Inja and a handful of other boys had called themselves comrades, teenage supporters of the long-jailed Nelson Mandela, invisible on distant Robben Island. They had spouted Marxist slogans. Willing to offer their blood to end apartheid.

There were few of them, back then. This part of the country, kept in deliberate poverty by the white government, was the land of Zulu chieftains and tribal lore. Most of the chiefs had made deals with the whites, in exchange for a pathetic stipend, a stinking hut, a thin cow or two, and dominion over people even worse off than themselves. Young men who stood up in defiance were whipped. If that didn't stop them, they were killed. Their bodies dumped in front of the huts of their weeping mothers.

So Zondi and Inja and the rest had lived in fear. And when Inja came to them one day and said they had been infiltrated by a government spy, they didn't ask for much in the way of proof. Jola, who ran with them, had been seen sitting in a car with a cop, smoking a cigarette. They caught Jola on a footpath down in the valley. He denied everything, his eyes white with terror.

Inja struck the first blow, with a cane-cutter's machete that lifted a flap of flesh from the boy's arm. The air thick with the smell of blood and fear. After a moment's hesitation, the others joined in. With knives and sticks and axes. Zondi found a rock in his hands, brought it down on Jola's head. Saw the skull split beneath the tight black curls, showing white bone. Lifted the rock, a veil of blood and brain matter dangling from the dimpled underside. Brought it down again. And again.

When they were done, Zondi stepped back, looked down at his red hands still gripping the rock. Dropped the stone. His breath coming in gasps. The dust hanging heavy in the air. The thing that lay in the sand no longer resembled a boy.

The first and last time Zondi had killed.

Now he felt the weight of inevitability. He was the outsider and he would pay the price for what had happened twenty years ago. Only three of the six youths who had killed Jola had survived: Zondi, Giraffe and Inja.

Inja was Lucky's enemy. A powerful one. That defined him, gave him a role. Enemies were useful in this valley that had no need for peace. And Giraffe was a rich man by local standards, so accommodations would have been made. But Zondi had no place. He had given that up years ago.

Zondi saw a flare of approaching headlamps in the rear window of the taxi. Heard the low growl of a powerful engine. The taxi driver said something over his shoulder and Lucky looked up as the lights swung by.

An automatic rifle fired hard and loud and the side windows of the taxi shattered. Lucky aimed his pistol through the broken glass, muzzle flashes strobing his face. Then he made a sound like an old man gargling and folded forward, landing on top of Zondi, something wet smearing Zondi's face. The driver shouted. More gunfire. More glass.

Zondi made a grab for Lucky's pistol. As his fingers found the grip, the taxi spun and somersaulted. Zondi flew around the rear of the minibus, in an embrace with the dead man. Smashed his head against something hard. Bit his tongue. Glass exploded over him, metal shearing and tearing, the seats breaking free of their bolts and gang-tackling him. The warm night air finding its way in through torn metal.

The taxi sparked on the gravel as it slid to a stop. Zondi tasted dust, invisible in the blackness. Heard a wheel still spinning on blown bearings and something dripping onto the metal beside his head. Then nothing.

Zondi opened his eyes, looking up at a million bright points of light, like pinpricks in a velvet curtain. Stars. Far brighter than he'd grown used to in the city. And the moon, a flaring disc. No, not the moon. A flashlight, shining down on him.

He was on his back, under a crush of weight he realized were the uprooted seats of the taxi. The minibus lay on its side and Zondi was staring up through the rectangle that had housed the sliding door. Two figures dangled down through the doorway. He heard voices. Male. Teenagers. Too young to be the gunmen.

'Yaw, yaw, yaw. They are meat, man.'

'Jump in and get their stuff. I see a gun.'

The light was blocked for a moment and the taxi shook as a figure dropped down and landed beside Zondi, heavy boots smacking the metal close to his head, crunching on broken glass.

As the beam moved Zondi saw Lucky, lying dead. The boy took his watch. The kid frisked Lucky and held up a skinny black arm, fist clenched around a wad of cash. 'Look, my brother!'

Heard the other boy laugh and say, 'Make fast before somebody comes on.'

Then the beam moved onto Zondi. He didn't shut his eyes fast enough.

'Hey,' the kid holding the flashlight said. 'That one is still alive.'

The boy standing over Zondi swung a boot and kicked him back to black.

chapter 28

THE ARMORED VEHICLE RATTLED THROUGH A VILLAGE THAT LOOKED LIKE sticks and straw blown in on a desert wind. The villagers – women, children and shriveled old crones – watched from inside the huts. Eyes white in the darkness.

They saw the rotting bodies of their men tied to the sides of the armored car. Saw Goodbread and his crew standing up out of the vehicle, shouting, drunk on palm wine and blood. Heard screams as the guerrillas lying in ambush fired on them.

Goodbread awoke wet with fever, scrambling himself upright, reaching for his AK-47. Fingers finding only the 9mm pistol beside him on the sofa. The shouts that woke him those of farm laborers on a tractor, not the enemy in a long-forgotten bush war.

Goodbread looked across at the man lying on the bed. On his stomach, arms flung wide. Breathing deeply. Still dressed in the striped pajama top and the bloody jeans. Feet bare and soft looking. His son had wanted to talk the night before, demanding answers from Goodbread after the cops had left. Pouring the bottle of Jack Daniel's down his throat like it was some kind of balm for grief. Knocked him down and knocked him out cold.

Not before he'd cursed Goodbread as every kind of wrongheaded sonofabitch in God's creation. Goodbread had sat silent, impassive. Taking it. Reckoned he owed his boy that much.

Goodbread smothered a cough, not wanting to wake Dell. Stood and walked across to the sink for a drink of water. He'd also slept in his clothes. Sat awake, truth be told, smoking in the dark. Gun at his side. He'd slipped into a fevered slumber for maybe a half-hour. Now the sun burned hot behind the yellow curtains above the sink.

He shifted the drapes, looking out at the day. Saw the green fields and the milk cows. The propellers of the wind farm turning lazily in the distance. A breeze found its way through a crack in the glass, flapping the X-ray he'd taped there to keep the wind out.

An X-ray of his chest. Showing his bones and the white masses that bloomed in his lungs like desert flowers. Taped up there to keep the wind out, sure. But also as a kind of meditation. A reminder. So each morning when he opened the drapes he'd know he had one day less to live.

Goodbread took the acetate film between his fingers and pulled it free of the glass. Opened a drawer beneath the sink and hid the X-ray. He didn't want his son to see it. Didn't want to get into that now. He heard a groan and saw that Dell was busy waking up to his own nightmare.

Goodbread coughed, spat bright red blood onto the silver metal of the sink. Ran the faucet, watched the blood and mucus swirl away down the plughole. He had thought that his last battle was going to be against his own body. But here he was, locked and loaded. Ready to face the old enemy.

DELL OPENED HIS EYES to the cramped room with the unplastered walls. Saw the gaunt old man silhouetted against the acid-yellow drapes. Flashbacks finding Dell through the fog of a hangover.

His father walked toward him, holding out a smeared toothglass of water. Dell took it and drank it back in one draft. Put the glass down on the cement floor beside the empty bottle of Jack Daniel's.

Goodbread said, 'You hit that bottle like you bore it a grudge.'

'We need to talk.' Dell's voice like sandpaper in his throat.

'Sure we do. But first I need to take me a shower. It's in

the building next door. I'll walk you there when I'm done. Meanwhile, I'm going to ask you to kindly keep the drapes shut, and stay away from the window. I don't want the laborers to see you.'

Dell nodded. The old man went toward the door, carrying a skinny towel and a bar of soap. Like a prisoner.

'I have to take a leak,' Dell said.

'Piss in the sink.' Goodbread went out, shutting the squealing door.

Dell drilled a stream of urine into the plughole. Zipped himself and heard a soft knock on the metal door. Froze.

'It's me.' The blonde woman's hoarse voice.

'Come in,' he said.

The woman entered, bringing with her a momentary blast of hard daylight before she shut the door. She carried two plates, one on top of the other, covered with metal foil. A plastic shopping bag dangled from her arm. She set the plates down beside the sink.

'Your dad in the shower?' She wore no make-up this morning, and she looked old and used up.

'Yes.'

'I brought youse some breakfast.' He could smell sausages and eggs. Made him want to puke. She took the bag from her arm and held it up. 'There's some clothes in here. My husband's. He was about your size.' Put the bag down on the sofa. 'Don't worry, I washed them.'

'Thank you,' he said.

She looked at him. 'How you feeling?'

'I'm okay.'

'Those cops last night… Hope they didn't scare you?'

'I nearly shat myself,' he said.

She laughed, showing yellow teeth. 'Don't worry with them. They're useless. They know bugger all.'

Dell nodded and sank down onto the bed. The old blonde sat on the sofa, unpacking the contents of the bag. Trousers. Shirt. Underwear. A pair of heavy work shoes. She looked up at him through tired eyes. 'I heard what happened. That the *kaffirs* killed your family.'

There it was. The word that had defined his life as a white South African. *Kaffir*, from the Arabic *kafir*. Unbeliever. But taking on a whole new meaning in apartheid South Africa. Hate speech. Way worse than nigger or coon or any of the others. Using the word branded you a white racist. Simple as that. Dell had got into countless fist fights with those who used it. Usually got the shit beat out of him, but still. And here he sat. Saying nothing.

'They killed my husband too, you know?' She laid the khaki trousers over the back of the sofa, picking a piece of lint from one leg. 'He went up to the Free State, to his brother's farm. To help with the harvest. The *kaffirs* came with guns and shot him and his brother. Stole their truck. We buried the two of them on the same day. Cops did nothing. Just two white men dead. Just another farm murder.'

'I'm sorry,' he said.

She shrugged, moving a strand of dry yellow hair from her face. Got to her feet, wincing as a pain in her back caught her. 'It's a war. No matter what they say. There's still some of us fighting.' The woman walked to the door, limping slightly and turned to face Dell, a hand on the doorknob. 'God bless you,' she said.

A smile touched her thin lips, furrowed from years of smoking. She opened the door and stepped out in the light. Closed the door, and he heard her feet crunching on the gravel as she walked away.

chapter 29

SUNDAY WALKED UP THE HILL TOWARD THE HUT, BALANCING A PLASTIC water container on her head. The container was heavy, holding three gallons, but she moved with sure-footed grace, only occasionally having to lift her hand to steady her burden. She had been down to the communal tap, twenty minutes away. Had to wait in line while the women filled their buckets and gourds. Listened with half an ear to their laments about taxi wars and sickness and poverty. Relieved when she heard the water drumming into her container.

With each step she took, her mood lightened. Today was the day she would be free. Free of the aunt who had used her as a servant these last ten years. Free of the old dog who had bought her for his bed.

She passed three scrawny goats, legs grown uneven from having to cling to the slopes as they foraged for food. Made her think of her aunt, who had suffered revenge after meddling in the affairs of a neighbor. The woman had paid a witchdoctor to curse Ma Beauty, and her leg had withered almost overnight. Or so she said.

Today was the day Ma Beauty went down to Bhambatha's Rock, to collect her disability grant. Sunday had hoped the woman would already be gone. But when she saw smoke curling from the chimney of the hut, she knew her aunt was still at home, making herself the thick brew of tea she drank every morning. Threw in stinking herbs and powders from her own witchdoctor, to protect her from evil spells.

Sunday would have to see Ma Beauty one last time. *One last time.* The three words made her smile as she looked out over the dry and torn valley. Tomorrow she would wake in Durban. By the ocean. She had never seen the ocean. Never been farther from here than Dundee, an hour's drive away.

Sunday felt a mix of terror and excitement. Especially when she thought of Sipho. She saw his smile, saw the long fingers of his hands on the wheel of the car. He looked so healthy. He'd told her he took medication, the pills the people of her area were so superstitious about, and ate clean food. Said that if a person was careful, they would live to be old.

And he practiced what he called 'safe sex'. Had explained this to her earnestly, as he translated one of his pamphlets from English, showing the pictures of the plastic things like balloons. She had felt her cheeks grow warm and she'd had to look away.

Sunday felt a confusion of feelings when she thought of him. Like she wanted to laugh and run and hide at the same time. She wondered whether he felt the same way about her. He sought her out, didn't he? Every time he was up from Durban.

As she neared the hut, she told herself to stop being stupid. She wasn't running away with Sipho. He was helping her to escape from the old dog. That was all. She had to focus her mind. This way no time for daydreaming.

Sunday ducked into the hut and placed the water container on the floor. Her aunt sat huddled beside the fire, iron teapot bubbling.

'Morning, Ma,' Sunday said.

The woman grunted, rubbing at her withered limb. 'My leg it is paining. You must come with me to town.'

Sunday felt a hollow space open up in her heart. 'But Ma, I have to work.'

Her aunt shook her head. 'These are your last few days before your wedding. They will expect you to be busy.'

'I need to get my pay.' The only money she had. The money that would get her to Durban.

'Pick it up tomorrow.'

'Please, Ma…'

The old woman grabbed the flesh of Sunday's leg, her bony fingers pinching like a scorpion. 'You! Where do you think you are, girl? In the city? That you can disrespect an elder like so?'

Sunday stayed impassive. Refused to show pain.

Her aunt put a hand to the wall and pulled herself to her feet, breath coming in gasps. 'Now hurry, you. I want to go early to town so I can buy myself shoes for your wedding.' Looked down her nose at Sunday. 'That a girl like you should be so fortunate I will never understand.'

So Sunday walked her aunt down the hill, having to put up with her moans and muttered oaths, supporting her weight as they negotiated the rocky path. As they reached the road a taxi pulled up, and a couple of women waiting on the red sand climbed inside. The co-driver stood with his hand on the sliding door, urging Sunday and her aunt to hurry, slamming the door closed after them.

Ma Beauty squeezed herself into a seat, making room for Sunday. The driver was already gunning the engine when Sunday sprang up and pulled the door open, jumped down onto the sand. Closed the door after her. Watched as the taxi took off, her aunt's monkey face – mouth shouting soundlessly – disappearing in the spray of dust.

Sunday had never disobeyed the woman before, and it left her feeling exhilarated as she ran back up the hill, sweating in the heat. She had an hour to pack her things and get down to the Zulu Kingdom. For her last performance.

Sunday stripped and washed herself. Dressed in her best white panties, jeans and pressed T-shirt. Then she packed all her belongings in a paper shopping bag. Another pair of jeans. Two T-shirts. Two panties. Her Zulu Bible. Placed the charred photo album on top of her clothes. Leaving behind her wind-up radio and her thin pile of dog-eared schoolbooks. She would have no use for them where she was going.

Sunday left the hut. She stood for a moment looking out across the valley toward where her family had been murdered. Saying goodbye. Then she walked down the hill.

chapter 30

DELL, WEARING THE DEAD MAN'S CLOTHES, WAS AT THE WHEEL OF A WHITE pickup. A Toyota double cab. Like a negative image of the truck that had smashed the Volvo over the cliff. He drove, his body on automatic. Willing the pain and grief away. Numbing himself. Each broken white line flashing by was a marker, taking him closer to the man who had killed his family.

His father sat at his side, a map spread across his knees, mumbling directions, the greenery giving way to flat semi-desert scrub now they had crossed the mountains. Dell saw two brown kids running at the side of the road, waving at him, teeth shining, and he understood that his children would never reach that age. His knuckles turned white on the wheel, and tears blurred the road until he wiped them away.

Back at the farm Goodbread had returned from the shower, wet hair sticking to his scalp. He'd checked that no laborers were in sight, and he'd covered Dell's head with the blanket and taken him to the bathroom. Told him to shout when he was done.

The shower was as spartan as the room his father lived in. Unplastered cinderblock. No windows. A curtain smelling of mildew. A shower head that dribbled tepid brown water. It was the first time Dell had been in a shower since the morning of his birthday. Standing under the water, after he'd peeled away the bandage that bound his ribs, sluicing off the blood and the grime and the prison cells, made him feel closer to human.

He dressed in the khaki work trousers, check shirt, and heavy brown work shoes. There was no mirror in the bathroom but he knew his transformation was complete. He looked like one of them. One of the white men he had spent his life fighting.

He shouted for his father, and the old man covered him again and led him back to the room. Dell shook the blanket off. 'I'm not going to tell anybody where this place is.'

Goodbread laughed. 'That's what you say now.'

'Meaning?'

'If we're captured they'll question you. And bet your ass they won't be polite. You'll tell them whatever they want to know, take that as gospel.'

'And you won't?'

Shaking his head. 'Reckon I've had more experience.'

Dell sat down on the bed and stared at the old man. 'I want you to be honest with me.'

'About what?' Goodbread sat opposite him, on the sagging sofa.

'Why you're doing this.'

'You're my son. They were going to kill you. I reckon I had but two choices: shut my eyes or get involved in your business.'

'Bullshit,' Dell said. 'You're still fighting your old war, aren't you? You and that bunch.' Pointing toward the house.

'My war is long over, boy.'

'But you miss it, having a license to kill black men?'

'I have sent white, yellow, black and brown men, equally, to their reward. It was never the color of a man's skin that concerned me. It was the color of his politics.' Goodbread fixed him with a stare. 'That you chose to marry a dark-skinned woman and father a pair of mulattos never troubled me. But the fact that you embraced Marxism at a time when WW3 was a button-push away, now that irked me mightily.'

The old Goodbread in full flight. And it was too much for him. A coughing spasm shook him and he lifted himself from the sofa and went over to the faucet, drank water, fought for air. After a minute he composed himself and returned to his seat.

'What's wrong with you?' Dell asked.

'Had me a flu in the winter. Takes longer to shake when you're old.' He lit a cigarette, hands trembling so badly he was in danger of killing the match. Sucked nicotine. Closed his eyes. Smothered a cough.

'Okay. Talk to me. What's your plan?' Dell said.

The old man opened his watery blue eyes. 'It's real simple. We're going to take us a ride up to Zululand. Get our hands on Inja Mazibuko. Get him to confess to killing your family.'

Dell stared at him. Shook his head. 'You're fucking crazy.'

'You got a better idea?'

'Yes. I call my lawyer. Get some media attention. Work this thing out.'

Goodbread wheezed a laugh. 'Oh, you've got their attention, boy, don't worry. But there's one thing I know for damn sure...'

'And what's that?'

'Stick your head up and there's no way in hell you'll live long enough to talk to no media.'

Dell tried to find an argument. Failed. 'And you think we'll be able to capture Mazibuko?'

'Yessir, I do. He'll tap into his informer network. Ask questions. Get the answer that I've already put out into the wind: that we're across the Namibian border. He'll know damn well I have connections up there. Last place he'll expect to see us is in his own backyard.'

'And if we capture him, what do we do?'

'I reckon that's when we call in your media.'

Dell sat and watched his father smoke. Saw the tremor in his hand. 'Level with me. What are our chances? An old man and a fucking pacifist?'

'You still calling yourself that after what they did to your kin?' Dell said nothing and Goodbread took a long drag on his cigarette, the ash flaming red. Then he shrugged and sighed smoke. 'Well, could be they shoot us down like dogs long before we get there. Or Mazibuko and his crew are sat waiting with their AKs hot and ready to go. Question is, do you want to die knowing you did nothing? I surely don't.'

So Dell had let himself be led out to the truck, covered with the blanket until they were a half-hour away from the farm. Then Goodbread had pulled over. Let Dell drive ever deeper into the brown landscape, the road unspooling ahead of them.

They rounded a curve and Dell saw three police vehicles parked on the shoulder, cops in dayglo vests standing in the road. The sparse traffic in front of their truck slowed. 'Fuck.'

'Easy,' Goodbread said. 'They're only pulling taxis over.'

It was true. Dell could see a couple of minibuses at the roadside, the cops questioning the drivers. 'What if they stop us?'

'They won't.'

'You going to start shooting?'

Goodbread laughed. 'Got nothing to shoot with, boy.' Dell looked across at him. 'Too risky to be on the road with unlicensed firearms this close to Cape Town.'

They were up to the roadblock now. A brown cop wearing a bib with orange and lime-green chevrons looked at them with sleepy eyes and waved them on. Dell accelerated, watching the cops shrink to nothing in his rearview.

'So, we're going after Mazibuko unarmed?'

His father spoke as he lit another cigarette. 'We'll pick us up some ordnance on the way. Don't you fret about that none.' Sucking smoke.

'What makes you so sure he'll go home? Inja?'

'Because, boy, he's getting married this Saturday. Taking him a fourth wife, in the Zulu way. Already posted out the invites.' Smiling like a skull, his old man's yellow teeth too big for his face. 'Reckon he has a surprise wedding gift coming down the pike.'

INJA'S MOOD WAS AS SOUR AS HIS STOMACH. HE STOPPED THE RENTAL Volkswagen near the wind farm, the giant propellers slicing the morning sun. He opened the door and shot a hot jet of puke onto the sand. Wiped the sweat from his brow, slugged back half a tin of lukewarm Coke. Burped. Finished the Coke and threw the can out. He had a map open on the seat beside him, directions scribbled on the page. He oriented himself and drove off.

Inja hadn't slept. He'd taken a taxi from the shack where he had eaten the sheep's head, across to a cheap hotel near the airport. Then he had spent late into the night on his phone, the Motorola heating up his ear like he was sitting too close to a fire. Worked his way through his contacts in the police and the netherland that linked the cops and the underworld like connective tissue.

Spoke to black men who had worked as cops during the apartheid era, who still lived in fear of reprisals for collaborating with the Boers and were eager to find favor with Inja and his all-powerful chief. Traitors who had links with the kind of people who would hide the white man and his father.

Finally, just after dawn – his throat dry from threatening and cajoling – Inja had been given an address. A farm two hours outside Cape Town where Goodbread had been seen. His informant telling him the local cops had checked the place out and found no sign of the escaped man. Local cops Inja wouldn't trust with a cow dead ten days.

As Inja followed the narrow asphalt road that carved its way through the unfamiliar green landscape, his phone rang.

He answered it, wedging it between shoulder and ear as he drove. He grunted a few times and hung up. Some good news, at least. His men back in Zululand had taken revenge for the taxi that had been ambushed. Killed a rival driver the night before outside Bhambatha's Rock. The brother of an old enemy. Good news, yes. But he should be at home, commanding his troops. The situation needed his guiding hand.

Inja overshot the gate to the farm. Reversed, crashing through the gears, then set off up a rutted sand road, his guts banging up against his ribs. Puke rising again. He reached for a spliff in his top pocket. Fired it up and hit it hard. The drug settled his stomach. Slowed things down. Gave him time to steady himself for battle.

Inja saw black men out in the fields, small specks in overalls. A red tractor rattled in the distance. He approached the house, an old stone place with a porch. He stopped at the rear, sat with his doors closed and windows wound shut, waiting for the farm dogs that he knew would appear. And there they were: two ugly beasts. Jumping up against his door, yellow teeth snapping, jowls leaving spit smeared across the window glass. Trained by these whites to tear at his black flesh.

He heard a man shouting commands in Afrikaans and the dogs retreated from the car, growling, Inja's scent in their snouts. He wound his window down an inch.

'Ja?' the Boer asked, standing in the doorway of the kitchen, hands on hips. A big man, about thirty, but already a gut swelling over the belt of his khaki shorts.

Inja flashed his badge. 'Can I have a word with you, sir?' Speaking English.

'They were already here last night. The cops,' the man said in Afrikaans.

Inja understood the ugly language – sounded like a throat disease to his ears – but he didn't speak it. 'I'm Agent Mazibuko, sir. I'm here with the task force on farm murders.' Fixed an ass-licking smile to his face.

The Boer looking surprised. 'What task force?'

'I'm here to liaise with the local farmers. To help stop this lawless element that is targeting you people.'

The man almost smiled. 'Okay. Get out. Don't worry with them.' Pointing at the dogs.

Inja cracked the door and the dogs growled.

The farmer said, 'Quiet!'

Inja stood up out of the car, ready to reach for his pistol. But the dogs stayed back, gargling low in their throats.

'Come in,' the Boer said.

The man led him into the kitchen and shut the door on the dogs. Two women sat at the table, finishing breakfast. One an old woman with yellow hair. The other was young, so white she looked like she had bled out. A dirty baby wobbled on her lap, and a small Boer boy-child looked up at Inja from his place at the table.

Inja smiled with a fine display of teeth. 'Are there any other people in the house, who would like to join our discussion?'

'What discussion?' the old yellow-head asked. She was shrewd, Inja saw. He knew she would be the one to question.

'Some farm murder task force,' the Boer said. Then he stopped talking when Inja shot him in the dimpled pink knee that protruded from the bottom of his shorts, the silenced pistol coughing like a polite African of old. The man sagged, grabbing at his knee, cursing some white god.

Inja had the pistol on the others. The young woman was about to scream. 'If you make a noise I'll kill you.' She shut her mouth. 'Take the baby from her,' he said to the old one.

The one with yellow hair took the infant and held it on her lap. The baby was a giant, with a head the size of a football. With his free hand Inja dug into his jacket pocket and came out with a handful of black plastic cable ties. He threw them in front of the younger woman.

'Now you are going to tie up this Boer bastard. His hands behind his back, and his ankles together.'

The farmer was gripping his knee. Cursing. The woman knelt beside him. Sobbed when she saw the blood pumping from her husband's shattered knee as he removed his hand. She took a moment to understand how to use the cable ties, then she secured his wrists. Stared at Inja, her hands shaking. He moved closer with the pistol. She tied the man's thick ankles. He leaned back against the wall, his face sallow.

'Now you tie the child.'

She did as he said. The boy was crying like only a little white brat could. Inja tore strips off a roll of kitchen towel and filled the child's mouth with paper.

'Put the baby on the table,' he said to the old yellow-head. She looked at him with hatred in her eyes, and sat the infant among the plates. It wobbled on its disposable napkin, fat and pink. Stank like shit. Inja held the silencer close to its head.

'Old woman, you listen to me or I'll shoot it,' he said. 'Tie up the young one.'

The yellow-head hesitated, then she did as he ordered. The young woman sat at the table, weeping, snot running from her nose as she was secured.

'Now sit down.'

The old one sat. The baby started to howl and Inja hit it on the head with the gun barrel and it toppled on its side among the dishes. Lay gasping. The old woman was out of her seat, coming at him with a bread knife. She had balls this one. Like one of those olden-time Boers who had dragged ox wagons over mountains and killed his ancestors with front-loader rifles.

Inja rested the gun barrel on the baby's temple, blue veins like rivers under its white skin. 'Drop the knife.' She stared at him, then obeyed, the knife clattering against a plate of congealed egg. 'Sit down.' She sat. 'Okay. Now. Robert Goodbread lives here? Yes or no?'

'No,' she said.

Inja lifted the gun away from the baby's head and shot the Boer man in the face. The farmer slumped forward, dripping blood and brain. The young woman collapsed onto the table, sobbing. The old one stared up at him, her mouth a slit.

'I ask again,' Inja said.

'Yes. He lived here.'

'And he brought his son here? Last night?'

He saw the lie moving into her eyes. Shot the young woman in the arm. She screamed and sobbed and prayed. Looked up at the old one through tears and stringy hair. 'Please, Ma. Tell him.'

'Yes. He was here. But they gone,' the old one said.

'Gone where?'

'Namibia.'

She looked to be telling the truth. Inja needed to be sure, so he shot the young woman in the head. Blood sprayed crimson across the picture of a Massey Ferguson tractor on the wall calendar behind her.

'I ask again.'

'They gone to Namibia. I swear to God.'

Namibia. Made sense. If this was true they would be across the border by now, the old white man and his son. Out of his jurisdiction. Inja found a new magazine in his pocket and slid it into the pistol. Cocked the gun. Pointed it at the boy-child.

'You're lying,' Inja said.

The woman stared at him. No tears in her eyes. Just hatred. 'They. Gone. To. Namibia.'

Inja shot the child in the head.

The old woman had her eyes closed, praying, 'Our father

which art in heaven, hallowed be thy name…'

'Shut up,' he said.

'…thy kingdom come, thy will be done, on earth as it is in heaven.'

Inja took a step back and shot the baby. The force of the bullet knocked it off the table and it lay next to its dead father like something discarded.

'Forgive us this day our trespasses, as we…' She stopped. And Inja had to laugh. No way was this Boer woman going to forgive *him* his trespasses.

He held the gun on her. Her eyes opened and she stared straight at Inja. Spat at him, 'Fuck you, *kaffir*. You'll rot in hell.'

He shot her in her yellow head. Emptied the pistol into the bodies of the three adults. The room stank of blood and shit and gunfire.

It was time for Inja to go home. He reloaded, then checked his watch. Just gone 9 a.m. He could be on a plane to Durban by 12:30. Pick up his car from the airport and be on the road to Bhambatha's Rock by three. Home in time for his wives to cook him tripe for dinner.

Inja opened the door and stepped out into the brightness. The dogs came at him and he killed them both. Then he walked across to the car, leaving as the flies arrived.

chapter 32

ZONDI SURFACED FROM BLACKNESS, SOMETHING DARK AND DENSE spiraling above him. He looked to his right, into the face of a skeletal corpse. The corpse lifted a clawed hand, sunken mouth chewing toothlessly. Moaning. Zondi raised himself onto his elbows, trying to work out where exactly he was in the afterlife, when a white face framed by long blonde hair entered his vision. Definitely hell.

The white woman spoke a stuttering, pidgin Zulu. 'You are okay?'

Zondi answered in English, 'Where am I?'

'St Mary's Mission Hospital. In Bhambatha's Rock.'

She spoke fluent English but with a strong accent. French. No, Belgian, he decided. The blonde, in a white coat, stethoscope dangling from her neck, squatted between Zondi and the moaning corpse. Zondi realized that he was in a ward so densely packed with suffering black humanity that he lay on a thin mattress on the stone floor beneath a bed, the springs coiled above him. Also realized he badly needed to take a piss. He started to pull himself out from under the rough blanket that covered his body.

'So I'm not dead?' The blanket fell away and Zondi saw he was naked. And semi-tumescent from his full bladder.

The blonde swallowed a laugh. 'No, you are very much alive, I think.'

Zondi covered himself, lying back.

'I'm sorry. Your clothes were torn and bloody. And we have run out of pajamas.' Waving a delicate hand at the packed ward. People sardined into every available space, the stench of shit and suffering and death throttling Zondi.

'Look, Doctor...?'

'Lambert.'

'I need to get out of here. Any chance somebody could go across to the rooming house and pick up some clothes for me?'

Blue eyes fixed on him. He saw she had beautiful skin, like white Belgian chocolate. *No, no, no,* he told himself. Tried to focus on the crucifix that gleamed at her collar bone. An elegant neck, made for love-bites. *Jesus.*

'You should not be leaving here. You have a concussion,' she said.

'I must leave.'

The doctor shrugged. The dark smears of exhaustion under her eyes told him she had more pressing matters to concern herself with. 'Okay. I will send an orderly. Come and see me at my office before you go.' She stood and walked away, maneuvring between the rows of black bodies.

The AIDS victim at Zondi's side sat up, and the shriveled dugs that dangled over the blanket, flat and leathery as saddlebags, told him she was a woman. She fixed her smeared eyes on him. 'God is good,' she said in Zulu.

'Yes, sister, God is good,' Zondi said. He lay back, thinking: *No. Whatever he is, he isn't that.*

chapter 33

DELL DROVE INTO A LANDSCAPE AS FLAT AND BROWN AS A CLOTH STRETCHED out to the horizon. Rusting windmills stood motionless over dry dams and exhausted khaki sheep slumped in the dust. The empty blacktop unrolled long and straight beside an abandoned railroad track.

Goodbread sat in silence at Dell's side. The only indication that he was awake, or alive, was his right arm rising like a metronome, bringing the endless cigarettes to his lips. Over the drumming of the tires Dell heard smoke being sucked in and sighed out. And an occasional dry cough.

This was a different Bobby Goodbread from the one he remembered, who was all bullshit and swagger, overheated by testosterone and bloodlust. Bragging about killing communists and busting Nelson Mandela. This was a silent husk, dried out, like the tumbleweeds that gave way in the wind of the truck's approach.

A faded road sign swam out of the heat haze, pointing to a small town a mile off the highway. Dell could see a church steeple rising amid low houses, and the hard shine of the tin roofed boxes the coloreds lived in.

'Turn in here,' Goodbread said, voice thin and cracked.

'Why?'

'To get us some firepower, boy.'

'I'm forty-eight years old. Somehow *boy* doesn't do it for me anymore.'

'That right? Then what would be your preference?'

'Robert. Or Rob.'

'Not Bobby?' A soft, dry laugh, lost in the ticking of the turn signal as Dell swung onto a gravel road. 'Head toward the gas station.'

'You know this place?'

'I had occasion to visit twenty-some years ago.'

They were approaching a town that seemed to be dying by inches. As if the closing of the railroad had taken away its will to live. The truck bumped over the tracks, passing a derelict train station and a couple of dark-brick railroad houses that had been stripped and looted. The walls of one singed by fire.

Dell pulled the truck into the Caltex gas station, the signage bleached by the sun. He stopped at the pumps and a colored man with a withered arm slunk over to them.

'You get us gassed up,' Goodbread said. 'I'm going to talk to a fellow inside.' Walked off toward the auto workshop.

Dell sat in the truck, smelling the gasoline, the counter on the pump clicking. The mosquito whine of a car speeding by on the highway. Otherwise nothing but the oppressive silence of the country.

The cripple poured water from a plastic bucket onto the windshield, and as he drew a rag across the glass he revealed Goodbread in conversation with a thickset middle-aged white man in a mechanic's overall. The man wiped his oil-stained hands on a dirty cloth, shooting glances over at the truck.

Then he nodded and shouted something into the dark mouth of the workshop. A blond boy of eight or nine ran out. Barefoot. Skinny legs protruding from gray shorts. Wearing a T-shirt with the South African rugby emblem on the front.

The mechanic pulled together the two iron doors of the workshop and padlocked them. Then he and the boy followed Goodbread to the truck. The man opened the rear door and sat, the boy sliding in after him, looking at Dell from under his pale fringe. Dell saw he had eyes as blue as robin's eggs.

Dell paid the attendant. Heard the man in the back talking

in Afrikaans, telling the pump jockey he'd be back in an hour. The mechanic leaned forward, speaking to Dell. 'Go past the cop shop, then take a right.'

Dell drove by the police station, a dark cop with a paunch standing in the doorway, watching them with no expression. Dell turned into a road of brown houses with Dutch gables. Nobody on the street.

The boy started humming the intro to a TV show the twins used to watch. The mechanic told him to shut up. He did. The houses dribbled away and the road continued out into the emptiness. Dust swirled up around them and Dell closed his window. Heard his father coughing. Battling for air.

After ten minutes the mechanic leaned over the back of Dell's seat and pointed a dirty finger toward a farm gate set into a barbed-wire fence. A FOR SALE sign hung on the fence, faded and rusted, with a bullet hole drilled through the middle. Dell stopped at the gate and the boy jumped down and opened it, the hinges tearing through rust.

Dell bumped the truck over a cattle guard. No sign of cattle. Stopped and waited for the boy to close the gate and run back to the vehicle. Took off toward a house that sat near a gap-toothed windmill. As they neared the house, Dell could see it was unoccupied. And had been for a long time. The roof sagged and the windows were boarded up.

'Park by the back of the house,' the mechanic said.

Dell stopped the truck and the men stepped out. The boy moved to follow his father, but the man shook his head. 'Wait here.' The boy stayed in the vehicle.

The mechanic led them across to the garage. A rusted metal door with a new padlock and silver chain. He unlocked the door and swung it open. The garage was empty but for a steel cabinet and a workbench standing against the far wall. The mechanic walked to the cabinet and opened it, speaking to

Goodbread over his shoulder.

'What does the major need?' Another of the crew who had followed Goodbread through Namibia and Angola. Making the world safe from communism.

'I want a pump-action, a rifle and two pistols.'

'Not a problem.'

The man took the selection of weapons from the cabinet and laid them on the workbench. Goodbread picked up the shotgun, inspecting it.

'While the major chooses, I just want to have a word with my boy.'

Goodbread nodded and the man walked out, toward the truck, disappearing from view. Goodbread reached into the cupboard and found a box of red shells. Broke open the shotgun and loaded it. Then he hugged the wall and squinted through the gap between the garage door and the hinge.

'Boy, follow me.'

Goodbread was walking. Suddenly a younger man again. The way he'd been when the cops had arrived the night before. Energized. Dell followed his father toward the truck. The mechanic stood by the rear bumper, his back to them. Turning toward Goodbread. Putting something in his pocket.

Goodbread said, 'Who you phoning, Jan?'

'No, nobody.' Trying a smile.

'Give your phone to my boy,' Goodbread said.

'Major, come on, you know me...'

Goodbread pumped the shotgun. The man reached into his pocket and took out the phone. Hesitated, then handed it to Dell, who looked down at the glass face of an aging Samsung, smeared with oil from the mechanic's fingers. Hit the green redial button and put the phone to his ear. A static hiss and then ringing.

A lazy voice answered. 'Police.'

Dell killed the call, wondering whether this was the fat constable he had seen filling the doorway of the police station. 'The cops,' he said.

'I didn't even get through,' the mechanic said.

Goodbread stared at him, shook his head. 'You sorry sonof-abitch. How much are they offering for us?'

The man shrugged. 'TV said fifty thousand.' Scratched at his stubble. 'My wife's gone. I got debt.'

'Real touching. If I had me a guitar I'd sing along, and that's the God's honest truth.' He coughed. 'You and me need to take a walk, Jan.'

'Major. Please.'

The boy was alert now, sensing danger. Half-sliding from the truck. 'Pa?'

Voice as high as a girl's.

'Stay there, Deon.'

The child obeyed.

'You walk with me and nothing will happen to your boy,' Goodbread said. 'Understand?'

The mechanic nodded. Looked at his son. Lifted a hand. Dropped it. Seemed about to say something, then he swallowed his words and turned and walked around the house, Goodbread a step behind him. Dell and the boy watched them disappear.

'Where they going, uncle?'

Dell couldn't find words. Saw those blue eyes staring up at him. Saw his dead children. The boy blinked at the blast from the shotgun. Dusty birds exploded from the roof of the house, black as shrapnel against the sky. Another bang. Then Goodbread walked back toward them, smoking pump-action dangling from his hand. Dell saw the boy was crying. Silently.

'Get in front, Deon,' Goodbread said in Afrikaans. The boy did as he was told, obedient as a gundog. Goodbread leaned the shotgun against the front seat. 'You wait here with the boy,' he said to Dell.

Dell slid in behind the wheel. The boy was shaking, and tears tracked the dust on his face. Dell marveled at the layers of hell that were being revealed to him, day by day.

Goodbread returned carrying two more handguns and a rifle, his pockets bulging with ammunition. He got into the truck, the boy sitting between him and Dell. 'Okay, let's go.'

'Where?'

'Back to the highway.'

'What about him?' Dell gestured with his head toward the child, who stared out the windshield, crying silently.

'Just drive.'

'I won't let you hurt him.'

'What the hell do you think I am?'

Dell could offer no answer. He started the truck. When they came to the gate, Goodbread stepped down and opened it and closed it after them. Got back in and they bumped toward town. Dell found a backstreet that skirted the cop station, and then they were past the town and back on the blacktop.

They drove for almost an hour in silence. The child shivered like he was freezing. In the distance, Dell saw a car pulled up under the shade of a thorn tree. As they drew closer he could make out a man, a woman, and three children sitting at a stone table, eating.

'Drive on until they can't read our license plate,' Goodbread said, looking back over his shoulder.

Dell watched the picnickers recede to small dots in his rearview.

'This will work,' Goodbread said.

Dell pulled over onto the shoulder and Goodbread cracked his door and stepped down. Motioned for the child to follow him. 'You go down to that auntie and uncle. You hear me, boy?' The child nodded, looked at them both, then started walking, feet bare on the hot gravel.

Goodbread was back in the vehicle, door slapping shut. 'Drive.'

Dell drove.

chapter 34

ZONDI FELT DIZZY. SHUT HIS EYES FOR A MOMENT, BLOCKING OUT THE sunlight that blasted in at him though the windows of the hospital corridor. Had to steady himself against the wall. Took a breath and got a lungful of disinfectant and the bitter smell of death and disease.

All around him were wasted men and women in candy-striped pajamas. Shuffling along the corridor with thousand-yard stares. Slumped on benches. On the floor. In wheelchairs. Gaunt, hollow cheeked. Skins patterned with lesions. Coughing through lips gummed by yeast infections thick as churned butter.

South Africa has the highest rate of HIV in the world. And Bhambatha's Rock was at the epicenter, smack in middle of the worst-infected area. One in three people carried the virus. Years of ignorance, superstition, government apathy and misinfor-mation had erased a generation, leaving babies to be raised by grandparents. A plague almost biblical in its ferocity.

Zondi was dressed in jeans and a clean shirt. A fresh pair of Reeboks on his feet. His head throbbed and his body ached. But he was walking out of here. The people around him were not. He came to an unvarnished wooden door with a card pinned to it: Dr M. Lambert. *Marie? Martine?* He knocked.

'Yes. Come in, please.' That accented voice.

He opened the door and found the blonde doctor sitting behind a metal desk, writing a report in a brown file. More files stacked beside her. A plastic bottle of mineral water and two glasses stood beside the files.

'Have a seat, Mr...?'

'Zondi. Disaster Zondi.'

She looked up at him, frowning. 'Disaster, like something terrible?'

He sat. 'Yes. It's a long story.'

She allowed a distracted smile, and rubbed at blue eyes smudged with fatigue. 'How are you feeling?'

'I'm okay.'

'Then you are lucky. The men you were with in the taxi are dead.'

'I know.'

'A trucker found you this morning and brought you here. Maybe you must talk with the police. Over in Dundee.'

'Of course,' he said. No way in hell.

The doctor was toying with a piece of paper. He saw it was the fax of the wedding invite. Torn and bloody. She held it up. 'This was in your pocket, when you were admitted.' A pause. 'You are here to attend this wedding?'

'Maybe.'

'From whose side of the family are you?'

'The girl's.'

'Okay. And she is how old?'

'Sixteen, I think.'

She tapped the invite. Hesitating before she spoke. 'This man. The groom. He was a patient here, not so long ago.'

The doctor stopped talking. Zondi waited for her to continue, but she didn't. She rummaged in the desk drawer and found a container of pills and put them in front of him.

'For your headache.' She poured some of her bottled water into a glass and pushed it across to Zondi. 'Take two pills now.' Standing. 'If you show symptoms like nausea and dizziness, please to return here immediately. Understand?'

'Yes.'

'Good.'

She lifted the files from the desk and dropped them into a steel cabinet. Slammed the door shut. One file remained on the scuffed surface of the desk. 'I must go now, to ward rounds.' The doctor switched a smile on and off and left the room, closing the door after her.

Zondi sipped at the water. Didn't touch the pills. Looked at the buff-colored folder, reading upside down: MAZIBUKO M. He slid the file across the desk and turned it to face him. Scanned it. Inja Mazibuko had been admitted to the hospital three months before with a bullet in his leg. Zondi turned a page. Came across the result of blood work. Didn't need a medical degree to see that not only was Inja HIV positive, but his T-cell count was shot to hell. He had full-blown AIDS.

Zondi understood now why Inja was marrying the girl who looked so much like her mother.

chapter 35

SUNDAY FELT AS IF SHE WAS IN ONE OF THOSE DREAMS WHERE TIME MOVED as slowly as a stream of dark mud. She sat on a blanket in the dust, weaving at the wooden loom, the betrothal beads whispering to her every time she moved.

Richard droned away in English, telling the small crowd of sweating white people that they should follow him to the beer ceremony that would conclude the tour. After she served the beer Sunday would hurry to where her bag waited in the hut. She would change her clothes and walk out to Sipho's car. And freedom.

Sunday looked up from her weaving, staring past the pink faces with their sharp noses and pale eyes. Seeing something unusual. A black tourist. A tall man in expensive jeans and Reeboks. Standing at the edge of the group. She heard Richard speak to him, and he answered in Zulu. But he was from the city. For sure, in those clothes.

As she left the loom and walked toward the ceremonial hut, she felt the man's eyes on her. But when she turned he looked away, the sun dancing like fire on the frame of his sunglasses.

Z**ONDI LOOKED AT THE GIRL** serving beer to the tourists and saw her mother. After killing Jola and fleeing to Johannesburg, Zondi had purged himself of his longing for Thandi, his first and only love. A kind of emotional cold turkey. Stumbling through drunken nights with fast Soweto girls in backrooms stinking of unwashed bodies and Vaseline and beer. There were times where he'd nearly weakened, jumped on a bus back to this valley where he would have been put to death.

Four years later, when he took his life in his hands and came home to bury his mother, he had seen her. She lived in a hut on a hill, married to a man who spent most of the year in Durban, polishing white women's stone floors to a mirror. Thandi told Zondi she was childless. *A barren woman*, she said. A disappointment to her husband.

Of course Zondi slept with her. In her mud hut, on a blanket on the dung floor. Thandi passive and silent after the Jo'burg girls, who had shouted their lust at the ceilings. The deeper Zondi pushed himself into her, the farther away he slid. He had won a bursary to study politics in Johannesburg. Ran with a crowd of intellectuals and radicals. Many of them blonde and hungry. Thandi had stayed marooned in a valley unchanged in hundreds of years. Jets rumbled overhead, but the people in their shadows lived the same way their great-grandparents had lived.

Zondi went back to Johannesburg without saying goodbye to her. And never returned. He'd heard, five or six years later, that she and her husband had been murdered, part of one of the ongoing clan feuds in the area. Heard that Thandi hadn't been barren, after all.

Her daughter came to him and knelt, extended a clay gourd for him to drink from. He almost spoke to her. Stopped himself. This wasn't the time. He took a sip of the sour sorghum beer. A taste that reminded him of the poverty of his childhood. His tongue attuned to single malt now.

He handed the gourd back and she looked up at him from under her eyebrows, muttered a 'thank you' in Zulu and darted away. Zondi's head throbbed. He felt breathless. Claustrophobic. Crouched and ducked through the low doorway of the hut, standing up into the dry heat that slapped him dizzy.

chapter 36

'**W**HY DID YOU HAVE TO KILL HIM?'
     His son's voice woke Goodbread, and when he coughed his eyes open, he was back in the distant dust of his childhood, in the high desert of West Texas. The land burned bare by the drought that had come in the wake of World War II. Took a moment to understand this was a different dry landscape blurring by through the windshield of the truck.

'What you say, boy?'

'You heard me,' Dell said.

Goodbread cleared his throat, battled to give voice to the dusty words. 'Reckon he left me no choice. He could identify us.'

'The kid will tell them, anyway.'

'Tell them what? He was maybe eight years old. What's he going to say more than we're two men in a white pickup truck?'

'And that cop in the town saw us.'

'I'll wager he was dreaming of his girl's lunch meat. Couldn't give a description worth a sack of shit.' Goodbread hadn't spoken in hours. And the talking left his throat sore. He drank some water and fired up a cigarette. Sucked smoke.

'Has it always come so fucking easy to you?' His son again.

'What in the hell are you talking about now, boy?'

'Killing.'

Goodbread didn't reply. Smoked and stared out at the road that stretched straight as a wire to the horizon.

Dell said, 'Ah, fuck it,' and fiddled with the car radio, searching for a newscast. He'd been listening obsessively for reports of their whereabouts. A voice cut through the static, speaking in that grating, guttural Cape accent. The newsreader talking about yet another farm murder. North of Cape Town.

When Goodbread caught the name *Althea Vorster* he turned up the volume. The woman, her son, his wife and two children. All dead. And he knew to a bone certainty whose handiwork this was.

A coughing spasm seized Goodbread and he felt blood wet and warm in his mouth and on the palm of the hand he lifted to his face. He turned his head away, stared out over the sand and scrub as he brought his breathing under control. Wiped himself clean on a handkerchief.

Dell stilled the radio, looked at him. 'The woman who cut my hair?'

Goodbread nodded. Gasped for air. 'Now that shitwad has got me angry.'

'You weren't angry before?' his son asked.

The old man shook his head. 'No. Before he killed your kin. Now he's killed mine.'

ZONDI SAT IN HIS BEEMER IN THE CAR PARK OF THE ZULU KINGDOM, ENGINE running, AC cranked high, windows shut against the heat and the dust. Sipping water from a plastic bottle. His head hurt like hell, as if his brain itself was aching. And he felt a weird dissociation, like he was lagging half a step behind himself.

The term *contrecoup injury* came unbidden. Caused, he remembered, by the brain smashing into the bones of the skull. He flashed on images from a crash-test movie he'd caught early one morning on the Discovery Channel, sitting drinking single malt, numb after a night of dislocated sex. Watching cadavers strapped behind the wheels of speeding cars sent into high-speed collisions. Heads exploding through windshields in sprays of glass, hoods of cars crumpling like foil. Lovingly rendered in balletic slow motion. Saw himself flying around in the taxi, his skull connecting with the hard metal surfaces.

He was sleepy, his chin sagging toward his chest. He sat up and poured water into the palm of his hand and wiped his face. Felt the AC chilling his wet skin. Through drops of water he saw the girl walking across the sand toward him, carrying a paper shopping bag with string handles. Dressed in those shapeless jeans poor people wore. Her T-shirt threadbare but desperately clean, with ironed creases so sharp you could cut your hand on them. Zondi opened the door and stepped out into the wall of heat.

When she was almost abreast of him, the girl smiled the same smile her mother had used on him twenty years ago. He turned and saw a young guy, maybe eighteen or nineteen, leaning against a small, dented Nissan. Wearing one of those

I'M POSITIVE T-shirts AIDS activists sported to proclaim their status. Smiling back at the girl. The boy took the bag from her and opened the trunk and stowed it. Slammed the lid and the two of them got into the car.

She looked too happy, Zondi decided, for him to intrude now. He slumped down behind the wheel of the Beemer. He'd come back tomorrow. When he was rested. When he felt more in control.

Truth was, he was shit scared. Terrified to open a door he'd bolted when he'd fled this valley long ago. He shut his eyes, sucking up a lung full of refrigerant from the BMW's AC. Heard the Nissan splutter into life. The old car bumped out of the parking lot, throwing up red sand at the late afternoon sun.

THE TOUR GUIDE WATCHED the car drive away. This was wrong, he knew, the betrothed of *Induna* Mazibuko alone with that little troublemaker from Durban. Richard had chased him away from the cultural village many times before, when he had come with his condoms and his pamphlets and his lies about disease.

Richard had changed out of his skins, wore a pair of sweat pants and a check shirt. Sandals made from old whitewall tires. He reached into the pocket of his sweats and found his Motorola. He had no way of reaching *Induna* Mazibuko directly, but he had the number of somebody close to him.

Richard prodded at the keypad with a thick finger as he watched the car disappear through the gates, and turn toward the main road. Heard the voice of the *induna*'s sister shout a greeting at a volume that pained his eardrum.

chapter 38

DELL SAT ALONE AT A TABLE IN THE DINER, WATCHING THE SKY DARKEN TO the color of congealed blood. His father was in the truck, parked across the road. He didn't want food. Said that Dell would be less conspicuous alone. Dell was amazed that he could eat. He'd only picked at the breakfast that morning, the one served to them by the blonde woman. But in the hours that had passed he'd found himself starved.

The colored waitress brought him a greasy steak sandwich and fries, and each mouthful seemed to make him hungrier until his plate was empty. He was the only customer in this little Formica time machine that seemed to have survived intact from the early sixties. And the small town outside the window hadn't changed much, either. Across from where he sat, Dell could see a dusty park and an open-air public swimming pool, run down and deserted.

Dell called for the check, and the waitress went to the cash register to prepare it. Goodbread came in. Didn't look at him as he headed across to the men's room. The woman took Dell's money and went to make change, moving at small-town pace. By the time she returned and Dell pocketed the money, his father still hadn't emerged from the bathroom.

Dell needed to take a piss, so he pushed through the swinging door. A porcelain urinal and a stall. The door to the stall was half open. His father lay on the floor. Dell shoved the door and stepped in. Saw blood on Goodbread's face and on his shirt. The old man was sucking air, the skin across his sunken cheeks a bruised blue. Dell grabbed him under the arms and lifted him, amazed at how light he was. Sat him on the seat of the toilet.

Bent him forward. Heard his breathing ease a little.

Dell grabbed a wad of toilet paper and crossed to the basin. Wet the paper and went back into the stall and wiped his father's mouth. There was nothing to be done about the blood on the shirt. Goodbread's breathing was more regular and some color had seeped back into his face.

'You okay?' Dell asked.

'Yes.'

Dell tried to get an arm under him. 'Let me help you back to the truck.'

The old man shrugged him off. 'I'll make my own way. You go.' His voice a whisper.

Dell walked out. Crossed the road and stood looking into the ruined swimming pool. It was half full of rotting garbage. He could see the frame of an old bicycle and the stiff carcass of a dog in the bed of waste.

He remembered reading about this place, around the time apartheid ended. The Afrikaners who ran the town had emptied the pool and smashed its tiled walls and floor with sledgehammers to make sure it would never hold water again. Refusing to share the rectangle of blue chlorine with the dark people from across the railway line.

Dell turned and watched his father cross the road. The old man looked like a ghost. Goodbread climbed up into the truck, shut the door and beckoned him. Dell make his way back to the pickup, cranked the engine, and drove down the main street. Goodbread fought for breath, gulping air through his mouth.

'Lung cancer?' Dell asked

'Yes.'

'How long have you got?'

'A month. Maybe two.' Words coming with difficulty.

'That why they let you out?'

'Uh-huh. Compassionate parole.' Laughed. The laugh triggered a coughing spasm.

Dell had nothing to say. He turned the truck toward the highway.

chapter 39

THE LITTLE CAR STRUGGLED UP THE LAST OF THE INCLINES THAT WOULD TAKE them out of the valley and onto the Durban road. Sunday sneaked glances at Sipho as he drove, the low sun silhouetting his fine features, almost girlish beneath his short-cropped hair. He felt her eyes on him and turned to her.

'Are you okay?' he asked.

'Yes. Thank you.' Looking away, quickly. Her cheeks burning.

'You're really sure you want to do this, Sunday? *Induna* Mazibuko is not a man you want to anger.'

'Of course I'm sure.'

As she spoke she took the betrothal beads from around her neck, and snapped the string of cotton and dried grass. The plastic beads pooled in her hands. Sunday wound down her side window and threw the beads out, saw them bouncing on the sand road, black as rabbit turds. There was a taxi a little way behind them, and it amused her that its wheels would crush them. She laughed, and felt lighter. She wound up the window and saw Sipho glancing at his rearview mirror.

'Do you have any family, in Durban? Who you can stay with?' he asked.

'No.' Sunday felt a sudden panic. She had an image of Sipho dropping her off in the middle of the giant city she had seen only on the pages of magazines.

He worked the gear lever with his long-fingered hand, and the engine whined, the car hugging the hairpin bends. They seemed to be moving no faster than the goats ambling along at the roadside, with their bearded old men's faces.

'Don't worry. You can stay with me. My family, I mean.

We've got a house in KwaMashu.' He looked at her. 'You know KwaMashu?'

'I've heard of it.' She'd seen pictures of the township sprawling over low green hills, small houses and shacks packed close together.

'You'll have to share a room with my sisters. One is about your age. And one is still at junior school.'

'Thank you,' she said. 'You are very kind.'

'Oh, you'll earn your keep, don't worry. My mother does hairdressing from the house. Maybe you can help her.' Smiling at Sunday. Then looking at the rearview, smile fading.

Sunday glanced over her shoulder. The taxi was close behind them, but not overtaking. Unusual for one of these drivers, who were impatient enough to pass slow-moving traffic on the suicidal curves. Sunday turned, about to ask Sipho a question, when they rounded a sharp bend and she saw a car parked sideways across the road. A big red car, like a jeep. *Induna* Mazibuko's car.

Sipho braked. The taxi behind stopped, boxing them in. The small car stalled and there was a moment of silence that went on for ever. Sunday could hear Sipho's keychain scraping against the steering column. Heard his breath. Swore she could hear her heart stop, and then start again, pumping blood through her veins.

Then the hard smack of car doors behind her. And the door of the jeep opened and the old dog stepped down. She heard Inja's shoes crunch on the gravel as he walked to her door and opened it. 'Get out.'

Sunday shrank back from him. He grabbed her by the arm and pulled her from the car. She fell to the sand, the skin of her knees tearing.

'Leave her!' Sipho shouted, standing. Four men from the taxi were at his door and one of them took him by the throat and stuck a gun to his head.

Sunday knelt, the gray shoes of the old man before her on the dirt road, sun kicking off the brass buckles. 'Bring that rubbish here,' he said.

The men dragged Sipho around the car and forced him to his knees beside Sunday. Inja had a gun in his hand, silver against his dark skin. He put the barrel to Sipho's head. The boy was expressionless, staring straight ahead.

'Has he fucked you?' Inja asked Sunday. 'Broken you? Put his filth in your blood?'

She looked up at the old dog, a black shape against the red sky. 'He has not touched me.'

Inja pushed the gun hard against Sipho's temple, almost shoving him off balance. 'Be truthful now, girl. Or I will shoot him.'

'I swear to God. I am speaking the truth.'

'And to where were you going? With him?'

'To Durban.'

'And what about our wedding?' She said nothing. 'You are a disrespectful girl.' He cleared his throat, spat onto the sand. 'Or have you fallen under a bad influence?'

'It was my idea,' she said.

'Is this true, AIDS man?' Inja asked, smacking Sipho lightly with the gun barrel. Sipho said nothing.

Sunday tried to catch Sipho's eye. To find a way to show him how sorry she was. But he stared out over the valley at the sinking sun.

An explosion. Sunday felt a wetness on the bare skin of her arm. Something hot on her cheek. She saw the boy topple forward, his face turned toward her, blood bubbling from his mouth. Light fading from his eyes. Another shot and his body jerked and a little river of blood flowed from under him, soaking into the parched sand of the road.

Sunday tried to scream, but she could find no voice.

Two men grabbed and lifted her, carrying her toward the taxi. Threw her in the rear and slammed the door. As the taxi reversed and turned, she saw Inja and the other men standing over Sipho's body. Inja said something, laughed, and kicked the dead boy with one of those ugly gray shoes. Then the taxi took the bend and Sunday could see no more.

chapter 40

INJA SAT ON THE CEMENT PORCH OF HIS HOUSE, WATCHING AS A BLANKET OF darkness was thrown over the valley. Usually the end of the day was a time of pride and reflection for him. When he would look down on the hard hills and the dry red earth from which he had sprung – a skinny runt, a bastard, unwanted and scorned, growing up as an illiterate herdsman – and congratulate himself on what he had become. An *induna*, with a fleet of taxis, fertile fields of Durban Poison, and two surviving wives with mightily dimpled thighs, each with her own hut here in his kraal. The father of a brood of children so numerous he had lost count.

But tonight he felt hollow and dissatisfied. His appetite was gone again, the plate of steak, tripe, and maize meal all but untouched on the concrete beside his chair. Even his brandy and Coke tasted sour as goat's piss.

He belched, rubbed at his stomach. Listened to the sounds of the night. The thin wail of one of his children out in the gloom. A man's laugh, quickly stifled: one of the guards patrolling the perimeter of the compound. Inja felt more than heard the thrum of the generator that powered his house, the focal point of the kraal, where he slept alone. His wives lived in huts lit by candlelight, and cooked over open fires, in the way of their ancestors.

He threw back his drink. 'Woman!' he bellowed.

The duty wife for the night, who crouched on the floor inside his house, waiting to serve him, hurried out and knelt before Inja. Not looking him in the eye. Wearing a red and black beaded hat, her heavy body wrapped in a plaid blanket despite the heat.

'More brandy. And take this swill to the pigs.' He shoved the plate of uneaten food toward her with his shoe. She lifted his plate and glass and backed away from him, bowing, until she disappeared into the house.

His cell phone sang in his pocket, loud as a cicada. High enough up in the hills here to get a signal. He removed the phone and saw the caller ID. The moment he had dreaded.

'Yes?'

'Call back.' The line went dead.

Inja walked into the living room, dominated by a giant TV that flickered, mute, and a bulky brown leather sofa and chair set, still swathed in the transparent plastic it was shipped in. He dug into the drawer beneath the TV and found another cell phone, loaded with an anonymous pay-as-you-go SIM card. He dialed the number he had memorized.

The voice said, 'Hold on.'

Shuffling and muttering and then another voice. One used to issuing commands. 'Tell me it is done.'

For a moment Inja considered lying. Knew it would be suicidal. 'They have crossed the border. To the north.'

'Jesus. I don't like this loose end.'

'*Nkosi*, there is no cause for concern.' *Nkosi*. Chief. Also the name of God.

'I'm trusting you on this. If you're wrong, there will be consequences.'

'I understand.' He cleared his throat, his tone more wheedling. '*Nkosi*, as you know, I am to marry in two days' time. Since you will be here, in Bhambatha's Rock, it would be the greatest honor if you would grace us with your presence.'

Inja shut up when he realized the phone was dead in his hand. He let the instrument droop to his side and stood staring blankly at the flickering TV. Then he opened the back of the phone and removed the little yellow card. Closed the phone, dropped it into the drawer and went back out onto the porch.

A fresh drink waited for him beside his chair. He took a box of matches from his pocket and set fire to the SIM card, threw it out into the night, watching it flare and fade like a dying glow-worm.

Fear nagged at Inja's innards. The knowledge that the escape of the white men would tell against him. He depended on the goodwill of the chief, his mentor these many years. The man who had helped him to become all he had become. The minister of justice. Living far away in his house in Pretoria, but a man from these parts, a royal Zulu. One of the few Zulu chiefs who hadn't collaborated with the Boers to hold on to his crust of power. When he was forced into exile by the white men, Inja had gone with him.

Back then, in the late eighties and early nineties, the chief had purged the ranks of the freedom fighters in the training camps in Zambia, Angola and Tanzania. Convinced they had been infiltrated by apartheid spies. There were no trials. The chief would point a finger and Inja would pull the trigger. Dump the bodies in unmarked graves. Proud to serve his master.

When Nelson Mandela walked free and the apartheid regime fell, the chief began his rise within the new government. And his dog was always in the shadows, ready to do his work.

The chief was now one of the most powerful men in the country, more powerful even than the president, who was his stooge, it was said. He had patiently collected dossiers on ally and enemy alike, and he terrified men into absolute loyalty. When they wavered he whistled, and Inja came running. But he knew if he misstepped it would be his body thrown into a ditch far out in the valley.

Inja stood with his back to the cool whitewashed wall, and tried to breathe through the fear and the fever that heated his blood. Yellow light from the doorway at his side spilled out across the sand, in an elongated rectangle that brought a pine coffin to his mind.

He tried to shake these morbid thoughts, looking at the new hut, the half-thatched roof beams just visible against the night sky. The house of his fourth bride. He had torched the house that had belonged to the wife who had rotted to nothing before she died. Commissioned locals to build this one for the virgin he would marry on Saturday.

Inja thought of her in the car with that polluted pig and a fury rose in him. He had wanted to fall upon her at the roadside, force himself between her thighs, feel his manhood rip that little skin inside her. Then leave her dead beside the trash she had wanted to abscond with.

But he had held back. Heard the counsel of his *sangoma*, that only by marrying this virgin in the way of his ancestors would he free himself from the curse that had turned his blood to poison. He needed her. Simple. Only she could save him.

Inja sat, trying to calm himself. He watched flying ants commit suicide against the naked bulb that hung above his chair. Tiny explosions of wings as the hot glass fried them. He closed his eyes. The after-image of the light bulb burning into his retinas.

chapter 41

TWO SHRILL BLEATS WOKE ZONDI. HE'D SLEPT LIKE THE DEAD. EVEN the pumping music and drunken shouts from the tavern hadn't disturbed him. But his cell phone message alerts startled him awake. He lay, disoriented for a moment, in the blackness of the room, hearing nothing now but the oppressive quiet of the country, the tavern long closed. Thought he'd imagined the digital yelps.

The phone, lying beside the bed on the beer crate that served as a table, had been mute since he arrived. He fumbled in the dark, lifted its glowing face and saw one skinny bar on the signal strength indicator. Some freak of the elements: the microwaves bouncing off a mountain or a cloud. He dialed and listened to a mechanical voice speaking faintly African-accented English, telling him he had one message. One single fucking message. An indication of his pariah status. He hit play.

Heard a voice say, 'Call a man about a dog.' A chuckle and then nothing more.

Zondi played the message again. He recognized the voice. M. K. Moloi. A one-time colleague of his who had disappeared into a political think tank a year ago. A flashy man of thirty who was aligned with a newly formed alliance that had split from the ruling party. Men who were in opposition to the justice minister.

As Zondi tried to call M.K. the signal evaporated. He stood up from the bed and hit the wall switch. The low-voltage bulb dangling from the ceiling dribbled its sickly blue light down on him. He paced the cramped room, holding the phone out like it was a dowsing rod. Nothing. He tossed it onto the bed.

Zondi scratched at himself. He'd slept on top of the covers, dressed in a pair of sweatpants and a T-shirt, but he itched where the bedbugs had fed. And his head throbbed, like some Zulu drummer was hard at work inside his skull.

The light hurt his eyes so he killed it. Sat down on the bed. Listened to the night sounds – a dog barking, a muffled cough that could have been human – and thought about the message. Felt certain that whatever happened now was preordained. Beyond his control.

chapter 42

GOODBREAD SLUMPED IN THE FRONT OF THE TRUCK, LOOKING UP AT the stars, like a hot white rash out here in the middle of nowhere. Heard the rumble of a rig down on the highway, its headlamps raking the bush that hid the pickup from view, sending dappled light across the interior of the cab.

You're on a hiding to nothing, that's for damn sure. Talking to himself. Prison habit. Years in solitary confinement. Not loud enough to wake his son, who slept in the rear of the truck, his long legs hanging out over the open tailgate.

Goodbread ducked below the level of the dashboard and lit a smoke, killed the match before he sat back up. Kept the cigarette cupped in his hand so the glowing ember would be invisible. Behaving as if he was on night ops a lifetime ago. In some godforsaken rice paddy or a stretch of desert scrub.

Goodbread felt a coughing spasm coming and he opened the door, reached across for the rifle at his side, wanting to get away from the truck so he didn't disturb his son. The dome light kicked in, making him a sitting target. He lifted a shaking hand to kill it.

Jesus Christ.

He slid from the truck, gripping the rifle. Ended up standing with his knees bent, head hanging down, hot blood spilling from his rotten lungs onto the sand between his feet.

Admit it, old man. You're done for.

Goodbread felt his knees give way like he'd been poleaxed, and he found himself kneeling in the dust, jamming the stock of the rifle into the earth to stop himself falling on his face. He sucked air. Choking. Bright lights spinning before his eyes like a mirror ball in a Saigon cathouse. Used the weapon to push himself to his feet.

He looked back toward the Toyota. Didn't look as if he'd woken the sleeping man. The spasm was over, and his breath was coming easier. But he still felt as if he was suffocating. Out here in all this space, with all this goddam air, and he couldn't seem to get any of it into his lungs.

After he was released from prison Goodbread had seen a doctor in Cape Town. Man told him he should be hospitalized. He'd walked out without saying a word. Went and holed up on Althea Vorster's farm. Her dead husband, Hendrik, had served under him in Angola. When Goodbread went to prison the Vorsters had been the only people who stayed in touch with him. Sent him packages that arrived torn and looted at his cell.

After Hendrik was murdered Althea kept up the contact. Insisted he come and stay on her farm after he was released. The old bottle-blonde had been sweet on him, Goodbread guessed. Muffled a laugh. If she'd been expecting anything from him, she'd gone to her grave a disappointed woman. The years in prison and the disease eating his lungs had long ago robbed him of any firepower down below.

Althea had known he was sick, but had never questioned him. Let him alone to do his dying. He had reckoned he'd wait for the day it got too bad. Take the truck and drive out into the desert. Flatten a bottle of Jack and suck on a shotgun. Then this mess came along.

Goodbread sat down on the warm sand and took a stainless-steel hip flask from his trouser pocket. Drank bourbon and stared out at the stars. Thought about a vengeful God. The one he'd been taught to fear as a boy back in the ramshackle churches of West Texas.

Spoke to that God now, old fool that he was: *Just give me a few more days.*

He could tell himself he was atoning. Find grand words to explain that he was on this last mission to get justice for his boy. Truth was, he was terrified. Him, a man who had taken more lives than he could count, didn't know if he had the balls to pull that trigger and take his own. Saw himself trapped in a bed, an oxygen mask stuck like a limpet to his face, dark women in white uniforms prodding at him as he drowned in his own snot.

But this was a chance to go out like a man. He'd never felt fear in battle. And he was driving them into one, up the road a ways. Knew there was a bullet waiting for him in Zululand. Knew he'd welcome it.

chapter 43

SUNDAY'S BLADDER, FULL AS A SACK OF FERMENTING BEER, WOKE HER. SHE
kept her eyes closed. Tried to burrow deep into the rough
blanket, avoiding the thin daylight that reached out from the
single window. Tried to stay unconscious where nothing could
touch her. Where she wouldn't have to wake up and face the
reality that she had killed Sipho, surely as if she had pulled that
trigger herself.

Sunday sobbed and sat up. She had slept on the blanket
on the dung floor, the fat body of Auntie Mavis blocking the
doorway to the hut. The woman lay on her back and snored,
sounding like a wasp's nest being smoked out. Last night the
men in the taxi had brought Sunday here to the old dog's sister.
Where she would be held prisoner until her wedding day.

The hut was no bigger than the one Sunday had shared with
Ma Beauty, but it was crammed full of furniture. A sofa and two
chairs. A TV perched on top of shelves filled with dusty little
ornaments. A white dancer in a frilly dress, balancing on tiptoe,
her arms above her head. A seashell with DURBAN painted on
the side in flowing blue letters. A little white wooden rabbit
with a pink bow on its neck. Plastic flowers. The walls were full
of photographs in ornate frames, all of Auntie Mavis smiling,
posing with her brother or with her arms around children
Sunday assumed belonged to the old dog.

Sunday stood, squeezed herself around a wooden dining-
room table and upholstered chairs. She had slept in her jeans
and T-shirt, slipped her feet into her tennis shoes. She stepped
over the fat woman and opened the door.

The hut was on the slope of a hill close to town, and Sunday could see the taxis already bumping toward the jumble of buildings. A man sat outside the door, his back against the mud wall of the hut, chin to his chest as he slept. The squeak of the door roused him and he opened one yellow eye.

'Where are you going, girl?' he asked, grunting as he pulled himself to his feet. He was a big man. Slow. With a belly that bulged from under his T-shirt, a pistol stuck into the waistband of his jeans.

'I need to use the toilet,' she said. Pointing down toward the communal pit latrine, chimney poking up into the dawn sky like a crooked finger.

He coughed and spat, waved a hand for her to get moving. She walked down to the outhouse, the big man at her heels. She could hear him yawning, and a sound like steel wool on a wooden board as he scratched at the tight curls of dark hair on his belly.

Sunday went into the latrine and closed the door. A gap at the top gave her a view of the pink and orange sunrise. The latrine stank even worse than the one she and her aunt used. Sunday finished and wiped herself on the scraps of newspaper she had brought from the hut.

She opened the door and saw the man standing pissing, steam rising from where the jet of urine hit the sand. He made no move to cover himself, and shook his thing before he folded it back into his pants and zipped the flies.

He waved his hand again. 'Go.'

She walked back up the hill. A girl of about ten, in a dress so torn it left more of her skinny body naked than covered, stoked a wood fire beside the fat woman's hut. A neighbor's child, Sunday guessed. Used as a slave by Auntie Mavis, who stood in the doorway of the hut, dressed in a fluffy nightgown. The fat woman walked toward the fire and Sunday saw she carried the shopping bag that held Sunday's things. Auntie Mavis threw

Sunday's jeans and underwear onto the fire.

Sunday broke into a sprint, the big man lumbering after her. As she reached the fire she saw the woman dip a fat hand into the bag and lift out the remains of the photo album.

'No!' Sunday shouted. Her cry scaring a bush shrike from the roof of the hut.

Sunday lunged at Auntie Mavis, but the big man grabbed her from behind and enfolded her in a bear hug, holding her kicking feet off the ground. She watched as the flames ate the book, finishing the job of the fire ten years before, reducing the photograph of her mother to curling ashes.

The fat woman stepped up to Sunday, lifted a heavy arm and slapped her across the face. Tears sprang from her eyes. She blinked them away. Determined not to let this rhinoceros see her cry.

'You are a little slut. Just like your mother. Now go into the hut and take off those clothes so I can burn them also. Then wash yourself of your filth.'

The big man set Sunday down inside the hut and Auntie Mavis closed the door from outside. A bucket of water stood on the floor. A dress like a sack, in some coarse rural fabric, was draped over the back of the sofa. Flanked by a pair of outsize brown panties and a white bra. Sunday had never worn a bra, and knew her small breasts would be lost in that contraption.

She stripped off her jeans, panties and T-shirt and kneeled down and washed her face in the bucket. The door opened and the fat woman took her clothes and slammed out again. While her face was wet, Sunday allowed the tears to come, and she felt as if they would never stop, would flow down the hill and flood the parched and ugly town that festered in the valley below.

chapter 44

WHEN ZONDI AWOKE, SUNLIGHT POKED THROUGH THE HOLES IN THE DRAPES, and he could hear the taxis honking for business on the main road. His body itched, his head ached, and he was powerfully thirsty, but he felt stronger than he had the day before. Less dislocated. He reached down for the plastic bottle of water beside the bed and emptied it. Checked his phone. No signal.

He took his toiletry bag across to the sink and lifted out a fresh bar of Roger & Gallet soap. Stripped naked and ran the single faucet. Cold water. The basin was stained and stank from being used as a urinal. An eroded chunk of Sunlight soap lay beside the faucet, a stylized rising sun molded into the surface. Zondi had no intention of letting the soap anywhere near his skin, but he lifted it to his nose and smelled his childhood.

For generations this soap had been used to wash bodies and clothing and linen in rural South Africa. His earliest memories were of his mother carrying him on her back, held close to her flesh by a blanket. She would sing to him as she went about her chores. Her voice, the warmth of her body, and the scent of the soap sending him to a place more peaceful than he had known since.

Unable to resist the temptation, he scrubbed the bar of Sunlight under the water, forced away images of the countless assholes and groins the soap had visited, and lathered his body, feeling the bedbug bites like Braille beneath his fingers. Rinsed and toweled himself. He ignored the bottle of Hugo Boss cologne lying in his bag, not wanting to mask this smell that made him feel almost happy.

Zondi flossed, brushed his teeth and dressed in a fresh pair of Diesels and a linen shirt. Shook his Nikes to dislodge any scorpion that had nested in them overnight, and slipped them on. Zipped his duffel bag and left the room.

He locked the bag in the trunk of his car and crossed to the phone container. Vusi kept vigil over the telephones. He smiled and stood when Zondi entered, keen to sniff another banknote.

'These phones,' Zondi said, pointing to the instruments. 'Do they display their number if I call a cell phone?'

'No, sir. Nothing shows up.'

Zondi nodded and took the phone farthest from the door, dialed M. K. Moloi's number. It was answered after two rings. 'Moloi.'

'You know who this is?' Speaking English.

'Uh-huh. Are you still in Bhambatha's Rock?'

Zondi, taken aback. 'Yes.'

'At a pay phone?'

'Yes.'

'Give me the number there and I'll call you.'

Zondi read out the digits printed on the wall above the instrument. The line went dead and he replaced the receiver. Within seconds the phone was purring.

Zondi lifted it. 'How did you know where I was?'

Heard a chuckle. 'You're in Zululand, my friend. And you know how it is with you Zulus: you're either born an assassin or a spy.' Moloi was a Tswana. Another breed entirely.

'What do you want?' Zondi asked.

'Your trip down there, it have anything to do with our canine friend?' Moloi had spent a few years at Harvard, and there were traces of Boston in his accent. An affectation that had always irritated Zondi.

'No,' Zondi said. His cards tucked close to his chest.

'Be advised that we have our eye on him.'

'Who's we?'

'A faction that respects the rule of law.' Another chuckle. 'He was down in Cape Town for a few days. Taking care of business. Or rather a businessman. You getting me here?'

Zondi was. Ben Baker. A chink in Inja's master's armor that had needed to be secured. 'Loudly.'

'All I'm saying, good buddy, is that if you stumble over anything interesting you loop me in. It could be to your advantage.'

'Sorry. I'm out of here today.'

'Pity. Anyway, let's have a drink when you're home. Matters of mutual interest and all of that good stuff.' Zondi was left with the dial tone in his ear.

He walked out and stood on the sidewalk, not seeing the dust and the filth and the goats and the taxis. Seeing lines that were being drawn up in Jo'burg and Pretoria. A battle was looming. No blood would be shed, but it would be ruthless all the same.

chapter 45

WAKING UP WAS THE WORST. DELL HADN'T REALIZED HOW DEPENDENT he'd become on the warmth of his wife's body, the wriggling aliveness of the twins as they snuck in early and burrowed beneath the blankets to join their parents. He turned off the memory.

He sat on the tailgate of the truck, eyes still gummed with sleep, scratching at his stubble, staring out over hundreds of roofless little cinderblock boxes that spread across the dry veld. Empty doorways and windows without glass. Anything of value looted and hauled away. A stalled housing development for the rural poor. Invisible when he'd driven the truck off the road the night before, so exhausted he was almost comatose.

He looked for Goodbread and saw the old man over in the scrub, crouching. Probably taking a shit. Used to bushwhacking. Dell reached back into the truck and found water. Had a drink. Rinsed his mouth and spat onto the sand. He hadn't brushed his teeth in a couple of days and his tongue felt like it was growing a carpet of fur.

He heard the chime of glass and saw his father walking toward him, carrying three dusty beer bottles in each hand. Watched as he set the empty bottles on a mound a few paces from the truck. Goodbread reached beneath his shirt, produced a handgun and cocked it.

All Dell knew about guns was that he wanted nothing to do with them. He'd never so much as touched one in his enforced stint in the military. Or since. Yes, he'd used his fists over the years. Not very well. And he once threw a half-brick at a cop during an anti-apartheid march. Missed. So, a pacifist. Kind of.

Definitely no guns. Ever.

When his friends, aging liberals pissed off after endless burglaries and hijackings, went and bought guns, he'd shaken his head. Flat out refused. Just like he refused to change his stance on the reintroduction of the death penalty. Murder by the state was still murder.

He heard the weapon firing twice in quick succession, and two bottles exploded. Then the old man waved him over. Dell hesitated. 'Come on, boy. I reckon it's time.'

Maybe it was.

He walked across to his father. Goodbread held the gun out to Dell and he took it. Feeling the surprising heft of the weapon.

'Shoot one of them bottles.' The old man pointed a trembling finger at the empties on the mound.

Dell lifted the gun and aimed. Tense as he squeezed the trigger. Felt the compressed power of the thing bucking in his hands. Missed.

Goodbread said, 'Just imagine you're pointing your finger at the bottle. Squeeze the trigger. You're not jerking yourself off, boy.'

Breathed. Relaxed. Lifted the gun and pointed it. Squeezed. Glass exploded. Arced the barrel to the next bottle and the next. Hit all four targets.

'Jesus,' Goodbread said. 'Either that's one hell of a piece of dumb luck or you're a natural, son.' Smiling his death's-head smile. 'At least you got something from me.'

Dell handed the gun to Goodbread, butt first. 'So, you reckon you still a pacifist?' the old man asked, feeding rounds into the magazine.

Dell, back in the mortuary for a moment, said: 'No.'

'Bottles are one thing. You going to be able to pull that trigger when flesh and blood is in front of you?'

'Yes.'

'You sure now? You not going to get yourself all dizzied-up from turning the other cheek?'

'No.'

His father held the loaded weapon out to him. 'Then I believe this is yours.'

Dell took the gun.

chapter 46

ZONDI SAT IN AN EATING-HOUSE ON THE MAIN ROAD OF BHAMBATHA'S Rock. His BMW was parked outside, gassed up and ready to take him home, starbursts of hard light kicking off the windshield, patterning the grimy ceiling of the diner. He was going to eat breakfast and then he was going back to Jo'burg. He owed a debt to nobody. Least of all a peasant girl he didn't even know.

The place was already doing good business, plastic tables full of noisy men busy with plates of food. Zondi ate maize porridge, spinach, potato and beans. The food was good, bringing back more memories of his childhood, and he found himself setting aside his plastic fork, and eating with his hands, forming little balls with the maize and the gravy.

The room went quiet as if somebody had hit a mute button and Zondi looked up to see a group of men block the light as they stepped into the doorway. Recognized the skinny man surrounded by five of his crew, automatic weapons dangling from their hands. Vusi from the phone kiosk was prodded into the eating-house by one of the gun barrels. His face slack with fear.

Inja swept the room with his arm. 'Everybody out. Move! Move!' That big voice, coming from the runt of a man.

People were already standing up from tables, hurrying toward the door, toppling plastic chairs in their haste.

Inja's finger skewered Zondi. 'Not you, my friend. You sit.'

Zondi stayed where he was, hands on the tabletop, swallowing a mouthful of food. The staff left their stations, none of them daring to look Inja in the eye, and followed the last of the patrons out. One of Inja's men closed the door, and in the silence

Zondi could hear fat bubbling in a pan back in the kitchen.

Inja sat down opposite Zondi, shot the cuffs of his check sport coat, put his elbows on the table. 'Zondi.'

'Inja.'

Zondi hadn't seen Inja Mazibuko in the flesh in more than twenty years. Not that there was much flesh to see. The man was older, but if anything he seemed even more spare than he had as a teenager. His face gray. His eyes yellow and bloodshot. A white residue caked his cracked lips like scum on a pond.

'What are you doing back here?' Inja asked.

'Just visiting.'

Inja sucked his teeth, nodding. Jerked his head toward Vusi. 'He says you were in the phone shop with a fax of my wedding invite. Asking questions.'

Zondi looked up at Vusi, who couldn't meet his eye. Saw the sweat rolling down the man's face. Listened to the fat spitting in the kitchen. Heard a meat fly circling somewhere behind him.

Inja reached up and grabbed Vusi by his shirtfront, pulled him down toward the table, his chin banging on the plastic surface, squashed face turned to Zondi. Eyes glazed with fear. Inja ducked his right hand beneath his jacket and came out with a .44. Jammed the barrel into Vusi's ear. 'Is he lying?'

Zondi could hear the rush of Vusi's breath, and saw his eyes widen, staring at him. Pleading. Zondi shook his head. 'No. He's not lying. Let him go.'

Inja nodded. Lifted the gun away from Vusi's head. 'Okay. Fuck off, you.'

Vusi pushed himself to standing and took off toward the door, leaving a trail of drops behind him. Zondi saw a puddle of piss beneath the table, rivulets reaching out toward his Reeboks. Moved his feet under his chair.

Inja put the gun down on the table. He snapped his fingers, speaking to one of his men, never taking his eyes off Zondi.

'Get me a Coke. Cold.' The man hurried toward the fridge. 'My betrothed. You know who her mother was?'

'It's difficult to miss.'

'Yes.' The man was back with the Coke and Inja cracked the tab and took a long draft. Burped. Wiped his mouth on the back of his hand. 'So what is your interest in this girl?'

'I have no interest.'

Inja stared at Zondi, then he smiled like a feral dog. 'You're a liar, Zondi. You're a liar.'

'Why would I lie?'

Inja tapped his index finger against his skull. 'Because I've just now worked you out, my friend.'

'Ja?'

'Ja.' Sitting forward. 'You think she's your child, don't you?'

'I'm not sure,' Zondi said.

'And what if she is? Are you here to collect the dowry?' Laughing. But no humor in his dead eyes. Drinking. Closing his eyes. Opening them, smeared and unfocused for a moment. Then finding Zondi, who said nothing. 'You are not going to get in my way, are you, Zondi?'

'No. I'm leaving, heading back to Jo'burg.'

'Good idea. This is no place for you. You're city now. Soft.' Slumping in his chair, rubbing his temples. 'I'll look after her, Zondi. She'll want for nothing. She is a lucky girl.'

'I'm sure she is.'

Inja stood. Zondi could smell him, something sharp and sour and almost metallic. The smell of disease. Inja picked the gun up from the table, reached forward and put the front sight under Zondi's chin, forcing his head upward.

'Because we were once friends, Zondi – comrades – I'm letting you get into your car,' jerking a thumb at Zondi's BMW parked out in the sun, 'and drive your ass back to Jo'burg. I see you again, I'm not so kind. Understand?'

'Yes,' Zondi said, his voice coming out muffled and strained.

Inja released Zondi's head and holstered the pistol. Nodded. Hitched up his crème trousers and walked to the door, his men falling in behind him, ordnance clanking. Zondi watched them get into their vehicles and leave in a display of red dust.

You win, he heard himself say. Not sure who he was talking to. Not Inja. That much he knew. Then Zondi realized that he was talking to himself. Not the man of nearly forty, but the boy he had once been. And if it was a debt he was here to repay, it wasn't to the woman long dead. Or to a girl who was a stranger to him. It was to that boy. To atone, maybe, for the things that he had done to turn him into the man he had become.

chapter 47

DRIVING THROUGH A DIFFERENT LANDSCAPE. ROLLING SUGARCANE FIELDS, like a thick green carpet spreading across the rolling hills. A different heat, too. Moist. Humid.

'How far away are we?' Dell asked.

'Reckon we'll be there early afternoon.'

'Want to tell me your plan?'

The old man said nothing, stared out over the landscape. Then he sighed, sat up a little straighter. 'The girl Inja Mazibuko has chosen as his bride. She's young, barely sixteen…' Words dying in a coughing spasm that rattled to a wheezing end. Goodbread wiped his mouth. Gasped. 'Heard it told she works at some tourist attraction, up in Zululand.'

'So?'

'We're going to take her. Catch Inja wrong footed. Draw him out.'

'Take her?' Dell stared across at him. 'You're saying we're going to kidnap this girl and use her as bait?'

'Yes.'

'No fucking way.'

'You getting all squeamish on me, boy?'

'I'm not going to let you put another innocent person in the firing line. You said we're going after Inja. I'm up for that. But not some girl. Forget it.'

'I have no great desire to risk anybody's life, son. But do you think we can just ride on up to Inja's homestead and get him to come along with us, meek as you please? He's a goddam warlord. Sitting up there with a mess of weapons and an army of crazy dope-head Zulu warriors. This is the way it's going down.'

'Fuck that.'

The roofs of a town broke the cane fields. Dell nudged the turn signal and took the truck off the highway onto a narrow road scarred by potholes.

'What you doing, boy?'

'I'm going to find a phone. Call my lawyer. Then I'm going to the police station and I'm handing myself over.'

'Reckon that's a good idea?'

'Yes.'

''Cause I surely don't.'

Dell said nothing as they headed into the town on a road flanked by pine trees, slowing when speed bumps drummed under their tires. They passed a faded pink billboard saying STOP AIDS, LOVE LIFE. It had been used for target practice.

Dell drove toward a church steeple that threw its shadow across low cinderblock buildings. Saw a Coke sign painted on the window of a store, eased the truck to a halt. Double-parked next to a minivan, two Indian men unloading bundles of newspapers from the rear.

Goodbread fixed Dell with his torn eyes. 'You're going to get yourself dead, son. And the law will never trouble Inja Mazibuko.'

Dell slid the pistol from the waist of his khakis and threw it into Goodbread's lap. Cracked the door. 'Take the truck and go.' He slammed the door and walked. Heard the scrape of gears as the truck drove away. Didn't look back.

Dell entered the store. Half-empty shelves of canned food, toilet paper and detergent. A swarthy man sat slumped behind the counter in the draft of a lazy fan. A woman in a pinafore and headscarf shouted Zulu into a pay phone mounted on a wall in the rear. The Indian men dumped the newspapers near the cash register and walked out with the unsold pile from the day before.

While he waited for the phone Dell picked up the *Mercury* from Durban. The headline suggested that Ben Baker's death was a hit. Denied by the cops, who were calling it a home invasion. Dell flicked through the pages to see whether there was any news of the man his father had killed the day before. Nothing.

'Hey.'

Dell looked up, saw the store owner, a Greek or a Portuguese, watching him over the counter. Chewing on a length of dried sausage. 'You think maybe this is a bloody library?'

Dell dug in his pocket and came up with two coins, threw them onto the counter in front of the man. Heard the Zulu woman still busy on the phone. He laid the newspaper across a shelf of chips and tabloid magazines, carried on turning pages.

Saw his mugshot on page four under the headline: KILLER REPORTER IN NAMIBIA? He looked wild eyed. Deranged. Knew the story was only getting this much ink because he'd been a newsman. His ex-colleagues on a *schadenfreude* binge. Dell's pic was flanked by a blurred snapshot of Goodbread from his glory days. Dell shifted his arm, revealed the color photograph beneath: a knot of mourners around three coffins. One large. Two tiny. Felt his gut contract as if somebody had grabbed it in their fist. Saw Rosie's parents, the woman's face buried in the old man's shoulder. Before he knew it Dell was walking back out the door, sheets of newspaper whispering to the floor behind him.

The truck idled in a parking bay, his father at the wheel. Dell opened the passenger door and sat. Goodbread said nothing, put the car into gear and they took off down the road.

'Give me the gun,' Dell said.

chapter 48

SUNDAY FELT LIKE A THIN SLICE OF BALONEY BETWEEN TWO CHUNKS OF bread, flanked by the big man and Auntie Mavis as the old truck bounced into Bhambatha's Rock. The man stank of bad breath and unwashed feet. And something else, a dark, sour smell, as if he hadn't wiped himself properly. Auntie Mavis, overflowing her pink dress, sweated through layers of cheap perfume, and Sunday could feel the dampness of the woman's arm as her dimpled flesh danced over the potholes.

Sunday spoke a silent prayer to her mother. Begging for her to come. To guide her. But Sunday feared that her mother had forsaken her, the last of her burned away with the book. Sunday hadn't heard her voice or felt her presence. No tingling up the spine, no cool breeze catching the back of her neck.

Sunday felt more alone than she ever had. There was nobody she could turn to in this town that lived in fear of the old dog. The police, tired of being slaughtered, had long ago shut the station house and moved to faraway Dundee. The law in Bhambatha's Rock was made by Inja Mazibuko.

'Come, girl, stop your bloody dreaming!' The fat woman stood up out of the truck and set off for the sidewalk, looking like the hot-air balloon Sunday had seen one day, floating pink and magical across the sky.

Sunday followed Auntie Mavis into a small building on the main road, feeling ugly in the sack of a dress that hung on her. The dressmaker, a woman as old as the rocks on the hills, waited at the door. She was one of the few who still remembered the pure traditions, handed down from her mother and her mother's mother before her.

The old crone bowed her already bent spine. Fawning over Auntie Mavis, toothless mouth drooling at the vision of the dog's money flowing into her pockets. Sunday knew she had hours of torture ahead, while the old woman poked and prodded at her, and remodeled the clothes on her body, uncaring if the needles drew blood.

The big man closed the door and sighed as he lowered himself onto a wooden stool by the window, staring out into the street, scratching his balls, the gun at his hip.

The dressmaker clucked her tongue and her young assistant, a mournful-looking girl Sunday's age, lifted away a sheet to reveal the wedding garments laid out on a tabletop. The embroidered shawl. The tall red bridal hat. The beaded black bra. The short tasseled skirt. The veil of beads that would be woven into Sunday's hair the morning of the wedding and remain there until her dying day. Telling the world that she was the property of Inja Mazibuko.

chapter 49

DELL DROVE DEEPER INTO THE HEAT. HUMIDITY SO THICK YOU COULD CHEW on it. Goodbread said the AC tore his lungs, so Dell had the windows rolled down. Still felt the water dripping freely from his body. The old man didn't seem to sweat, sat like a dried-out husk, staring through the windshield, smoking endless cigarettes.

Dell followed the coast road, along the edge of Africa. To the left the cane fields, to the right the Indian Ocean. He caught glimpses of water, flat and greasy, through the fungus of condos and golf estates – the privileged hunkered down behind razor wire and electric fences, staring off toward far Australia and wondering why they hadn't got the hell out when their currency still meant something. The hungry poor getting closer by the day, their shacks flung up against the perimeter walls of the rich men's enclaves, their shit turning the streams and lagoons black with disease.

Dell avoided the urban tangle of Durban, where he'd spent the first ten years of his life, heading inland, toward a place he'd never been. Far from the eight-lane toll road. He switched on the radio. A Durban station, blasting out Bollywood show tunes for the descendants of the cane cutters the British had brought in by the boatload from south India a hundred years ago.

The cane gave way to rolling hills. A town blurred by. Dell looked across at his father. 'Remember this place?'

'Yes.' Coughing, rousing himself from his trance. 'Changed a lot over the years. Was just a dirt road back then.'

'So all that stuff about busting Nelson Mandela? It was true?'

'You calling me a liar, boy?' Looking across at him, some of the old swagger back in his voice.

Dell shrugged. His father laughed and smothered a cough. Pointed a gnarled, nicotine-stained finger past the houses and the fields, to a road that ran parallel to the freeway. 'Happened right there. August of nineteen sixty-two. Mandela was on the run. Had been for months. The South African security police were after him, but they couldn't find their dicks in their breeches. I told them that he'd been down here, visiting a Zulu chief named Luthuli. That he was pretending to be the chauffeur of an old white commie faggot. We waited, me and the Boers. Saw the car coming along that road. Mandela wasn't even driving. Old homo was. White man driving a black man in this country back in sixty-two?' Laughed. Wheezed. 'The South Africans stopped the car and Mandela gave himself up with no fuss at all. Went away for twenty-seven years.'

'How did you know where he would be?'

Goodbread was sitting up straight now, more like the man Dell remembered. 'I was CIA, boy. My cover was junior consul in Durban, but I was working for Langley. I'd infiltrated the commies and fellow travelers here in Natal. Jews. Indians. Some educated Zulus. It was all too goddam easy. One of them gave Mandela up for fifty dollars.'

'He denies that, you know? Mandela. That he was betrayed. Says he was just careless.'

'He's a gentleman.'

Dell looked across at the old man, searching for signs of sarcasm. Finding none. 'Did my mother know who you really were?'

'Didn't you ask her?'

'She wouldn't talk about you.'

Goodbread sighed. 'No, guess she wouldn't.' He watched the road a while. 'At first she knew nothing. When we met, she was a college student in Durban, thought I was just some small-time desk jockey. I told her after we were married.' He laughed. 'Said she was proud of me.'

'That didn't last long.'

'No. Can't say it did.' He shrugged. 'I had a young man's appetites, that's true. And I did things of which I'm not proud. God knows, if I could undo a bunch of them I would. But if you think it was all whoring and carousing, boy, you're dead wrong. There was a war to fight.'

'Don't dress it up, old man. You just ditched us and fucked off.'

'What would you have had me do? Drag a woman and a baby off to goddam Vietnam? I left you and your mother here where it was safe, and went and did what had to be done.' Goodbread lit another cigarette, drawing smoke into his wrecked lungs, exhaling with a rattle of phlegm. 'As a father and a husband I displayed little aptitude, that I will allow. But I would like to believe that I followed my calling. Made a contribution.'

'You killed people. Plain and fucking simple.'

'Damn straight. Communists. It was a different world back then.' Talking around smoke, energized by his memories. 'Anyway, after Saigon fell I came home.'

'Bullshit. You went to Angola.'

'Close enough to keep an eye on you and your ma.' Dell shook his head and laughed. 'Why do you think you spent two years playing with your johnson in Pretoria while medics were dying like flies in the bush war, boy?' Dell looked at him. 'When I got pulled out of Angola and joined the Afrikaners, I used my influence with them. Kept your ass safe.'

Dell said nothing. It may even have been true. They didn't speak for a while and Dell thought the old man had fallen asleep. Then Goodbread fired up another cigarette. 'Your ma. At the end. Was it bad?'

'It was Alzheimer's. It's always bad.'

'I tried to get to her funeral. They wouldn't let me out.'

'Nobody wanted you there.' The old man nodded, smoked. 'You know, she forgot you were in prison,' Dell said. 'And why. Like she hit a delete button and those dead women and children were just gone.' Felt his father's eyes on him. 'She asked for you with her last breath.'

'Jesus.' Something caught in Goodbread's throat and he coughed.

'Maybe it was a kind of a blessing for her, losing her memory. I envied her, sometimes.'

Goodbread said, 'I'm sorry.' His voice wavered, an old man again.

Dell said, 'Tell me something...'

'What?'

'How do you live with what you've done?'

His father exhaled. More than smoke leaving him as he sagged away from Dell. Shutting down. 'I'll not speak of that, boy.'

'Why? You scared?'

'Not of you or any other man.' He squinted out through the glass, his eyes lost in an eroded landscape of wrinkles. 'But I do know I will be held accountable.'

Dell said, 'Please don't tell me you found fucking religion in prison...'

'Oh, I always had religion. When you grow up in Texas religion and firearms are part of your birthright.' He coughed, tears came to his eyes and he spat into a rust-brown handkerchief. 'But religion is like politics. People use it to their own ends. No, I found God.' Dell waited for the laugh or the sneer, but he saw the old man was serious. 'And if I hadn't of found him he would of found me.' He stared at Dell through his watery blue eyes. 'You can't hide, boy. Not never.'

NJA SPED ACROSS THE BRIDGE AND UP THE MAIN STREET OF BHAMBATHA'S Rock, blue light flashing on the roof of his Pajero, scattering goats and children and chickens. He had three of his soldiers in the car with him: one at his side, two in the rear. All carrying automatic weapons. And in his mirror he could see a pickup truck, with two men inside, eating his dust. This is how he traveled around here, especially in times of war. Always ready for battle.

But no matter how fast he drove he couldn't outrun the hidden enemy that had him sweating with fear. He'd grown used to feeling sick to his gut, but this was different, as if cane rats were gnawing away at his nerves. He had a sense of being eroded from within.

Inja, unhinged by panic, overshot the dressmaker's and when he stood on the brakes, the pickup almost rear-ended the Pajero. The two vehicles slid to a stop, sending a fall of thick dust over the hawkers who squatted on the sidewalk.

When the dust cleared, he saw his betrothed through the dressmaker's dirty windows, being fitted with her traditional bride's outfit. The sight of her calmed him. He sat breathing away his fear, marveling at her resemblance to the only woman he had ever truly desired.

Inja's sister stood looking at him through the glass and he waved her out. Watched her waddle toward the car. Him so small and that one with the ass of a rhino. He called her 'sister', but she was a cousin, in truth. The only person who had ever cared a damn about him. He pressed a button and the side window slid down.

She stared at him. 'Brother, are you ill?'

'No, no.' Waving her words away with a swat of his hand. 'Any trouble with the girl?'

'No, brother.'

'After she is done here, I want Obed to take her to the Zulu Kingdom. She must work this afternoon.'

'I thought her work there was done?'

'Why? She is not yet a married woman. Do as I say.'

'Yes, brother.' Inja closed the window, but the fat woman tapped on the glass.

Irritated, Inja lowered the window halfway. 'What is it now?'

'May I talk to you?' she asked. Speaking with the reserve that custom demanded.

'Talk.'

'Alone.'

Inja told his men to go and buy him a Coke, and they left the Pajero as she climbed up beside him. He caught a whiff of sweat and dirty privates above the scent of cheap talcum powder. 'Brother, can I speak my mind?'

'Yes, yes.'

'This girl. She is trouble for you.'

'No. In fact she is the cure for my trouble.'

'I fear when you look at her you see her mother. As if you don't remember that she is dead.'

He laughed. 'I need no reminding. I put her in the ground. Her and that floor cleaner she called a husband.' He shut his eyes a moment, savoring the sweet memory of his revenge.

'I beg of you, don't marry this girl. Let her aunt return the dowry and be done with it. Find another bride.'

'What nonsense is this, woman?' Inja asked, fixing his yellow eyes on her.

'I visited the *sangoma*. She threw the bones. She saw blood, my brother. Your blood. And a flame that ate your flesh.'

'Enough. You have said enough.' Felt his fear rising again like a fever. He reached across and pushed open the passenger door. 'Go now.'

She looked as if she had more to say, then she thought better of it and slid from the vehicle and wobbled back into the dressmaker's. Inja fought his racing pulse, staring at the girl through the glass. There was truth in what his sister said.

As a youth, he'd watched Zondi with this girl's mother. Lusted after her, but couldn't touch his comrade's woman. When he came back from exile he found her married to a useless man who spent his life on his knees before the Boers. Inja attempted to court her, but she'd scorned him. She hadn't lived to do that twice.

Inja had looked on as the girl grew into the image of her mother and when he'd approached her aunt with the marriage proposal he'd had a sense of a circle closing. The skinny woman who had reared the child knew who he was. Knew he had killed her sister. But she was greedy, and the promise of cows and money had washed away any familial loyalty.

He watched now as the girl was fitted with a high red hat. Could already see his white bed sheets caked with blood the morning after the wedding, the linen paraded outside his house by the women. Singing, ululating. Rejoicing in the consummation of the marriage. A consummation that would have healed him.

His men returned to the vehicle and Inja gunned the engine and took off down the road. He looked for Zondi's BMW. Gone. Had known he would run, like he had run twenty years ago. A man who had no stomach for blood. Soft, like a woman, in his city clothes.

The Pajero stopped outside the tavern where Inja would drink away his dread. Gamble with the men of the town at *marabaraba*, an African form of checkers, played on an improvised board with beer bottle caps as tokens. They would let him win game after game, until long after the sun had set.

chapter 51

THE TRUCK WAS SUCKED INTO A CURVE AND DELL SAW THE VALLEY SPREAD out below them. The lush cane fields, green hills and pine forests came to a sudden end, as if they'd been sprayed with Agent Orange. He was looking down on a land of red earth and red rock. No grass. No vegetation other than gnarled thorn trees and aloes.

The road, a ragged ribbon of asphalt, twisted down to the valley. The blacktop sparkled with broken glass, and the torn and rusted bodies of cars that hadn't made it down the pass littered the slopes. When a minibus filled his rearview mirror, Dell felt the cold chill of déjà vu, but the taxi muscled past with inches to spare, disappearing around a blind bend.

They reached the valley, the truck drawn down the switchbacks into the heat that burned Dell's lungs. Mud huts clinging to the rocky hillsides. Trenches of erosion carved into the earth like tribal scars. Dry riverbeds. The sprawl of rural poverty. They passed a store, a crumbling pile of pink cinderblocks. A woman in a blanket and beaded headgear stood in the doorway. She stepped back into shadow when she saw Dell's pale face.

He glanced across at his father, who sat smoking. Impassive. He could hear the sigh of the old man's exhalation. 'Aren't we helluva conspicuous out here?' Dell asked.

Goodbread shrugged. 'I'm told they get tourists on this road, going to what they call the cultural village. Zulus in skins and girls with bare titties. Apparently the foreigners pay good money to see that sorry shit.' The old man removed a piece of paper from his shirt pocket and unfolded it. 'This here's our bride-to-be. Just so you know who we're looking out for.'

Dell reached across and took the paper, holding it against the wheel with one hand, taking his eyes off the road to glance at the color printout of a wedding invite. Saw a girl in traditional costume, standing next to a man in a suit. The pimp who had watched while the cop interrogated him back in the Cape. The man who had killed his family.

Dell looked back out at the road. 'Where did you get this?'

'I served with some Zulus in the early nineties. One of them lives hereabouts, near Dundee. E-mailed it to me up at the farm. He's no friend of Mazibuko. Wishes him harm, I reckon.' A dry laugh. 'Funny thing is, it's not customary for Zulus to send out wedding invites. It's usually done by word of mouth.'

'What's that, then?' Tossing the page onto his father's lap.

'That's a man getting above himself. A man ripe to be cut down.'

Dell changed gear as they headed into a bend, looked across at his father. 'This girl, she doesn't get hurt. Are we straight on that?'

Saw his father jerk upright. 'Jesus Christ!'

Dell hit the brakes, but the tires found no traction on the gravel and the truck slammed into the bull that had ambled into their path. The animal was flung into the air, landing on the hood of the truck with a heavy wet smack, blood spraying across the windshield. The Toyota stood on its nose for a moment, then the rear spun, throwing the bull to the ground.

The truck sat stalled, pointing back the way they had come, red dust shrouding them. Dell looked out the rear window as the dust cleared. The bull lay on its side on the road, tributaries of blood flowing out onto the sand.

Dell turned the key in the ignition. The engine caught, then spluttered and died. 'Fuck.' He pumped the gas pedal.

Goodbread said, 'Don't you flood her now.' Dell turned the key again. Nothing. 'Give her a moment,' the old man said.

That's when Dell saw them, maybe ten Zulu men and boys, swarming down the hillside from a cluster of nearby huts. He caught the gleam of blades in their hands. He turned the key. Engine coughed and cut out. Dell felt for the gun in his waistband as the men reached the truck.

Goodbread slid out of the Toyota. Relaxed, but with a hand near the pistol under his shirt. The men surrounded him. Torn clothes, bare feet, dark skins shining with sweat. Blades in black fists. Dell heard the rattle of Zulu, tongue-clicks like small explosions in the mouths of the men. Heard his father reply in the same language.

Then Goodbread laughed and shook his head. A couple of the Zulus laughed too, and the old man leaned down into the window to talk to Dell. 'They want to know if we're of a mind to claim the meat. Told them no.'

The men fell upon the bull, started butchering it with cane machetes and pocketknives. Dell stepped out and walked to the front of the truck. The hood was dented and the bumper and bars were bent and red with blood. But the bull had come off worse. Dell watched as two small boys each grabbed one of the animal's horns, while a shirtless man – all ribs and sinew – started hacking off the bull's head with a rusted wood saw.

Dell got back into the Toyota, tried the key, and this time the engine fired. Goodbread lowered himself into the truck and slammed the door. Dell turned the vehicle, and drove slowly around the Zulus. One of them waved a bloodstained arm. Goodbread flapped a hand in reply. Dell worked the stalk of the windshield washer and twin jets of water hit the glass. The wiper blades smeared blood across their view, the color of the landscape that surrounded them.

'Welcome to the heart of goddam darkness, son.' The old man's laugh sounded like a death rattle.

chapter 52

ZONDI SAT ON A WOODEN BENCH UNDER A THORN TREE. HE WOULD RATHER have waited in his Beemer, with the AC cranked up to the max, but it was the only car in the parking lot at the Zulu Kingdom, and he felt conspicuous anyway. *So what's your plan?* he asked himself. The answer was simple: he didn't have one. He'd improvise.

A small yellow bus, with a tour company logo painted on the side, lurched up the road and stopped with a squeak of hot brake drums. Zondi waved away the dust, the fine red grains settling in the folds of his crushed linen shirt. How had he lived here, all those bloody years ago? Simple. He hadn't known any better.

Zondi watched as a group of skinny Orientals filed out of the bus, and stood in the shade of the vehicle, casting anxious glances up at the blowtorch sun. A woman in a baseball cap barked at them in Japanese. Or maybe Korean. They formed an obedient line and followed her into the kraal, camera lenses flaring in the sun.

Zondi heard an old pickup truck rattling to a stop. Saw the girl get out, swamped by a shapeless poorhouse dress. She looked sad. Somehow older than the day before. A big man, running to fat, fought his way out of the driver's seat. As he stood his T-shirt lifted, and Zondi caught the hard shine of a pistol at his waist. The man followed the girl toward the beehive huts. He was pigeon toed, and he walked with his head and chest flung forward, as if he were crossing a finishing line.

Okay, and now what's your fucking plan? Zondi asked out loud, watching the big man disappear behind a reed fence. Feeling out of his depth here.

Zondi had never been at the sharp end of law enforcement. His skills lay in the meticulous collection of data, building mantraps of fact, conjecture and association under the corrupt and the venal. He'd left the wet work to others who were better equipped.

He eyed his Beemer, thought of settling his ass on its leather seat and getting the hell out of there. Then he sighed and stood and followed the girl and the gunman into the kraal.

IT WAS ONE OF THOSE PLACES Dell had always avoided. A tacky little tourist trap that looked like a bad movie set. A few beehive huts enclosed by a fence of sticks. An entranceway guarded by the skull and horns of an antelope.

A Zulu man with a beer gut, dressed in tire sandals and bits of skin, stepped out of one of the huts, wearing what looked like a feather duster on his head. He held a stabbing spear in his hand, waved it at the heavens, bellowed a war cry and made as if he was going to turn one of the little Orientals into a kebab. Then he laughed and the tour group giggled nervously. Fired off a barrage of flashbulbs in reprisal.

Dell followed at the back of the group, his father walking ahead, his bush hat pulled low over his eyes, doing an impersonation of a senior citizen on vacation. Dell saw another man on the fringes of the group. A man who looked as out of place as Dell felt. Tall black guy. Definitely city. Designer cargo pants and shades. Clean white Reeboks. A slim watch on his wrist. The guy caught his eye for a moment, then he walked on to where the girl from the wedding invite sat on a grass mat, weaving knotted strands of cloth on a wooden loom.

She wore a beaded skirt, a red and blue choker around her slender neck. Her breasts covered by a bib of animal skin. More beads wrapped her calves, and seedpods encircled her ankles. The kind that would sound like cicadas when she danced. Dell couldn't see her as a bride. She was a child.

The girl ignored the tourists, kept her eyes on the cloth. She looked up just once, toward another Zulu guy, also in Western clothes. A big man in a T-shirt and jeans that bagged at his butt. He leaned against one of the huts and yawned, then he scratched his ass. Dell glanced across at Goodbread. Saw the old man's eyes on the big guy, then back on the girl.

It was just a recon, his father had said. To check out the lay of the land. Suited Dell. The rush of adrenalin that had come after they hit the bull had drained, and he felt tired. Hot. Grief bubbling up from some bottomless underground reservoir. He wanted to go and lie under a tree somewhere and not wake up.

SUNDAY SERVED THE BEER. Brought the gourd to the rich black man who had been there the day before. He shook his head and she moved on, wondering who he was. She had seen him sitting beside the shining car, watching her when she arrived. Sunday thought of that black fax machine swallowing the wedding invite in the phone kiosk. *Stop dreaming*, she told herself.

Sunday moved on to serve the small yellow people who chirped like birds and made faces when they tasted the beer. They reminded her of her aunt, with their thin bodies and the skin stretched tight as drum hide across their high cheekbones.

The last two people to get the beer were a tall white man with dark hair, who drank and wiped his mouth with the back of his hand, nodding, and an old man as white as the bones of a carcass left lying in the sun. His hand shook as he took the gourd, and she heard his teeth smacking the clay rim. But he drank long and deep and when he was finished he looked at her with his pale eyes and thanked her in Zulu.

Richard did as he always did, throwing back a full gourd and burping loudly, standing with his swollen belly bulging out over his skins, smiling with teeth like rows of yellow corn, while the foreigners took snaps. When they were done he led them out of the ceremonial hut to buy souvenirs. Sunday sat a while, alone in the dark coolness.

Then she left the beer enclosure, and went across to the small hut where the ugly clothes the fat woman had given her were waiting. Sunday was standing naked, except for her panties, when the hut went dark and the big man ducked in through the low door.

She covered her middle with the dress. 'Uncle, I am not ready,' she said.

He stood, picking his teeth, staring at her. She could smell the sourness rising from his skin like the fumes from a pit latrine. He laughed. 'Don't worry, girl, when I feel the hunger, I feed on a thing with meat on its bones. Hurry, now. Finish.'

Sunday turned her back. Pulled on the dress over her head, the fabric coarse on her skin. Stepped into her tennis shoes, anxious to be out of the hut and away from this man looming behind her, his breath coming in wet grunts.

ZONDI WALKED TO HIS BMW, hearing it chirp as he used the remote to open it. Stood leaning on the roof, watching the big man and the girl heading toward the truck, the girl hanging back, looking down at her old shoes as they scuffed through the sand.

Zondi saw the two white men walking toward a Toyota double cab with a dented hood. The younger man got behind the wheel. The old man stood and lit a cigarette. His eyes flicked across Zondi and then over to where a hawk circled the red hills. Something about the old man was familiar, and Zondi started running his database. Stopped when he saw the big gunman shambling away toward the bathrooms, leaving the girl sitting alone in the truck. If he was going to do it, it would have to be now.

Zondi pushed away from the car, took a step toward the girl, not sure whether he was walking back into his past or forward into some fucked-up future. Stopped as the yellow tour bus bumped past, wiping her from view.

GOODBREAD DREW SMOKE into his lungs, held it for as long as he could, felt the soothing warmth as the nicotine rush hit. He hadn't been able to smoke during the beer ceremony, all the thatch and dry wood ready to blaze like kindling. He exhaled, heard the dry squeak of his breath, like the blades of a rusty windmill coming to rest. His eyes on the circling buzzard, black against the burning sky, but watching the big, loose-fleshed man with a pistol under his dirty T-shirt. Saw him hand the girl into the battered pickup.

Watched the other dark man, too, leaning with his arms on the roof of the BMW. Well dressed. City written all over his tailored shirt and expensive shoes. Something setting off alarm bells. A cop maybe? Didn't look as if he was armed, though. Goodbread could always tell. A man held himself differently when he was packing a weapon.

He saw the bodyguard walking away from the truck, toward the bathrooms. Saw the black man watching the girl across the gleaming roof of the Beemer. Goodbread knew there couldn't be no dress rehearsal.

The small tour bus smoked to life, sweating tourists sucking AC like they were in an oxygen tent. As the bus rattled by, Goodbread felt the dust kick into his lungs. Fought a cough. Then he was moving. Telling his boy to start the truck.

Showtime.

DELL YAWNED AS HE TURNED THE KEY of the Toyota and heard the engine fire, released the hand-brake, waiting for his father to get in beside him. But the old man headed over to the other truck, the brown one, dented and pimpled with rust. Moving fast. The pistol was in his hand, held flat against his khaki work pants.

Jesus Christ.

Dell was awake now. Saw Goodbread open the door of the old truck, the girl looking up at him, shaking her head, his father's hand white on her dark skin as he pulled her from the vehicle. The girl cried out. Goodbread had the gun at the girl's head, and Dell saw her eyes widen and her mouth open and close again.

Then Goodbread was walking her to their truck, left arm around her, holding her close, pistol to her ribs. They were nearly at the Toyota when the Zulu guide, still in his skins, spear in hand, came running across the parking lot.

'Leave her, you white bastard!'

Goodbread turned, gripping the girl with his left arm. Lifted the pistol. The Zulu kept on coming, bearing down on Goodbread, stomach wobbling over his leopard-skin loincloth, the spear raised above his head, ready to throw. Goodbread shot him in the head, and the spear left the Zulu's hand and jammed into the dirt just short of Goodbread's feet. The tour guide fell flat on his face, leopard skins flapping up to show his red underpants.

Dell reached across and pushed open the passenger door of the truck. Goodbread shoved the girl onto the seat, coming in after her. Coughing, fighting for breath. Dell reversed, forced the gear lever into first, hit the gas. Goodbread's door slapped shut.

The bodyguard ran out of the bathroom, still buckling his jeans, reaching for the pistol at his hip. Letting go a shot that starred the windshield. Getting closer, pistol staring straight at Dell. A bullet slammed into the metal of the doorframe beside Dell's head with a sound like a hammer on an anvil.

Before he had time to think Dell lifted the gun from his waistband, stuck his arm out the window. Fired. At first he thought he'd missed – saw the big man still aiming – then red bloomed on the gunman's white T-shirt. He opened his mouth in surprise and blood flowed down his chin as he toppled slowly as an imploded building, legs going first.

Dell heard Goodbread shouting, 'Go, boy! Go goddammit!'

He floored the gas, bumped over the dead man, nearly mowed down the tall black guy in the expensive clothes, who sprinted toward them. Swerved around the tour bus that sat becalmed in the sea of dust, and slalomed out toward the main road.

chapter 53

SUNDAY HAD NEVER BEEN SO CLOSE TO WHITE PEOPLE BEFORE. SHE'D always kept her distance from the foreigners, now she was squashed in the front of the truck with the two white men, the younger one hitting her knee with his hand as he smashed through the gears. He was panting, sweating. Stinking of fear. The old one fought for breath like he was drowning, one hand holding onto the dashboard, the other gripping the gun that slipped away from her ribs as he coughed.

The driver threw the car into a curve, flinging Sunday up against the old man. She smelt something like sickness on him. Saw the sun shining through his hairy ears, veins like red worms near the surface of the skin.

'Where are you taking me?' she asked in Zulu. The younger one ignored her and the old one was too busy coughing blood, big drops that shot from his mouth onto his trousers, to answer.

Then her mother answered. Drew her eyes to the piece of paper that lay on the floor of the truck, under Sunday's frayed tennis shoes. The wedding invite. But different somehow. Printed on thin paper and the colors were blurred and smeared. So this is how it must have come out of the machine. In Pretoria. And now Sunday knew. Her mother hadn't deserted her: she'd sent these white men to save her.

DELL LOOKED IN THE REARVIEW. Caught glimpses of the road through the red cloud that pursued them. The truck ramped a hump, airborne for a moment, and he could see back over the dust, saw the BMW gaining on them. As the Toyota hit the gravel, the girl was hurled up against Dell. A whiff of woodsmoke and

Sunlight soap. He elbowed her aside, nearly lost the truck on a bend, battled to control it. Beemer closing in. He wasn't going to beat it for speed.

The girl looked back over her shoulder, speaking rapid Zulu. Clicks like gum being popped. Dell didn't understand a fucking word. Goodbread fought the coughing spasm back down into himself, grabbed at Dell's arm with fingers as bony as a skeleton, pointing out toward the plain.

'She says, turn here. Onto the track.' Words strangled on phlegm and blood.

Dell saw two rough scratches in the hard, rocky surface, leading off into a Martian landscape of ruts and furrows. 'Jesus, and then?'

'Just do it.'

And he did, wrestling the wheel to the right, almost losing the truck, back yawing. Floored the gas and felt the tires grip and they were flying onto the track, loose rocks striking the underside of the Toyota like small-bore fire. Looked in his rearview. The Beemer was honest-to-God coming after them.

Who the fuck is that black guy?

The truck flew over a mound, landed hard, and Dell was staring up at a rocky gradient. The slope of a torn and eroded hill. He stopped, forced the Toyota into four-wheel drive, muttered something that may have been a prayer. Hit the gas.

The tires spun, churning dust, until the rubber found traction, gripped, and the truck hauled itself up the rise, hood framed against the bleached sky. And then they were over, skidding and slewing down toward a dry river bed. Dell checked the rearview, which served him up a blurred and vibrating landscape in reflection. No BMW.

ZONDI STOOD ON THE BRAKES as he saw the incline, felt the car go, ended up at ninety degrees to the slope. Stopped in a spray of gravel. Left stranded like a sand shark washed up on a beach. Ate dust. Watched the fat ass of the truck disappear over the ridge.

Fuck.

He turned the BMW, avoiding rocks and aloes, and drove slowly back the way he had come. Picked up speed once he was back on the gravel road. Started running his database again. Thought he had a hit on the old man. He needed the Internet. But first he needed a gun.

Inja upended the square of cardboard, crudely marked with blocks in diminishing size, sending tokens and money flying. Then he tipped the table, beer bottles and whiskey glasses crashing to the concrete floor of the tavern.

The men who had been losing to him backed away, looking for shelter in the shadows of the dim room. Inja tugged his pistol from his trousers. Pointing it at the unfortunate who had brought him the news.

The man cowered on his knees, hands held up above his head in prayer. Eyes closed. '*Induna*, please. I beg of you, *Induna*.'

Inja stared down at the man, then took the weapon away from his head, looked at the gun as if he'd never seen it before. Holstered it. His breath coming in rasps. Saw the men backed up against the walls, none of them daring to look at him. His vision blurred, the room wavering before his eyes, as if he was staring at it through flame.

When Inja spoke, his normally rich baritone was hoarse and thin. Barely a whisper. 'Get every man,' he said to his flunkey. 'Each and every one. Arm them and send out search parties. Let them round up people from all corners of the valley. Find out where these white bastards took her. If people won't speak, shoot their children. And keep shooting them until they do speak.'

THEY WERE IN A CAVE. THE TRUCK HIDDEN ON THE PLAIN BELOW, BEHIND A ridge of spiky rocks that rose like a ribcage from the earth. Dell sat with his back against the cool stone wall, staring into the gloom at the rear of the cave. His memory serving him up action replays of the moment he'd pulled the trigger back at the tourist village. Blood flowering on the big man's shirt. His legs giving way. The wet bumps as the truck drove over his body.

Dell heard his father and the girl talking in Zulu. Goodbread crouched in the mouth of the cave, binoculars to his eyes. Scanning the parched landscape, a rifle leaning against the rock at his side. The girl sat beside him. Watchful. Goodbread gave the glasses to the girl. She lifted them and dropped them in shock at the sudden magnification. Goodbread laughed, said something, and she lifted them again. He showed her how to focus them for her young eyes, then he came over to Dell. Sat down beside him. Offered his hipflask, hand unsteady. Dell shook his head.

'Drink, boy. You just lost your damned cherry.'

Dell didn't respond. Goodbread sighed and took a long pull, teeth rattling against the mouth of the flask. 'You saved your life by shooting that man. And my life, not that it's worth a good goddam. And the girl's.'

Dell stared at his father, saying nothing. Saw the blueness under his cheekbones. Heard him fighting for air. Looked across at the girl, squatting, binoculars fixed to her eyes.

Goodbread spat a chuckle. 'Girl's got the notion in her head that we're angels, sent by her dead mamma to save her from the hands of Inja Mazibuko.'

'What did you tell her?'

'Hell, I'm not going disappoint the child. Plenty of time for that. Good thing is, we don't have to worry none about her running away.'

'So what do we do now?'

'We wait, boy. For the dog to sniff us out.'

'And then?'

The old man sighed. Coughed. Gasped. 'Son, we left two dead men back there. Reckon that changes the game some.'

'You mean there's no going back? No riding into town with Inja Mazibuko tied to a horse, ready to tell the sheriff the truth that'll set me free?'

'Don't reckon that's going to happen.'

'You knew it wasn't going to happen. From the start.'

The old man shrugged his bony shoulders. 'It was always a possibility.'

'You're a dead man. What do you care? You're just looking to go out guns blazing. The legend of Bobby fucking Goodbread.' Shaking his head at the old man, who stared at him from under parchment-thin eyelids, saying nothing. 'You don't have the balls to kill yourself, do you?' Saw his father flinch. 'So, what is this? Assisted suicide?'

Goodbread drank from the flask. Wiped a hand across his mouth. 'You looking for justice, son?' Dell said nothing. 'There's the justice you find in a courtroom. And there's the justice you find for yourself.' Lighting a cigarette. A wet rattle in his lungs as he sucked smoke. 'There's a good chance we're not going to walk away from this. But we can take Inja Mazibuko down with us. Reckon that's justice enough.'

'So we kill the dog?'

'We kill the dog.'

'And what about his master?'

Goodbread sighed. 'Let's not be overambitious now, boy.'

Dell nodded. 'Tell me how it's going to work.'

'We wait him out. Reckon he'll move in on us. After dark. We're holding the high ground. And we've got the girl. Should be able to take him down.'

'And that's your plan?'

'Yes, son. That's my plan.'

Dell stared at his father. Then he held out a hand. 'Give me that drink.' He took the flask and drank long and deep, felt the booze burn its way down to his gut.

chapter 55

ZONDI DROVE ALONG THE DIRT ROAD, FAR FROM THE TOWN. MILE AFTER MILE of eroded badlands, shimmering under a blazing sky. Years since he had been out here, but nothing had changed. Women and girl-children walked with water containers and faggots of firewood balanced on their heads, sliding glances at his shiny city car. Young men rose up out of the earth at the roadside, shirtless, sinewy torsos pale with dust. Staring after him with eyes dulled by weed. He waited for the crack of a weapon. An explosion of glass. Nothing.

Zondi drove on, the BMW throwing a long shadow across the sand, and he saw himself at eighteen, standing over Jola, rock raised above his head. The youth's body patterned with blood from the stab wounds, his eyes white in his dark face. Mouth screaming out a plea that Zondi couldn't hear above the beating of his own heart.

Up ahead a mound of torn metal caught the sun, the light kicking off mangled car bodies piled high against the sky. A small cinderblock building with unpainted dung-brown walls hunkered down behind the car wrecks.

Zondi pulled off the road and stopped next to a rusted wire gate that sagged off a wooden post. No fence. Just the gate, standing like a useless sentry. He stepped out into the heat. Passed the gate, followed a path that led through the car wrecks, toward the open door of the building. Went inside.

It took a moment for his eyes to adapt to the windowless gloom. A room empty of furniture. Two men squatted on the cement floor, watching him. The hot embers of joints glowing in their mouths. The air heavy with weed and sweat and paraffin. A radio, somewhere out back, thumped Zulu pop.

Twists of metal and hand tools lay scattered around the men. An anvil. A ball-peen hammer. A hand-cranked drill. Zondi didn't know what they manufactured now, but when he was a child this was an armorer's workshop. Where homemade rifles were fashioned from scrap metal. No call for those, now that stolen weapons flooded the area, arming the warriors for their feuds.

The younger man stood. He was Zondi's age, but no taller than a child. One shoulder rode up close to his ear, the other dragged low as if an invisible hand was forcing it down.

The hunchback exhaled a plume of smoke. 'And look at this, Father,' he said to the man who stared up at Zondi. 'Look at what has come home.'

The squatting man closed one nostril with his thumb, and snorted a string of mucus onto the floor next to Zondi's shoe. Repeated the procedure with the other nostril. 'So the coconut returns,' he said, sniffing.

That's how they saw him, these people: dark on the outside, white on the inside. Fuck them.

The older one grunted and lifted himself to his feet. Dressed only in shorts. Barefoot. A powerful man with a hard gut and the scars of many battles etched into his skin. Zondi could see the light from the doorway shining through the empty holes in his uncle's earlobes, stretched so long that they hung almost to his shoulders. An outmoded Zulu ritual. The old man's ears had been pierced as a child, and each year the lobes had been stretched with thicker sticks, until he had been able to wear bone earplugs the circumference of a Coke can.

Zondi's father's ears had looked the same as he lay in his unlined pine coffin, dead after a faction fight. Stiff black suit. Starched white shirt. The ornate earplugs the only splash of color.

'What are you doing here, son of Solomon?' his uncle asked.

A formal greeting edged with sarcasm.

'I need a gun,' Zondi said. 'I'll pay.'

The old man laughed, showing Zondi the few teeth he had left. Yellow and crooked, fringed by a beard of tight white curls. He had to be at least eighty. Looked twenty years younger. 'And who, boy, are you going to shoot?'

Zondi shrugged, 'Maybe nobody.'

'Maybe Inja Mazibuko?' His uncle smiled. 'The dust carries words in this valley, boy. You know that.' Laughed. Shook his head, the lobes flapping like bits of silly putty. Then he stopped laughing, clucked, staring at Zondi but talking to his son: 'He lights the fire in the wind, this one.'

Zondi was in no mood for this rural Amos 'n' Andy routine. 'Tell me, Uncle, can you help me with a gun, or not?'

The old man scratched at his beard, then he nodded. 'Yes, yes.'

'How much?'

'You're my brother's firstborn, how can I take your money?' Looking at Zondi's wrist. 'Give me your clock.' Holding out a hand, nails long and brown, hard as thorns.

Zondi hesitated. Shrugged. Unclipped his Breitling and held it out to the old man, who snatched it and turned the face to the light, grunted, then put it in his pocket. 'Get him a gun,' he told his son.

The hunchback disappeared into the yard. Zondi's uncle stood in the doorway, looking out at the road. Nodding at the dusty BMW. 'That your car?'

'Yes.'

'You can't drive around in that thing. Not if you make war on Inja Mazibuko. Take the Ford.' He pointed toward an ancient pickup that sagged in the shadow of the building. Paintwork faded to the color of the sand. One mismatched door a pale blue. Front bumper gone.

Zondi knew the old bastard was right. He was too much of a target in the Beemer. 'And what do I have to give you for that?' he asked.

The gap-toothed smile. 'Nothing. You just leave your car keys. As deposit.' He held out a hand again, palm upward. Zondi dropped his keys into the hand. Knew he'd never see his BMW again. What the fuck, he was insured.

His cousin was back, carrying a pink plastic bag. Zondi took the bag, felt its weight, opened it to see a Z88 9mm pistol and four boxes of ammunition. The sidearm used by the South African police. A cop had sold it to them. Or they'd killed him for his weapon.

The old man spoke to his son, 'He is taking the Ford. Start it up.'

The hunchback lurched out to the truck. Zondi went to his BMW to get his duffel bag. By the time he returned, the pickup was smoking like a steam train, his cousin crouched up front, pumping the gas.

Zondi waited until the twisted man slid out, and got behind the wheel. The truck stank of gasoline and something rank. Like a body had decomposed in it, and the fluids had soaked the upholstery and the carpets. He tried to wind down the side window. The winder spun, and the glass fell like a guillotine into the door. He fed the rattling engine gas, and bumped out of the yard, watching the men in the rearview mirror that was tied on with wire. His uncle laughed, shook his head, and his cousin swung his hunchback from side to side.

Zondi turned the wheel and headed back toward town. The stolen gun jabbed his ribs. He felt as if this place was reclaiming him. Inch by inch.

chapter 56

NJA STOOD NAKED UNDER A THORN TREE, ALL SCRAWNY SHANKS AND dangling eggplant-colored penis. Smoke boiled around him as an obese woman in a bra and skins threw herbs onto a wood fire. Her face, made ghostly by white paste, was lost in the fumes.

The woman bowed, handing Inja a clay gourd filled with shit-colored liquid. The smell burned his nose when he swallowed, the medicine as bitter as death. Immediately he felt dizzy, and sank to his knees. A violent spasm seized his gut, and puke spewed onto the sand. Sweat sprang from his body like morning dew and he spat strings of vomit. Fought for breath. Another spasm hit him and he heaved again. And again. Until he was empty. Purified.

The smoke cleared for a moment, and Inja could see an ancient man, as furrowed as the eroded earth, squatting outside a mud hut. The skins of a monkey and a snake pegged above the doorway. A frayed red flag, the sign of a witchdoctor, dangled like a tongue from a wooden pole rising above the hut. The *sangoma*, dressed in hide and beads, muttered in Zulu, blessing a butcher's knife with a long, flat blade. He stood, the knife hanging heavy from his hand, and made his way to where Inja knelt beside the fire.

The *sangoma* sliced Inja twice, horizontally, across his bony chest. Shallow cuts, but blood ran down Inja's torso, pooling in his lap, dripping onto his thighs and knees. The witchdoctor chanted as he twisted open a metal shoe polish tin. Dipped his fingers into the black paste, made from charred herbs and animal fat. Battle medicine that could turn bullets to water, so they said. Smeared the mixture into the cuts on Inja's chest. Inja felt a sharp stinging, as if wasps were at his flesh.

The *sangoma* shouted an order and two youths emerged from the smoke, dragging a protesting goat, paws tied with baling wire. They manhandled the animal toward the tree and slung it, kicking and twisting, over a low branch above Inja's head. He felt the scrape of the goat's threshing hooves on his shoulders. The animal released its bowels in a fall of sour dung. The woman was chanting now, a high-pitched keening, in a duet with the goat, which screamed its fear.

The old witchdoctor dragged the blade of the knife through the ash, then he used the blunt side of the steel to trace a black cross onto Inja's back. The woman's chant grew louder, her face swimming through the flame, eyes dipped back in ecstasy, yellow as gobs of fat. The *sangoma* grabbed the goat by its snout and exposed its neck. Slit its throat with one quick movement of his arm.

Hot blood geysered down onto Inja, running over his head, dripping down his body. He turned his face up toward the dying animal and opened his mouth to receive the blood. He drank and was filled. Inja saw his father and his father's father before him. His ancestors guiding him back to the river of power. Entering him through the liquid, giving him strength for the battle ahead.

At last the goat drooped lifeless over the branch. Bled out. Inja stood, his body crimson with gore, staring into the flames, the woman's chants louder and more frantic. Then her wails floated away with the smoke, and she sank to the ground. Silent.

Inja lifted his eyes from the fire when one of his gunmen entered the yard and prostrated himself.

'Yes?' Blood caked Inja's tongue as he spoke.

'*Induna*, she is found,' the man said, his forehead in the dust.

SUNDAY WATCHED THE OLD MAN with white hair coughing, his ribs heaving beneath his shirt as he crouched at the front of the cave. Rasping like a sick dog. His lips were drawn back in a grimace, and she could see the blood on his teeth. Water dripping from his forehead, running into the deep grooves in his face. He lowered the binoculars and she looked into his faded eyes.

Sunday found the plastic bottle of water and handed it to him. He fought for breath, the loose skin on his throat almost mauve in color. Drank from the bottle, coughed water and blood onto the sand between his shoes, drank again. Wiped his mouth on the back of his hand.

'Give me the glasses, grandfather,' she said. He handed her the binoculars. 'You rest. I will keep guard.'

'Girl, you call me if you see anything. Anything. You hear?' Speaking her language well enough for her to understand, but in a cracked voice foreign to her ear.

She nodded and he sat with his back to the rock, the rifle cradled in his arms. The other man lay deeper in the cave. His eyes were closed, but she knew he wasn't asleep.

Sunday lifted the glasses, rotated the grooved focus ring, and the landscape jumped at her. The sudden magnification didn't shock her this time. She swept the barren landscape, seeing her life spread out beneath her. The hill where her parents had died. The hut where she lived with her aunt. The town, lying like a pile of bricks baking in the sun.

Sunday moved the glasses over the sand road that led from the cultural village. Followed a taxi throwing up dust, thought she could hear the whine of its engine. She panned the glasses with a vulture as it hung in the air, almost level with the mouth of the cave.

An omen, she knew. As she watched the bird hover, she heard the man cough again, and she felt a breeze on the nape of her neck though there was no wind in this sheltered cave. She didn't look back, not wanting to see the spirits crowding around the old man, ready to take him to the shadowlands.

chapter 57

ZONDI DROVE THE RATTLING FORD OVER TO THE HOSPITAL. HE PARKED near the entrance, not bothering to close the windows or lock the truck. Slung his duffel bag over his shoulder and went into reception. Asked for Dr Lambert.

The Zulu woman behind the counter looked him up and down. 'You are a friend of hers?'

'Yes.'

'It's her afternoon off. She's out by the pool.'

The woman directed him down a corridor, and Zondi walked through the ranks of the diseased, bodies withering away inside their striped pajamas, glazed eyes watching death approach with mute African passivity.

Zondi exited the corridor and crossed a gravel courtyard toward a high wall and a gate marked SENIOR STAFF ONLY in English and Zulu. He went through the gate and found himself on a patch of dead yellow grass, ringed by aloes. Somebody's idea of a garden.

A small kidney-shaped pool of chemical blue water lay like a mirage in the middle of the grass. He saw a dark shape under the water. As he approached the pool, the blonde doctor broke the surface and stared up at him, wiping her eyes.

'Disaster Zondi.' No surprise in her voice.

'I'm sorry to disturb you, Doctor. I need a favor.'

She pressed her hands down on the tiles and lifted herself out of the water in an easy motion. Walked across to the towel that lay on a plastic lounger. She wore a black one-piece Speedo. When the late sun caught a few tendrils of blonde hair escaping where the swimsuit cut high in her groin, Zondi forced himself to look away, over at the burning hills.

The doctor dried her face. 'Are you unwell?' she asked.

Zondi looked back at her as she lifted the towel to her hair, and he could see a shadow of blue stubble in her armpits. *Jesus.*

'No. No. I'm fine. I just need access to the Internet. Maybe you can help me, Doctor?'

'Martine.' He could smell chlorine and sweat and tanning oil on her skin. She wrapped the green towel around her body. 'And what am I to call you? Please not Disaster.'

He smiled. 'Zondi will do.'

'Zondi. Okay.' She lifted a beach bag from beside the lounger, a stylized yellow sun and the word DURBAN stitched below the straps. 'I have the Internet in my room. But it is like a snail. Come.'

The doctor stepped into a pair of flip-flops and led him across the grass and into a low brick building, cool and dark after the heat outside. Wooden doors on either side of a polished stone corridor. She stopped at a door and unlocked it. Zondi followed her in.

She dropped the beach bag on the floor. 'Please excuse the mess.'

Mess was an understatement. He'd seen neater home invasions. Closet doors gaped, clothes spilled out like they were escaping their hangers. The bed an unmade tangle. Shoes, underwear, magazines, coffee cups and overflowing ashtrays littered the room.

The doctor crossed to a small desk by the window and booted up a laptop. He heard the cricket warble as she went online. 'It is a slow connection, so you must be patient.' She took some clothes from a wooden chair and threw them onto the bed. Pointed to the chair. 'Please.' Zondi sat, lowering his duffel bag to the floor. 'I'll go shower.'

She disappeared into the bathroom and shut the door. Zondi

heard the spurt of water and had to quell images of her wet, naked flesh. As he slid the chair closer to the computer the butt of the gun in his waistband stabbed into his abdomen. He removed the weapon and laid it on the table beside the keyboard.

The face of the computer was anonymous. No screensaver. Files neatly organized, in contrast to the room. Zondi called up Google. The Internet connection was as slow as the Belgian had promised, but it didn't take Zondi long to put the pieces of the puzzle together. As he suspected the old man who'd gunpointed the girl was Earl Robert Goodbread. Just about recognizable from the photograph taken at the massacre trial sixteen years ago. And the second man was his son. Robert Dell. The fugitive family murderer. Looking very different now from the mugshot on the monitor, where he was all long hair and patchy beard and wild eyes.

Zondi knew from the Ben Baker investigation that Dell's wife had worked for the fat man. Was screwing him on the side, in fact. It wasn't hard to join the dots. She'd known something that could incriminate the minister or his dog. Inja killed the woman and her children by smashing their car off a mountain road. Was sloppy in his work and left Dell alive. Then tried to cover his tracks by framing Dell. Goodbread broke Dell out of jail and they were coming after Inja. The girl was the bait. Easy for Zondi to figure out what had happened. No idea what he would do next.

Zondi shut down the search engine and deleted the browser history, erasing his tracks. He sat a moment and massaged his temples.

The bathroom door opened and the Belgian doctor emerged, followed by a tendril of steam and the smell of jasmine soap. She wore a white bathrobe, brushing her wet hair straight back from her face as she walked.

Her eyes flicked across to the gun lying beside the computer.

'So what are you, Disaster Zondi? Some kind of a gangster, or some kind of a cop?'

He reached for the 9mm and made it disappear beneath his shirt. 'I used to be in law enforcement. Now I'm just another citizen.'

'You are sure?' She sat down on the bed, staring at him, unblinking.

'Yes.'

She found a box of Gitanes beside the bed and lit one. Her eyes matched the blue of the pack. The room was very quiet and he could hear the cigarette paper ignite. Heard her inhale and exhale. Saw her eyes on his duffel bag beside the chair. 'Where are you staying?'

'Nowhere, really.'

'There is a room empty, next door. A doctor went back to Italy. His replacement arrives only in one week. I'm sure nobody will mind if you use it for a night or two.' She scratched beneath the clutter on her bedside table, squinting through cigarette smoke, and found a key tied to a piece of card. 'Here.'

He stood and took the key. 'Thank you.'

The doctor shrugged. 'It is nothing.' She crossed her long legs, the bathrobe falling away. Looking at him with those clear blue eyes.

And there it was. He felt the room tip. Felt himself sliding toward her. Zondi pulled his eyes away from hers and grabbed the edge of the desk. To anchor himself.

'I appreciate your help, Martine.'

She shrugged again, sucking on the cigarette. Inhale. Exhale.

Zondi shouldered his bag and walked toward the door, opened it, turned to her. She sat with her back to him, staring out the window at the sun low over the red hills. He went out and shut the door.

chapter 58

ZONDI SLUMPED BEHIND THE WHEEL OF THE FORD, ON A RIDGE OVER-looking Inja's compound, parked so the low sun didn't flare off the truck's windshield. He waved away a fly, drawn to the sweat that ran down his face. Pooled beneath his armpits and glued the shirt to his back. His own stink mixing with the vapors rising from the Ford's torn upholstery.

An image of the Belgian doctor floated in from nowhere, her full lips pouting as she sucked on the cigarette. He forced himself to imagine those lips in twenty years' time, no longer plump, etched with deep furrows, her beauty a faded memory. It didn't work. He wanted her. Simple as that.

Zondi sighed and shifted in his seat. He looked down at the kraal, wishing he had a pair of binoculars. No movement since two vehicles had driven in and parked outside the main house a half-hour before. He watched the sun sinking ever lower. Knew that once darkness fell his plan would be useless. He laughed. *What fucking plan?*

When he left the hospital and found this vantage point, he'd convinced himself that Inja would lead him to the girl. The dog would have men all over the valley, searching for Goodbread and Dell and their captive. They were hidden somewhere around here. And they would have been seen, the way every-thing was seen in this valley of spies. All Zondi would have to do was follow Inja. But in the dark he'd have to use the Ford's headlamps, and that would make him a perfect target.

Zondi sat up. Three cars were on the move. Inja's Pajero and two trucks. The warlord and his army, bumping away from the compound toward the gravel road that circled the low hills like a frayed belt.

Zondi started the Ford. It moaned and spluttered, finally caught in a smoky rattle. He took hold of the steering wheel. Jerked his hands away. The cracked plastic was baked hot as a brick in a kiln. Cursing, he grabbed the wheel again, gritted his teeth, and set off after the convoy.

THE PAJERO DROVE ALONG A CATTLE TRACK on the fringes of the valley, where the poorest scratched a living from the plundered land. Inja sat up front, heard the wheels drumming on the sun-baked soil. Two gunmen in the car with him. Another six in the vehicles ahead and behind.

Inja hadn't washed since the ritual. His body, under his clothes, was caked with dried blood. It stank. Rich. Metallic. He held out his hand, fingers spread. Felt the blood cracking as his skin stretched. He wasn't shaking. He was strong again.

He fired up a spliff, sucked in the smoke. Held it until he thought his lungs would burst, then he let it explode from his mouth in a fragrant cloud. Felt it infuse his blood. Focusing him. His fingers touched the amulet at his throat. A string of beads and dried roots. From the *sangoma*. For protection. To give him power over the enemy who awaited him. The white men.

The track died, and the cars negotiated boulders and ditches until they came to the base of a hill of stone. One of Inja's men sat on a rock, AK-47 resting across his knees. Guarding an old, emaciated man, in torn khaki overalls and tire sandals, who squatted on the ground, hunched in on himself like a prisoner, empty earlobes brushing his shoulders.

Inja cracked the door and stepped down, ordnance clanking as his soldiers joined him. Inja's gunman stood, head bowed in greeting. The old man didn't move, stared off into the gathering gloom. Inja heard soft scuffs as a trio of skinny sheep appeared, searching the barren soil for feed.

'What did he see, this old one?' Inja asked, nodding at the shepherd.

'*Induna*, he says he was grazing his sheep down near Bourke's Cutting and he saw a truck. Two white men and a young girl. One of ours. They hid the truck and climbed up to a cave.'

'Stand, old man,' Inja said.

The shepherd stood. The old bastard couldn't meet Inja's eyes. 'Is this true? What you saw?'

Nodding, head bowed. 'It is true, *Induna*.'

Inja pointed at the sheep. 'These are yours?'

'Yes, *Induna*. They are mine.'

'You have more?'

'No, *Induna*. Only these.'

Inja drew his pistol and shot one of the sheep in the head. The animal toppled to the ground and the old man sighed. A sound of infinite suffering.

'Tell me the truth, grandfather. What else did you see?'

'I saw nothing more, *Induna*.'

The other two sheep had scattered at the shot, one of them trying to find shelter under the Pajero, its tick-infested ass sticking up to the sky as its hooves scratched at the sand. Inja shot it in the rear, and the sheep screamed, and tried to burrow deeper under the vehicle. He shot it again and it sagged to the earth. The third sheep bolted.

Inja said, 'Fetch that animal.' Two of his men ran off in pursuit. Inja turned back to the shepherd. 'Where do you live?' The old man lifted an arm and pointed up toward a mess of mud huts on the slope of the hill. 'Did you speak to anybody else of what you saw?'

'No, *Induna*.'

The soldiers returned with the sheep. One of them dragged it by the tail. The other had hold of the loose skin at its neck. The sheep bucked and twisted.

'Let it go,' Inja said.

The men stepped away from the sheep, and Inja shot it in the eye. It fell on its side, kicked twice and lay still. The shepherd looked at the dead animal without expression.

Inja said, 'Speak of this and it will be your stinking old backside I shoot next. Understand?'

The old man nodded, staring off into the darkness that seeped in over the valley. 'I am silent, *Induna*.'

Inja laughed to himself as he holstered his pistol. Yes, now the old bastard was quiet. But when Inja was a runt of a boy, men like this had scorned him. Mocked him when he fell on his ass during the stick-fighting contents. Called him a mongrel dog. Said that only incest could have resulted in such a poor specimen of manhood.

Inja walked back to the Pajero and one of his men held the door open for him. The SUV sat low as his soldiers joined him. 'Let us go hunt us some white meat,' Inja said.

The driver started the Pajero and they bumped across the rutted land, the other vehicles falling in behind. Inja saw the fat moon inching its way up over the hills. A wedding moon. At its fullest tomorrow night. The night of his nuptials.

chapter 59

DELL LAY WITH HIS EYES CLOSED. NOT ASLEEP. TRYING TO BRING THE faces of his wife and children into focus. But they remained at a distance. Soft. Instead he saw Ben Baker's thick white hands on Rosie's brown body.

He felt a nudge and opened his eyes to darkness. Made out the shape of the girl crouching over him. She handed Dell the binoculars and pointed toward the entrance of the cave, the rocks haloed by silver moonlight.

She went across to his father, who lay slumped against the wall. The rifle lying at his side. Dell could hear him fighting for breath, and knew things were bad when he saw the old man's lips weren't wrapped around a cigarette. Heard him moan and mutter.

The girl tore a strip of cloth from the hem of her dress and wet it with water from the plastic bottle. She wiped Goodbread's forehead, wiped at the blood and mucus that clotted his mouth. The girl spoke softly in Zulu, soothing the old man. Dell heard a word he understood. *Tata.* Grandfather. Goodbread grabbed at her wrist and he tried to fight her for a second, then he sank back as she whispered to him.

Dell went to the mouth of the cave. Crouched down with the glasses and scanned the landscape made bright by the moon that rose big as a soup plate.

BURNING UP. Like the flames of hell were licking at his flesh. A face coming at him. Black skin, silver light on the high cheekbones. A mouth speaking that language of clicks.

No longer in the cave, Goodbread rushed a kicked-down

door in a ghetto house outside Johannesburg. Surging with the squad of Zulu killers. A door opened behind him. He spun and fired, hearing the familiar conversation of the AK-47. A black girl, stepping out of a room, holding a baby. Trying to speak around blood. Couldn't. Folded. The baby fell on its back onto the stone floor, pedaling its yellow-brown sausage limbs. Howling.

Goodbread shouting, 'Hold your fire!' Reaching down for the naked, bawling infant.

But one of the Zulus beat him to it. Picked the baby up by a leg, and swung it, pulping its brains against the wall. Goodbread shot the man in his laughing mouth.

Chaos. A clusterfuck of photographers and news crews fought their way into the house. Flashbulbs detonating in Goodbread's face as he and the Zulus fled in an unmarked truck.

Goodbread struggled, strong hands gripping his wrists. 'Shhhhh, grandfather. Be still.' Felt cool water on his forehead.

But still back in 1994. A few months before the South African elections. The last kick of the dying mule that was apartheid. Faceless Afrikaners, working in secret – politicians, cops, military – to destabilize the country. Knew their days were numbered if Mandela came to power. Conspiring with the Zulus who had long collaborated with them. A squad of men brought up to Johannesburg from a faraway valley. Men who were birthed into blood. Goodbread led them in the attack on a house full of youth leaders and comrades. The old enemy.

But no enemy. Just women. And a baby. A goddam media ambush. Afterward the Afrikaners and their Zulu allies knew there had to be a sacrifice. To shut the media up. Goodbread had shot one of his own men, and what the hell, he was a foreigner. A glorified goddam mercenary. So they threw him to the wolves.

The prosecutors, the new guard – blacks and Jews – offered him a deal if he named his superiors. He declined and they sent him down for life. A pimply kid from the US consul came to see him, in a Pretoria prison. Told him he was a disgrace to his country. Goodbread laughed in his face and demanded to be taken back to his cell. Reckoned it was right and just that he rotted away for the rest of his God-given days.

Goodbread heard a voice calling his name. His son's voice. Goodbread coughed. Clawed his way back from the past. Felt his lungs tear and burn like they were aflame. Puked a mouthful of warm blood down his shirtfront. *Old man. Useless goddam old man.*

Heard his son again. Urgent. Spooked. 'Headlamps. Coming this way.'

ZONDI SAT ON A ROCKY RIDGE IN THE MIDDLE OF THE ERODED PLAIN, the Ford stowed behind an outcrop below him. The moon dangled over the empty landscape. The track Inja's convoy had followed to the shepherd's post lay like a pale scar in the moonlight.

Again Zondi waited. He'd heard the shouts of interrogation and the gunshots and the screams of the sheep. Knew Inja and his men would have to return this way, there was no passage over the hills that surrounded the plain. So he waited. Uneasy. Too close to old ghosts. He rubbed a hand against the stubble on his jaw, caught the scent of the Sunlight soap still clinging to his skin.

Thought of his mother. He never saw her alive after he fled the valley, and the money he'd dribbled down from Jo'burg hadn't stopped tuberculosis and poverty from taking her. She was buried not far from where he sat. Just the other side of the range of low hills that crouched before him. *Fucking godforsaken place.*

Zondi heard the low growl of engines and headlamps cut through the night, powdery dust motes dancing in their beams. He watched as the vehicles slowed. The Pajero stopped and the trucks fell in beside it. The revving of motors, snatches of shouted Zulu, and then the vehicles moved toward the hill opposite Zondi. The SUV driving straight ahead, the trucks fanning out on its flanks.

Inja was using the classic beast horn formation so beloved of the Zulus of old. The tactic that had left these plains sticky with British blood. Inja would attack from the center, and the two horns would outflank and surround the targets, cutting off any escape.

Zondi scrambled down the embankment and started the Ford, the engine grinding before it caught. He set off after the convoy. Running blind. Following the beams that speared the night.

THEY WERE CLOSER. Three sets of headlamps. Dell dropped the glasses and turned. His father knelt, trying to stand. Not making it. The girl whispering to him.

'We're getting out of here,' Dell said.

Goodbread stared up at Dell, just enough moonlight to see his dead man's face. 'Leave me.' A torn whisper.

Dell was tempted. Knew he and the girl stood a better chance if they abandoned Goodbread. But the girl grabbed one of the old man's arms, lifting him. Strong these women. From years of carrying water, and gathering firewood, while their men smoked weed and plotted revenge.

Dell reached down and took Goodbread's other arm, and between them they got the old man standing, his arms slung around their shoulders. Dell could feel his father's ribs fluttering like birds, fighting for every breath.

They left the cave and started down the slope, feet loosening rocks that clattered down to the valley. The bobbing headlamps were close now. The low growl of the approaching vehicles echoed in the hills. Then a spotlight kicked in, feeling its way up the rocks toward them.

INJA SAW THE THREE PEOPLE caught in the beam. The old one supported by the man and the girl. 'Don't shoot,' he shouted out the window of the Pajero, even as he heard a shot coming from the truck to his right. Idiots.

He shouted again, his voice drowned as the men in the vehicle to his left opened up. Before he could see whether any of the shots had found their target, the truck with the spotlight hit a rock and the beam bounced off the trio, scribbling a wild path up the hillside.

The shooting stopped and Inja climbed half out of the side window of the Pajero, bellowing: 'No fucking shooting, I said!'

He heard the scream of an engine and a light-colored pickup appeared from behind a hillock, speeding across the plain. Inja was almost flung from the Pajero as his driver swerved and floored the gas, in pursuit of the truck.

The LIGHTS OF THE THREE VEHICLES glared at Dell from the rearview. The pickup's headlamps danced crazily across the uneven landscape and he could hear rocks tearing at the underbelly of the Toyota. He swerved to avoid an eroded sinkhole, fishtailed, almost lost the truck, fought to find traction on the sand.

The girl sat at his side, gripping the dash, staring over her shoulder. Muttering some incantation. Maybe she was praying. His father was sprawled across the rear seat, panting like a dog.

The Toyota vaulted a ridge, all four wheels off the ground. Seemed to hang for ever, suspended in space, and Dell could see two moons staring down at him like predators' eyes through the bullet-starred windshield. Then the truck hit earth. The girl flew and her head smacked the roof with a dull clang.

'Seat belt,' Dell shouted. No idea if she understood. No time to strap himself in.

The door at the back of the camper shell burst open, and banged madly as the truck barreled forward. No lights in the rearview, and for a moment Dell thought he'd lost them. Then his headlamps dimmed through dust, and he saw the haunch of a yellow truck swerving in ahead of him. He fought the wheel hard right into a slide, and felt the back of the Toyota glance off the yellow vehicle, leaving the pickup yawing and weaving like a drunk.

A Pajero had got in front of them and the Toyota's cracked windshield disintegrated in a shower of glass. Dell thought they were under fire, but realized it was a rock, hurled by the rear wheels of the SUV.

The yellow truck was at their side, and the third vehicle came in at them from the right. The Pajero's brake lights burned red as jewels, and the flanking vehicles boxed them, a vise closing. Dell saw the passenger to his right withdrawing the snout of his AK-47 before it was sandwiched.

Dell stood on the brakes. The girl braced herself against the dash. His father's body smashed into the rear of Dell's seat. The Toyota skidded to a stop, flinging up a curtain of dust. Dell spun the wheel one-eighty and floored the gas.

Checked the mirrors for lights. Heard the girl scream. Saw a rock face looming. No time for brakes. A detonation of metal and glass and his chest smashed into the steering wheel. Hard enough to crush the wind from his lungs. He smelled smoke and the engine died. Fighting for breath he looked back. The Pajero turned in a dusty slide, shook itself like a wet dog, then charged forward again. The other two trucks falling in behind.

Dell tasted blood in his mouth. Spat. Felt for the pistol at his waist. Still there. The girl opened the side door and took off into the night. Dell reached for his door handle and shoved. Wouldn't budge. As he struggled across to the passenger side, the rear door of the truck swung open, and his father stood up, silhouetted in the fast-approaching beams. Firing the rifle on automatic.

INJA SAW THE GIRL FALL out of the Toyota, kneeling in the sand. Staring into their lights. Then she pushed up like a sprinter from the blocks and took off into the night.

'Follow her,' he shouted to the driver.

A hard rattle of an automatic rifle and the driver's window

exploded. The man slumped over the wheel, dead foot still tramping the gas, sending them full speed into the rear of the truck. Inja's head starred the windshield.

GOODBREAD WALKED TOWARD THE LIGHT. Felt the rifle bucking in his arms. His weak goddam old man's arms. Nearly dropped the weapon. Stitched a couple of rounds uselessly into the earth, then fought the rifle up and heard bullets drumming on metal. Glass shattered, and the SUV shimmied, then hurtled forward.

Passed by him so close that its wind tugged at his clothes, just before it rammed the Toyota. Another truck was loping across, spotlight flaring in Goodbread's eyes. He shot the light out. Kept walking forward. Firing. Empty. Hammer clicking like a Zulu tongue. Grabbed the hot magazine from the weapon. Dropped it.

Felt a bullet take him in the leg. Sank to one knee. Rammed the spare magazine home. Something hit him hard in the shoulder. Burned like a bastard. Raised the rifle and closed his finger and felt the weapon buck and chew and spit.

Then everything was quiet and slow and Goodbread felt the warm sand enfold him. He lay on his back, staring up at a terrible light that was at once the moon and something else entirely.

chapter 61

SUNDAY RAN INTO THE NIGHT. KICKED OFF HER SHOES, HER FEET FLYING over the rocks. Skin toughened by years of climbing these hills. Her arms pumped, breath strong and even. She was a born runner. Always something to run from, in this place.

She saw a slope ahead, rising black against the moon. If she could reach it she would be safe. No car could follow her. Forced more speed into her legs. Told her lungs not to burn. Not far now.

ZONDI HEARD THE GUNFIRE and the sound of tearing metal. A pause. Then the chatter of automatic weapons. Coming from below him. He'd been holding a parallel course to the vehicles that pursued the Toyota, trying to outflank them. Found himself above them now, bouncing across an eroded plateau lying silver in the moonlight.

He edged the old Ford close to the slope, ratcheted up the handbrake and left the truck. Door open, engine idling unevenly. He crouched low and approached the rocky edge. Looked down. Saw a pair of vehicles jammed together like mating dogs, while the two trucks roamed the plain.

One set of headlamps sent yellow fingers into the night and snagged a running figure. From the lightness of the runner, it could only be the girl. Sprinting across the sand, toward the slope. Toward him.

The truck surged after the girl, headlamps throwing a halo around her. Zondi drew the pistol and took a bead on the lights as they bucked and weaved. Too far for an accurate shot. He fired. Knew he'd missed. Saw the girl look back over her shoulder. Wanted to shout. Tell her to keep running. Saw her stumble.

SUNDAY FELT HER BODY leave the ground. Seemed to take for ever before she hit, the palms of her hands tearing on the gravel, the breath smashed from her. She sucked dusty air, pulled herself to her knees, saw lights warming the sand around her.

The truck was beside her, door opening, voices shouting. She tried to get up and run again, but a man's arms grabbed her and pulled her onto his lap. The truck flew away, door flapping like a broken wing.

She tried to fight the arms off. To fling herself out the door that swung wide. But the man tightened his grip around her ribs, squeezing the air from her lungs. She could smell his sour breath. Feel the rough scrape of his beard against her cheek. Sunday stopped fighting. Let herself go slack.

The man reached over and pulled the door shut and the truck bounced across to where the old dog stood waiting.

INJA WIPED BLOOD FROM HIS EYE. He had a gash on his forehead, but he was alive. The medicine had worked. The yellow truck slid to a halt, the girl up front, slumped in the lap of his soldier.

'Is she hurt?' Inja asked, stepping toward the truck.

The big soldier with a shaven head, skull bearing the dent of an old axe wound, pushed the door open with his boot and stood up, still gripping the girl, her bare feet dangling. 'No, *Induna*.'

'Put her down.'

The gunman lowered the girl. She stood a moment, head hanging, then she folded into a squat, skinny arms drooping onto the dirt. In the spill of the dome light Inja saw she was crying. 'Stay with her,' he said.

Inja went back to the Pajero and removed a flashlight from the glovebox. Whipped the beam around, taking stock. The driver was dead. The soldier in the rear gut-shot, lying with his face pressed up against the window glass, blood leaking from his lips.

Inja's beam found the body of the old white man, lying on his back on the sand, arms flung wide like he'd fallen from a height.

'Where is the other white man?' Inja asked.

His crew shrugged, waited for his fury. Inja stood a while, sniffing the air.

The big soldier approached him. 'Do you want us to search for him, *Induna*?'

Inja shook his head. 'No. Where can he go? He won't be able to hide his pale ass in the morning.'

Inja ordered his soldiers to remove the driver's body. Throw it into the rear of the Pajero with the dying man, who was weeping and pleading for water and for his mother.

Inja ignored him. Got behind the wheel of the SUV and started the car, jammed it into reverse gear. Heard tearing and grinding, then the Pajero was free of the Toyota. Headlamps smashed and blinded, but the car good to be driven. He left the SUV idling when he stepped down.

Inja crossed to where the old man lay, the beam of his flashlight bouncing off the dead eyes. He called for a knife. Took it from the soldier who held it out to him and passed the man the flashlight. 'Shine this on him,' he said.

Inja knelt beside the old man. Lifted the shirt, saw the pale, wasted body stitched with gunshot wounds. Loosened the dead man's belt and pulled the khaki trousers down past his hips.

He stabbed the blade into the old man's white flesh just above his pubes and pulled the knife up to the sternum. Disemboweled him. The way his ancestors used to disembowel their enemy, to make sure they could never return to haunt the battlefields. Then he moved the blade up to the old man's face and took out his eyes. So his spirit wouldn't be able to see Inja from the shadowlands.

DELL SCRAMBLED UP A HILL, loose rocks tumbling. Telling the men below where he was. He stopped. Crouched down. *Do I honest-to-God care?* Wondered what impulse still made him run. *Why not just stop and take a bullet?* End it all.

He sat with his back to a rock, holding the pistol. Waiting. At least he'd take some of them with him. Then he heard an explosion and the sky beyond the rocks glowed orange. He edged forward and looked down. The Toyota was burning, flames kicking high into the night. Doors slammed and the two trucks and the Pajero took off, the SUV running without lights.

Dell watched the flaming Toyota. Saw the Volvo tumbling. Burning. Back in the morgue as the fumes from the gasoline fire grabbed at his throat.

chapter 62

THE CONVOY RUMBLED UP THE TRACK TO INJA'S HOMESTEAD. HIS WIVES peered out of the doorways of their huts, children clotting their legs like ticks. When they saw Inja stand up out of the lead truck, they clucked the brats back inside and locked their doors. Inja put aside the thought that they would have danced if it were he lying dead in the rear of the Pajero.

His sister waddled down the steps from his house. 'Brother, you are bleeding.'

He swatted her fat hand away from his forehead. Looked across to where the girl sat between his two men, in the yellow truck. 'Sister, you take that girl. Stay with her in there until morning.' Pointing at the newly completed hut. 'I am locking the two of you inside. You don't close your eyes. Watch her. If she wants to piss or shit she does it in a bucket. Do you understand?'

'Yes, brother.'

Inja looked on as the big woman dragged the girl into the hut. He locked the door after them and turned to his men. Pointed to four of them. 'You stay here and keep guard. If I catch a man sleeping he will follow the swallows.' He drew a finger across his throat.

The men nodded and took up positions around the hut.

Inja addressed the last pair. 'Take those,' pointing at the bodies of his two soldiers, lying in a tangle of limbs in the rear of the Pajero, 'and bury them.'

The men looked at each other. The big man with the dented skull found the courage to speak. '*Induna*, they have wives and children that need to mourn them.'

Inja stepped up to his soldier, and even though he reached barely to his chin, the man took a step back, and dropped his eyes to the earth. 'And you? You have a family?' Inja asked.

'Yes, *Induna*.'

'Then you do as I say or they will mourn you. And once they have cried their tears and wiped their snot, I'll fuck your women and kill your sons. Understand?'

The man nodded and Inja walked up to his house. Feeling the stirrings of the sickness in him again, the weakness that robbed his limbs of power. Waited until the door closed behind him before he allowed himself to sink to the floor, the room spinning, sweat dripping from his forehead.

chapter 63

IT WAS LATE WHEN ZONDI GOT BACK TO THE ROOM AT THE HOSPITAL AND he felt hollow and meaningless. The drapes were open and moonlight washed the bare walls. He didn't switch on the light. Shut the door, took the gun from his waistband and put it down on the table beside the bed. The bedsprings creaked as he sat down. Wished he had a bottle of Glenmorangie.

He didn't know how long he sat there, in the dark, before he heard the slap of shoes in the corridor. The footsteps stopped at the room next to his, and a key scraped in a lock.

Before he could think, he crossed the room and stepped out into the corridor, catching the Belgian doctor as her door was closing. She paused, stethoscope gleaming between her breasts, the fluorescent light painting her white coat blue. Nothing was said. Zondi moved back, allowing her to step out, lock her door and follow him into his room.

He sat down on the bed and clicked on the lamp. She reached across him and killed it, a loose strand of her hair brushing his face. They were kissing, and he pushed her down onto the bed. Crouched over her. Pulled off her jeans and panties. Leaving her in a T-shirt and white coat that stank of chloroform and human waste and disease and death. He heard a metallic clink as she dropped her stethoscope onto the side table, on top of his gun.

Zondi found a condom in his wallet and she took it from him. Rolling the tube onto his flesh was the only foreplay. She fell back on the bed and pulled him into her. It was fast. Sex as an analgesic.

When it was done they lay side by side, and she found her cigarettes in the pocket of her coat. He heard the scrape of a match, caught the sulfur smell and watched her face turn orange as she lit the cigarette. She shook the flame dead and sucked smoke. The long sigh of her exhalation. Louder than her climax.

'So, Disaster Zondi, tell me about your name. It is a... nickname?'

'No. It's on my birth certificate.'

'Is that what you were, maybe, for your parents? A disaster?'

'They were illiterate Zulus. Knew no English. They thought a disaster was something good.'

The Belgian laughed smoke. 'Sometimes it is.'

She touched him and felt that he was ready again. The next time was slower, and she let herself go. Cried out. Then she lifted herself off him and dressed quickly.

'I hope you sleep well,' she said as she walked to the door. Like she was leaving a patient's bedside.

chapter 64

DELL SAT SHIVERING UNDER THE MOON THAT HUNG PALE AND UGLY OVER the torn landscape. Not shivering from the cold, because heat still rose from the hard earth and the rocks. He heard the ring of metal against stone and realized that he held the pistol in his trembling hand. He lifted the gun, studied its blue glow in the moonlight.

Dell opened his mouth and swallowed the barrel. Tasted the sharpness of the gunpowder, the bitterness of the metal, and something almost sweet that must have been gun oil. Felt the arc of the front sight pressing up against his palate. The slight serrations of the trigger under his index finger. Shut his eyes. Increased the pressure on the trigger. Wanting this release. His finger froze when he saw his family. Not the charred meat in the morgue: his wife and children as he remembered them. Laughing. Happy. Alive.

Rosie. Mary. Tommy.

Dell opened his eyes and slid the barrel from his mouth. His breath coming ragged and irregular. But he wasn't shaking anymore. Knew whoever he once had been, he was no longer. He wanted to die. But not yet. Not until he had reckoned with Inja Mazibuko.

Dell settled back against a rock. Listened to the night. Cicadas. A bird call. A distant whoop of some animal. He must have fallen asleep, because when he opened his eyes sunrise bled pink into the sky on the horizon. His mouth was dry, and he knew there was no water to be had.

Dell stood and started down the slope, toward the torched truck. When he heard a bark unlike a dog's, he stopped. Moved forward cautiously, rounding the blackened hood of the Toyota. A hyena was feeding on his father's entrails. The animal looked up at him, muzzle wet with blood. It bared its teeth.

Dell reached down for a rock and threw it at the scavenger. Hit it up near its ribcage, bones sticking through its dusty skin like corrugated sheet iron. The animal shuffled back a step and growled again. He could see its eyes: close-set, yellow, feral. Wearing its spotted fur like a bad suit. Dell's fingers found another rock and he hurled it, all of his rage and grief focused in the release. Hit the hyena up near its blunt snout and it yelped. Then it turned and slunk away, scrawny assed and knock-kneed, growling over its shoulder before it disappeared into a gulley.

His father lay sprawled on his back in a mess of viscera. A bullet had drilled a neat hole in his temple. His mouth sagged open, tongue showing blue, as if he were licking his lips. Meat flies clustered around the gaping wounds where his eyes had been. Dell looked up at the twists of charred paper floating in the sky. Vultures.

Guess I owe you this much, old man, he said as he grabbed his father's ankles and dragged him, rolling his body into a ditch, trying not to hear the wet slap of his entrails. Made sure the body fell on its front, so he didn't have to look into the gaping eye sockets.

Then he set to work covering the corpse with rocks. Even this early the day was hot, and soon he was sweating. Tongue swollen with thirst. He stepped back. A small mound of red rocks covered the body. He sat a while, catching his breath, thinking about his father, the man he'd always hated. Had anything changed? No. Nothing had changed.

Dell stood. He needed water. He set off toward a cluster of huts flung up against the slope of a distant hill, iron roofs catching the rising sun.

chapter 65

SHE LAY LISTENING TO THE DEEP BASS BOOM OF THE DRUM. THE DRUMMER stood outside the main house, sending a message out to the valley that this was the day that Sunday was to become *Induna* Mazibuko's fourth wife. Each smack on the cowhide brought her closer to the moment the old dog would take her.

She hadn't slept, lying awake in the hut. Hearing the snores of the fat woman, who had fallen asleep despite her brother's commands. The room stank of the woman's sweat and the slop bucket in the corner. Auntie Mavis had used it to empty her bowels before she slept, a foul and noisy business. Sunday needed to pass urine, but there was no way she could go near that bucket.

She closed her eyes and prayed. Praying away the stench and the monotonous pulse of the drum that seemed to mirror her heartbeat. Praying that she would hear her mother's voice. Instead Sunday heard a key in the lock and she sat up, wrapping herself in the blanket, as the door opened. Inja Mazibuko stood in the doorway, dressed in shorts and a T-shirt. As skinny as a cane rat. A pink Band-Aid on his forehead.

'Sister!' he bellowed in that voice that seemed to come from a bigger man. The fat whale surfaced grunting and moaning from the blankets, blinking her eyes at the light. 'Get this girl dressed and ready. The guests will be arriving soon.'

The old dog stared down at Sunday. She tried to stare back, but she couldn't, and she dropped her gaze. Terrified of the hunger in his eyes.

AS DELL NEARED THE HUTS on the hillside, he saw two figures, scratches of black against the red sand. Drawing closer, he saw they were a very old man in torn khaki overalls and a boy of maybe eight, wearing grown man's shorts cinched in at the waist, his fleshless torso white with dust. They were dragging the carcass of a sheep toward a makeshift handcart, a wooden box on a pair of bent bicycle wheels, the yoke stuck in the dirt. Two more dead sheep lay on the cracked earth, drawing flies.

The man and the boy strained at the carcass, trying to lift it up onto the cart, but neither was strong enough and the sheep slid back onto the sand. The old man squatted beside the sheep, drinking air, staring down at the dust. The boy stood over him, watching Dell approach through ancient eyes.

Dell's tongue was thick in his mouth, and he battled to speak the Zulu word that had somehow stuck in his memory from his childhood in Durban: *amanzi*. Water. He mimed drinking from a bottle. The old man looked up at him. Bloodshot eyes a roadmap of suffering.

Dell sank to his knees on the sand. '*Amanzi*. Please.' He found a crumpled banknote in his pocket and held it out toward the old man.

The Zulu shook his head, looked up at the boy and spoke. The boy nodded. Dell could see that the child's tight black curls were red-blond at the roots, the sign of kwashiorkor, a protein deficiency caused by malnutrition. The boy jogged off in the direction of the huts, his skinny legs like bell clappers in the frayed shorts.

Dell looked at the old man, who ignored him, staring into the distance, oblivious to the flies that homed in on his eyes and nostrils. Crawled over his distended earlobes. Dell stood and crossed to the sheep lying by the cart. It had been shot in the head. Saw the bullet holes in the other two carcasses. Didn't try to understand.

He squatted and got his arms under the dead animal, hot sand burning his skin. The sheep was a bag of bones and stinking, matted fur. He managed to lift it and drop it into the handcart. The weight of the carcass tipped the box back into the dust, leaving the T-shaped yoke silhouetted against the sky.

Dell sweated, amazed that he had enough moisture left in him to produce perspiration. He felt dizzy after the exertion and sat down, his back to the cartwheel, feeling the rim digging into his shoulder. When he got his breath back, he crossed to the second sheep. Not sure why he was doing this. Maybe it was his day for carcasses.

The old man watched Dell now, hands dangling between his legs. Dell grabbed the sheep by a hind hoof and hauled it toward the cart. This one was meatier, and he was struggling to lift it when he felt the old man beside him, saw the muscles in his arms as stringy as jerky. Between the two of them they heaved the sheep onto the baseboard of the cart. Dell went for the third, dragging it back, and they manhandled it aboard. They both sank to the ground, the old man nodding and muttering thanks.

A shadow touched Dell and he looked up to see the boy standing over him, holding out a plastic Coke bottle filled with water. Dell snatched it from the boy's hands and tipped it to his mouth. The water was warm and brackish but he drank until he'd emptied the bottle, liquid spilling over his chin, running down his neck onto his shirt. When he dropped the bottle to the sand, he felt a sharp cramp in his stomach.

Dell heard metal protesting as the old man and the boy dragged the handcart along the pathway up toward the huts.

The boy had placed a banana – split skin black and oozing – on a rock beside Dell. He lifted the banana and looked at it. And suddenly he was crying. Tears coming from God knew where in his parched body. Strings of snot and spit dangling like bungee cords from his mouth as he bawled.

ZONDI AWOKE THINKING OF his mother's funeral. Saw dusty men

clutching at frayed ropes, lowering her coffin into red soil that lay hacked open like flesh. An expensive casket, more than he could afford at the time, but still it had been scorned by his family.

Zondi sat up. *A coffin is a fucking coffin, man. You're sounding like the idiots in this valley.* The place was dragging him back.

He quit the bed, the doctor's sweat and Gitanes still clinging to the sheets. He showered and dressed. Packed his duffel bag. Left the room. Slipped the key under the Belgian's door and got out of there. Rattled away in the Ford, the town disappearing in his dust.

You're going to drive to Dundee. Report last night's mess to the cops. Hire a car and get the hell back to Jo'burg. Fight battles that are in your weight range. Telling himself this even as his hands turned the wheel, the Ford bumping off the main road, driving across the rutted earth to the place where he had buried his mother. Just over the hill from last night's bloodletting. Trying to push away flashes of the eviscerated old man, the burning truck, and the girl held captive in the convoy that drove off into the night.

Zondi stopped the Ford at the base of a hillock. Feet had worn a pathway up to a graveyard that perched on a fissured ridge, dry as chicken dust. He sat a while in the truck, waving away flies. As if he was waiting for something to tell him exactly what the fuck he was doing out here. Impatient with himself, he pushed open the door, and walked up the hill to talk to his dead mother.

Zondi arrived at the top of the footpath. Stood lost in the vast fungus of white wooden crosses that grew from the dust. Evidence of the plague that had swept this valley. He wandered among the makeshift markers and the fresh red mounds, until he found a solitary headstone. His mother's. A small lump of badly hewn granite that seemed ostentatious among these pauper's graves. Years after her death, still plagued by guilt, he'd commissioned masons in Dundee to carve and place the headstone. He'd sent money down from Johannesburg and promised himself he'd visit the grave for an unveiling ceremony. He never had. Zondi was ashamed to see that his mother's name was misspelled.

He squatted down. Awkward. Waved a fly away from his head. Looked out over the sea of listing crosses. He'd done this, as a boy. Spoken to the ancestors. But he was a man now, in his Diesels and his Italian sunglasses. Talking to the ancestors was commonplace in African culture. No big deal. And not just out here in the sticks. In Jo'burg slick execs in silk suits – newly rich from black empowerment coups – drove their Beemers and Benzes across to the sprawling Avalon cemetery in Soweto, muted their cell phones, and hunkered down to rap with the dead.

So there he sat. Not knowing where to start, or what to say. But knowing he needed something. Some help. *Think of it as a meditation*, he told himself. Like the Buddhists in their charnel houses. Opening themselves up to the notion of non-attachment. *You're dressing it up, man. You're Zulu to your bones. Just do it.*

He closed his eyes. Felt a breeze on the back of his neck. Opened his eyes. Still sensed the coolness on his skin, but the dust lay unstirred. That kind of breeze was a sign that the spirits were with you, or so the superstition went. He laughed. Unconvincingly.

Closed his eyes again. Heard something, almost like a footfall. Kept his eyes shut. Let it play out. Heard the rasp of a weapon being cocked. Opened one eye. Looked up into the dark mouth of a pistol and saw Robert Dell beyond it. Wild eyed. Dusty. Caked with dried blood.

chapter 66

THE BLACK GUY STAYED COOL. NOT STRESSING. 'PUT THE GUN DOWN.'

Dell kept the pistol on him. 'Who are you?'

'The name's Disaster Zondi.'

'You're bullshitting me.'

'Would I lie about something like that?'

Dell had to concede the point. The guy was definitely city. Very Jo'burg in his Diesels and his designer shades. Spoke in that slightly Americanized drawl a lot of the black hipsters affected.

'Put that thing away, you're making me nervous,' Zondi said.

Dell's arm dropped, then jumped right back up again, like it was on a spring. 'Give me your gun.'

'I'm not armed.'

'Everybody in this fucking place is armed. Give.'

Zondi reached for his weapon and held it out, butt first. Dell took the gun. Not sure what to do with it. Kept it in his left hand. Felt dizzy. Lowered himself down onto the headstone.

'That's my mother's grave you're sitting your ass on.'

Dell stood. Swayed. Felt like an idiot. Jammed Zondi's gun into his waistband. Too many guns. 'Are you a cop?'

'Do I look like a cop?'

'Maybe one of those overeducated types the national prosecutor recruited.'

Zondi snorted. 'Okay. I was. Not any more.'

'What do you do now?'

'I'm on sabbatical.'

'Down here in the ass-end of the world?'

'I'm on a mercy mission.'

'The girl?

'Yes. The girl.'

'And what's your interest in her?' Dell asked.

Saw Zondi's eyes flicker behind the shades. 'She's the daughter of an old friend.'

'Yesterday, at that Zulu village, the girl didn't act as if she knew you.'

Zondi shrugged. 'I was about to introduce myself, then you and your cowboy daddy came riding in.'

Dell looked at him for a while. Trying to figure this out. 'You know who I am?'

'Yes.'

'Then you know what Inja Mazibuko did to my family?'

'I've got an idea.'

'And you want to take this girl away from him?'

'Yes.'

'Then maybe we're on the same side here.'

Zondi shook his head, little flares of sun firing the rims of his glasses. 'This isn't a fucking buddy movie, man.' He stared out over the landscape, watching a dust devil spin and weave. Looked back at Dell. 'What are you planning to do to Inja?'

'Kill him.'

'Inja's a warlord. You think you can just waltz in on him and plug him?' Dell said nothing. 'Do you even know where he is?'

'I can find him.'

Zondi stared up at him, impassive. 'That white skin of yours is like a beacon. You won't last till lunchtime.' He stood and held out a manicured hand. 'Can I have my gun back now?'

Dell thought about it, then gave him the weapon. Zondi started walking away.

'Where are you going?' Dell asked.

'To the wedding. You coming?'

Dell followed him.

SUNDAY SAW HER AUNT, thin as a twist of root, dragging her crippled leg as she danced and howled around the cooking fire. Saw the old dog, wandering scrawny and proud through the smoke, beads layering his bony chest, his loins covered by a short skirt of skins, animal fur circling his upper arms and calves.

Saw the dignitaries from the valley as they stood in line to pay their respects to the dog, bowing before him. Men in traditional clothes or black suits stiff as cardboard. Married women in red hats and beaded aprons, Reeboks and Nikes sticking out from under their blankets if they were wealthy, feet bare and cracked if they weren't.

Saw the unmarried virgins, heavy brown breasts bare to the sun, sneaking envious glances at the bride, wondering how such a skinny thing had landed the wealthy and powerful *Induna* Mazibuko.

And Sunday saw herself sitting on the straw mat, face covered by the veil woven into her hair, a symbol of her servitude to the old dog. Felt as if she was looking down from high above the kraal, circling the sky with the vultures. Like she was already dead.

ZONDI DROVE THE FORD back toward the main road, Dell rode shotgun. Zondi sneaked a glance at his passenger. He looked like shit and stank worse. Gray stubble clashing with the bad dye job. Bruises of exhaustion beneath his eyes. And Zondi had seen how Dell's hand had shaken when he'd pointed the gun at him. Worried that he'd pull the trigger without knowing it.

'Zondi?'

'Ja?'

'You believe the minister ordered the hit on Baker?' Dell asked.

'I'm a hundred fucking percent sure he did,' Zondi said.

'Baker was going to go public with a paper trail of all the bribes and payoffs in return for immunity from prosecution. Not even the minister could have dodged that bullet.'

Dell stared out over the empty landscape. 'So you people were watching Ben Baker for a while?'

This guy and his reporter's habit of asking questions were getting to Zondi. He wanted to tell him to shut the fuck up. Better yet he wanted to stop the Ford and throw him out. Leave his dead white ass behind. But some voice – surely to God not his mother's? – told him that he'd asked for help. And he'd been sent Dell.

Zondi looked at him. 'Where are you going with this?'

The white guy stared out the window. 'Baker and my wife were having an affair.'

'I know.' Dell watching him now. 'She featured in our surveillance reports.'

'For how long?'

'Maybe five or six months.'

'Christ.'

'Dell, did you love your wife?'

'Yes.'

'Then let it go,' Zondi said. 'Baker bought people. That was his thing. Believe me, your wife wasn't the only one.'

'I just can't see it, you know? Rosie and him. Hell, he wasn't even her type.'

'Let it go, man. She fucked up. Strayed. She would have come home.'

'Maybe,' Dell said. 'But she didn't have the chance to.'

'No, she didn't.'

They hit the main road and Zondi turned away from town. Saw a store sticking up out of the dust like a scab. Stopped the Ford a distance from the entrance.

'I'm going to get us something to eat and drink,' Zondi said, cracking the door. 'Stay here. And stay low.' He stepped out of the car and walked away.

DELL ALMOST FELL ASLEEP. Felt his chin bump onto his chest, jerking him awake. He sat up straight. Glimpsed a shape at his side window, reached for the gun. Saw a kid, face caked with snot and flies, whining in Zulu, holding out his hands like a begging bowl. Dell dug out the banknote the old man had refused and handed it to the boy. Mistake. Within seconds the Ford was mobbed by a crowd of begging children.

Zondi approached, carrying a plastic bag. Shouted at the kids in Zulu, fighting a path through to the driver's door. He slammed it and tried to start the car. The sound of rocks in a tumble drier. Finally the engine caught, and Zondi took off. 'Jesus, you really know how to stay invisible, don't you?'

He passed the bag across and Dell opened it. A dusty pair of plastic Hong Kong binoculars. Bottled water. A wrinkled apple and a few packets of potato chips that looked like they'd been on the shelves a while. A black peaked cap with the white skull-and-crossbone insignia of the Orlando Pirates soccer team. A pair of Ray-Ban knockoffs. And a can of black Cobra shoe polish.

Dell held up the can. 'What's this?'

'Smear it on your face and hands.'

'You're kidding, right?'

'No. You stick out, man. Just do it.'

Zondi reached down and handed Dell the rearview mirror that lay on the floor of the truck. Dell balanced the mirror on the vibrating dash and started rubbing the polish into his cheeks. He caught the sharp smell of turpentine and the paste burned his skin. He covered his face and his neck. Smoothed it over his lower arms and hands.

Saw Zondi looking at him. 'And what do I do now,' asked Dell, 'sing 'Mammy'?'

Zondi laughed, and after a moment so did Dell. Sounding strained, wobbling on the edge of hysteria. But laughing.

chapter 67

SUNDAY WAS PULLED BACK INTO HERSELF BY THE BELLOW OF A DYING animal. A man in a blue overall slaughtered a cow beside the fire, hacking at its throat with a butcher's knife, thick, bright blood patterning the sand.

Sunday was sick to her stomach with fear. She felt like running. Couldn't. The old dog's gunmen, rifles slung over their shoulders, patrolled the throng of guests that crowded her as she sat huddled on the grass mat. Inja stood by the fire, drinking. The heat haze made his body twist and dance like he was possessed. He turned to her and bared his teeth in a yellow smile.

Fat Auntie Mavis, stinking of brandy, dragged Sunday up off the mat, hissing at her. 'Wake up, girl! Come. It is time.'

Sunday allowed herself to be prodded toward the slaughtered beast. The crowd roared in anticipation as the butcher crouched and opened the cow's belly with his blade, letting the animal's insides spill out pink and glistening onto the sand.

Auntie Mavis reached beneath the blanket that wrapped her fat middle and produced a fistful of banknotes. Shoved them at Sunday. 'Do it, girl.'

Sunday took the money and squatted down beside the cow, feeling warm blood and sticky innards beneath her bare feet. Smelled the piss and the shit. Looked up at the faces in a circle around her, cheering, clapping, ululating. Her scrawny aunt at the front of the throng, wailing like a dying thing.

Sunday felt Auntie Mavis's bare foot in her ribs. 'Do it now!'

She slid her hands inside the stomach of the cow, arms sinking to the elbows in hot, sticky organs. Left the money inside the abdomen and pulled her arms free of the carcass. Stared down at the blood that dripped from her fingers into a puddle between her feet. Heard the crowd roaring approval. The ancestors had been bribed. She belonged to Inja Mazibuko.

THE FORD WAS PARKED UNDER a thorn tree, halfway up a hill in about as desolate place as Dell had ever known. Just the one kraal on a knoll below them, drumbeats rising up on the eddies of late afternoon heat.

Zondi stood scanning the landscape with the binoculars. Dell sat in the truck, door open, wearing the black cap and the sunglasses. The boot polish itched on his face, and ran down his chest in dark rivulets of sweat. He dug in the plastic bag and found the elderly apple. Took a bite. It was brown inside and tasted like flour. He threw the apple out the car window and rinsed his mouth with water. Stood up and walked across to Zondi.

'What's happening?' Dell asked.

Zondi lowered the glasses, shrugged. 'It's a Zulu wedding. Fat women in bras are dancing, and wasted men are smacking each other with sticks.'

Dell took the glasses, looked down at Inja's compound. The binoculars were weak and the lenses distorted, but he could see a knot of people involved in a ceremony in the circle of huts. Heard the drums and high-pitched ululating.

Dell handed the glasses back to Zondi and squatted in the sand. 'You're Zulu, right?'

'Ja. So?'

'You don't seem too crazy about your traditions.'

Zondi shrugged. 'Call me jaded, but I don't buy into this noble savage bullshit. It's the fantasy of white men and Zulu nationalists.'

'Like the minister?'

'Exactly.' Panning the glasses across the landscape.

'You from around here?'

'Way back.'

'So you knew him?'

'A little. He went into exile when I was a kid.'

'Tell me about him.'

'You're the reporter. You know the story.'

'I know the rumors,' Dell said. 'He doesn't do interviews. Says the white media demonizes him.'

Zondi laughed, lowering the glasses. 'What do you want to hear? That you take Bob Mugabe, mix in some Mobutu Sese Seko, add a dash of Idi Amin and you've got our next president?' Dell shrugged. Zondi lost the smile. 'Fact is, he's a fucking chameleon. When he talks to the poor, he's a poor man. Talks to the rich he's a businessman. Talks to the struggle veterans he's a comrade. But he's all about power. About as ruthless a fucker as you can get.' He set the glasses down on the hood of the Ford and stood with his hands in his pockets. 'If people get in his way he buys them off. If that doesn't work...'

'He whistles for the dog,' Dell said.

'Ja. But not for much longer.' Dell looked at him. 'Inja's got full-blown AIDS. And he's not on antiretrovirals. Believes in other methods.'

Dell took this in. 'You're telling me, him and this girl... it's one of these virgin cure deals?'

Zondi nodded. 'I've got to get her away from him before he consummates this thing tonight.'

'Jesus.'

'It's the way it's done down here.'

'Don't you have any influence with the authorities?'

Zondi laughed. 'What authorities? Inja's the law in this valley. The nearest cops are fifty miles away, too shit scared to set foot here. And what would I tell them, anyway?'

'That he's forcing the girl to marry him against her will.'

'He bought her, Dell. For a couple of grand and a few skinny cows. Doesn't matter what she wants. It's called tradition.'

Dell nodded. 'Okay. So what's the plan?'

'We wait until it's dark and everybody's drunk. Then we go down there and get her.'

'How?'

'We'll improvise.' Saw Dell's face. 'You got a better idea?'

'No.'

'Okay, then.' Paused. 'Dell, I know you want to take Inja out. Fine by me. But the girl is my priority. Understood?'

Dell nodded, then walked away. Looked out over the kraal far below. Marveled at just how fucked up things could get.

chapter 68

THE WEDDING MOON, FAT AND YELLOW AS BUTTER, OOZED UP OVER THE hills. Inja sat on the steps of his house, alone in the darkness, firing up a spliff. He sucked in the hot smoke, watching the drunken revelry below.

Men and boys fought each other with sticks, flickering shadows in the firelight. The elders feasted on his meat and drained away his beer. The festivities would carry on into the morning and beyond. It had cost him a lot of money. But it was good. The ancestors would be pleased.

Inja's only disappointment was that his chief, the minister of justice, had not put in an appearance. He was in the area, visiting his home in the valley. Addressing a rally in Bhambatha's Rock tomorrow night. Knew the chief's absence was a sign of his anger at the way Inja had mishandled the Cape Town mess. Inja sighed smoke. Damage control was called for. Obeisance would have to be made. But not tonight. Tonight was Inja's.

He looked across to where the girl sat beside his sister, the fat woman drunk, a plastic chair awash with her flesh. Dwarfing the girl, who was invisible beneath the veil, her skinny shoulders wrapped in leopard skin. Inja took a last drag on the spliff, flicked away the embers and walked over to her.

It was time.

SUNDAY SAW THE OLD DOG coming toward her through the smoke. She was too tired and empty now to feel fear. Auntie Mavis cackled at her side, saying something filthy about the rituals of the wedding night, a chunk of meat in her hands, tearing into the flesh with her teeth, juices flowing down her many chins.

Her plate piled with food on the mat next to Sunday's leg, cutlery lying ignored.

That's when Sunday felt the breeze on her neck, stirring the beads that hung from her hair. Felt her mother's presence. Heard her voice. Drawing Sunday's eyes to the small knife lying on the tin plate, the jagged blade orange in the firelight.

Sunday took the knife and sent it into the folds of her skirt. Then she stood as her husband reached her. Felt his hand on her arm, leading her toward his house. The women's voices, high and loud, rolled across the kraal in praise of Inja, calling on the ancestors to lend power to his manhood.

chapter 69

Zondi steered the Ford along the sand road toward Inja's compound. No headlamps. Driving by the light of the moon. Drumbeats and singing flowed in waves from the wedding party below them. Hopefully drowning the uneven racket of the truck's engine.

Dell was at his side, staring out into the night. Silent for once. A suburban whitey whose life had taken a detour into hell. Dell's eyes held a look, a particular kind of glaze, that Zondi remembered well from back in the struggle days. The eyes of people who had passed a point of no return. People who were ready to die. Unarmed kids who'd attacked squads of cops firing automatic rifles and pump-action shotguns. Grief-mad mothers who'd picked up rocks and charged the yellow armored cars that blocked the streets of the townships like fat clogging arteries.

Zondi had been in those mobs, but he'd always brought up the rear, ready to fade into the tear gas and the dust when the blood began to flow. So what the fuck was he doing now, on some Mutt and Jeff mission that could only end badly?

He stopped the truck on a slope about a mile from Inja's compound. Killed the engine. The handbrake creaked like old timber as he set it. The truck groaned and lurched forward a foot or two before the brake finally held.

Zondi looked across at Dell. 'You ready?'

'Yes. Let's do it.' No hesitation in his voice.

Zondi opened the door and stood up out of the truck.

Inja brought her into the front room. Sunday had never been in a house this big. With furniture like she had seen in the magazines her aunt read. A huge TV set flickered in the gloom, showing a beautiful black girl in a red dress driving a silver car with no roof. The girl sang. Silently.

Inja paused to lift a bottle of brandy from the table by the TV, then he took Sunday's arm and led her down a corridor. He opened a door and flicked a switch and electric light filled the room. A real bed, high and wide, with a bright pink blanket with long fluffy hair. He closed the door after them and set the brandy bottle down on the table beside the bed.

Inja crossed to another door and opened it, showing her a hard white space beyond. 'Here, girl. Use this.'

Unsure, Sunday stepped forward. Saw the light hammering off white tiles, saw a bath with taps and a toilet with a blue cover. The closest she had ever come to anything like this was the restroom at a gas station, and that had been filthy and stinking, the floor awash with overflowing waste.

Sunday walked into the bathroom and closed the door. Lifted her beaded skirt and slipped down the panties that the fat woman had given her to wear. Big ugly things. Bloomers. She raised the lid of the toilet and sat. Drilled her urine into the water. Checked that the knife was still in the waistband of her skin skirt, up behind her right hip.

She wiped herself, looked for a place to throw the paper. Realized she was being stupid and dropped it into the toilet bowl. Pressed the flush lever and jumped back at the explosion of water.

Stood at the basin and rinsed her hands, looking at herself in the mirror, this veiled person in a high red hat. Thought of the girl in the silver car on the TV and wondered about God and his choices.

Sunday wiped her hands on a towel that was so thick and so soft that she wanted to stand there for ever, holding it, letting it soothe her. But she dropped the towel in the basin and turned and went out.

When she walked back into the room, the old dog was lying on the bed, on his back. Naked. Sunday averted her eyes and he laughed. She'd seen unclothed men and boys, but never anything like this: his thing fat and hard.

He stood and reached for her, pushing her down onto the bed, and she felt his throbbing flesh leave a trail of slime on her ribs like a slug. He pulled the veil away from her face and then his hands were at the skins that covered her calves. He lifted one of her legs so her bare foot pointed at the ceiling, and bit into the meat of her calf hard enough to draw blood. She refused to scream. Waiting.

Inja's hands were at her skirts. He was breathing hard, and she could smell the foulness of his breath, and feel the warm wind of it on her face. He pushed his hands between her thighs and shoved them apart. Tugging at her panties. Her fingers found the blade and she brought it out and plunged it into his belly as he thrust his thing at her.

He made a sound like a gelded pig, and grabbed at the wound, as if he was trying to push the blood back into himself. She used her knees to throw him off her and stood, the knife still in her hand. Knowing she must use it again.

But the handle was slick with blood and when she lunged at him he brought up his arm, and the knife flew from her grip and hit the stone floor, spinning under the bed. Sunday ran for the door. Felt his fingers close for a moment on her ankle, then she kicked loose. He bellowed, his voice impossibly loud. Echoing in the big room.

Sunday flew down the corridor, toward the front door. Inja yelling, his bare feet smacking the stone as he came after her. She ran past the flickering TV, out onto the porch, ready to sprint into the night, when she was lifted off her feet and the big man, the one with the dented skull, held her. She heard the dog shouting from inside the house, getting closer.

Sunday and the big man stared at each other, eyeball to eyeball. She could feel his heart beating. Then he lowered her and stepped back into the darkness, fading away as if he had never been there. And Sunday ran for her life.

DELL FOLLOWED ZONDI over the rocky ground. They were close now. He could smell meat smoke from the fires that burned in the circle between a Western-style house and three huts. The clearing was jammed with people, their voices bubbling out into the night.

Zondi stopped him with a raised hand, and Dell made out the shape of a man sitting with his back against a tree, the moon kicking off a rifle barrel. They stood for a minute. Still. Then the man let loose a loud snore and slumped to the side.

Zondi crossed to the drunken sentry and lifted his AK-47, clicked the banana-shaped magazine free and threw it into the darkness. Laid the weapon on the sand beside the sleeping man. They walked on, toward the house. A man shouted, from somewhere below them. His voice distinct for a moment, then lost in the babble.

Feet on gravel. Somebody running at them. Zondi moved forward and grabbed the girl. She was ready to scream, but he covered her mouth, letting her see him in the moonlight. He took his hand away from her face and she gasped, drinking air. Put a finger to his lips and she nodded. They all turned as a man came around the side of the house, a man crouched low, hugging his belly. A naked man, bleeding, sprawling onto the sand.

Inja.

Dell was over to him, the pistol in his hand, the barrel jammed up against Inja's head. The moon bright enough for him to see Inja's face, catch the shine of his eyes, and the flash of teeth in the gaping mouth. Dell's finger closed on the trigger. Ready to end this thing.

chapter 70

BUT DELL DIDN'T END IT. AND NOW HE CROUCHED BARE-CHESTED OVER Inja, in the rear of the truck, chewing dust as the Ford bucked and swerved. Pressing his bunched shirt to the wound that pumped toxic blood from the naked man's belly, saying, 'Don't you fucking die on me, you piece of shit.'

Back there, behind the house, as he'd been about to pull the trigger, Zondi had knelt beside him and touched his shoulder. 'Think, Dell. Kill him and you don't stand a chance.'

Dell had looked up at Zondi. He didn't care about himself. He could kill the dog. But knew that he wanted the dog's master. Lowered the gun.

So here Dell was with Inja bloody and twisting beneath him like something newborn. Trying to save his life.

ZONDI DROVE, FOOT FLAT, Ford fishtailing along the sand road. The girl at his side silent, gripping the dashboard, her high hat scraping the roof of the truck. No rearview, so Zondi had to look back over his shoulder for headlamps. And to check that Dell hadn't killed Inja.

Seeing the wounded man had changed the game for Zondi. He had the girl. Fine. But now he could do more. Bring down the man who had put his boss in the ground. Who was pissing on everything Zondi believed in. If he could just keep Inja alive long enough, he could do it. Maybe.

He saw the mounds of the car wrecks gleaming in the moonlight. Looked back. No headlamps. Just Dell crouched over the wounded man.

'Father,' the girl said. 'Where are you taking me?'

Zondi was smacked back to the now. *Father.* Of course, it was just the Zulu way, a respectful form of address for an elder. But it reminded him that he had another mess to untangle. 'Don't worry, girl. You are safe.'

Fucking liar.

Zondi slowed and turned off the road, bumped the Ford past the dangling gate, stopped when the car bodies hid the truck from view. Not a safe place, this. But the only place he could think of where they could hide Inja while they tried to save his life.

Zondi banged on the iron door. Silence. Banged again. Heard grunts and muffled curses, then the door opened a crack and his hunchbacked cousin peered out at him, blinking away sleep. 'What you want?'

Zondi pushed the door open, feeling the twisted little man give way. A match flared and he saw his uncle's face in the glow of a paraffin lamp. The old man lay on the floor. Two mats and thin blankets thrown down in the midst of the tools and car parts. The room stinking of sweat and weed.

'What is this?' the old man asked.

Zondi drew his pistol, pointed it at the hunchback. 'Go and sit by your father.'

His cousin slunk over to the old man and sat down. Zondi's uncle shook his head. 'You dare to do this in my house?'

'Shut up.' Zondi kept the gun on them, walked backward out the door, called across to the truck. 'Bring him in.'

Dell dropped the tailgate and he and the girl lifted Inja out of the rear of the Ford. Dell taking him round the shoulders, the girl grabbing his feet. Carrying him into the room. They laid him on the floor, groaning, eyes closed, in the circle of light from the lamp.

Zondi heard the suck of his uncle's breath when the old man

recognized Inja. 'Are you mad? What hell are you bringing upon us?'

The old man stood, edging away from Inja, ducking under the length of plastic rope stretched across the room with an overall, a T-shirt and a pair of briefs pegged to it. Zondi tugged the T-shirt free of its peg and threw it to Sunday. 'Keep that on his wound.'

The girl hesitated a moment, then she knelt, and pressed the T-shirt to Inja's stomach. Zondi reached down and grabbed the blanket off his cousin's bed. Still warm from the man's body. He threw it over Inja's nakedness.

'Dell,' Zondi said, pointing to the wash line. 'Take down the rope. Cut it. Tie these two up.'

Dell unknotted the rope and clipped it into four pieces with the lineman's pliers that lay beside a hammer on the floor. He must have recognized the older man as the threat, because he went to him first. Zondi's uncle tried to fight, broad-shouldered and strong as a bull.

Zondi stepped forward and kicked him in the kidney. Not at all ashamed at how much pleasure it gave him. 'Old man, you keep still or I will shoot you.'

His uncle stopped struggling, sank to the floor, muttering about the vengeance of the ancestors. Dell tied the old man's hands behind his back. Roped his ankles. The little hunchback didn't put up a fight. Sat staring into a dark corner of the room while Dell tied him.

Zondi crouched beside Inja, who lay still as death. Touched a hand to his throat. He could feel an erratic pulse. Zondi stood and walked to the door. 'I'm going now. Don't let him die.'

SUNDAY SQUATTED BESIDE THE DOG, pressing the cloth to his stomach. Waiting. The white man, his face and arms painted black, streaks of dark color running over the pale skin of his chest, sat against the wall. Staring at nothing. Like he had in the cave. The gun on the floor beside him.

'Girl.' She looked up. The old man calling to her in Zulu. 'Girl, I know you. You are Ma Mavis's child.'

'Shut up,' the white man said.

'Take the gun from this white bastard. Free us. We are your people. This man will only do you harm.'

'I said shut up.'

'Listen to me, girl, or you will pay for this.'

The white man picked up a fistful of cotton waste from the floor, black with oil, and walked across to the Zulu. The old man tried to twist away, shaking his head, shouting, but the white man shoved the cotton into his mouth and left him looking like a foaming animal.

While the white man had his back to her, Sunday let go of the T-shirt and reached across for the saw blade that shone on the floor beside Inja's foot. Lifted the blade and laid it across the throat of the dog, ready to hack into him.

She felt a hand on her arm. Gripping her. The white man lifted her arm away from Inja's neck, and twisted her wrist. The blade fell from her fingers and clattered to the floor. He shook his head, said something to her in his language. He pushed her away gently, lifted the bloody T-shirt and pressed it against the dog's belly.

Sunday sat, the veil falling across her eyes. She reached for the blade again, saw the white man tense. Then she took off the hat, and lifted the blade, sawing the veil away from her hair. Freeing herself. The white man watched her, his arms trembling with the waves of convulsions that came from the dog.

ZONDI KNOCKED AT ANOTHER DOOR. This one opened to reveal the Belgian doctor. Her hair mussed, face creased with sleep. 'Disaster Zondi,' she said. Zondi glimpsed bare skin as she stepped back into the darkness of her room. 'I thought you had fled.'

He followed her in and shut the door. 'I need your help.'

The doctor crossed to the bedside lamp and warm light washed her nakedness. She stood watching him as she lit a cigarette, shaking the match dead. 'My help with what?'

'With an injured man.'

'Injured how?'

'He's been stabbed. In the stomach.'

'Then bring him in.'

'I can't.'

'And why not?'

'Because there'll be people looking for him. This would be the most obvious place.'

She stared at him, expressionless, sucking on the cigarette, cheeks hollowed by the inhalation. Spoke around smoke. 'You're trouble, aren't you, Disaster Zondi?' He didn't bother to reply.

The Belgian dropped the cigarette into a coffee mug and it whispered as it died. She unearthed a pair of panties from the clutter and stepped into them, her breasts hanging heavy.

'I'll be outside,' he said.

Zondi walked down the corridor, toward the pay phone mounted on the wall near the entrance. Scrolling his useless iPhone for a number with one hand, searching for coins with the other. He dialed, looking at his watch. Two a.m. Ringing.

Fucking answer.

'M.K.' Crisp, alert.

Doesn't the man ever sleep?

'You know who this is?'

A moment's hesitation. 'Yes. Give me your number.'

'No time. I have the animal we were discussing.'

A quick backwash of breath. 'You have it where?'

'Near its home. It's injured.'

'Badly?'

'Yes. But there's a chance.'

'Can you get it to Dundee at daybreak? I can have a chopper in place.'

'Why not land here?'

'Too dangerous. Can you transport the animal?'

'I think so.'

'Do it, then.'

The phone was dead in his ear. He hung the receiver back in the cradle, turned to see the doctor walking toward him, dressed in Levi's and Nikes, a man's white dress shirt unbuttoned over a gray top.

She said, 'I need to pick up a trauma bag. Wait for me in the car park.'

Zondi nodded, watched her walk away. Wondered who the shirt had belonged to.

chapter 71

DELL HEARD THE RATTLE OF THE FORD. BECKONED THE GIRL OVER TO keep pressure on Inja's wound, drew the pistol and stood by the door.

Feet on gravel then a knock. 'Open. It's me.'

Dell unlocked the door, and Zondi motioned him out. The truck was parked hard against the side of the building and Dell caught the sheen of pale hair through the windshield.

'How is he?' Zondi asked.

'Same. The girl tried to cut his throat, though. With a hacksaw blade.'

'Jesus.' Shrugged. 'She has her reasons.' Zondi looked toward the truck, then back at Dell. 'I don't want the men in there to be able to ID the doctor. Help me get them outside.'

Dell followed Zondi into the room. He checked that the girl hadn't tried to kill Inja again. She had not. She knelt, pressing down on the T-shirt, which was sodden with blood.

Zondi laughed when he saw the old man's mouth over-flowing with cotton waste. 'And this?'

'He was hassling the girl.'

'Big on the oral tradition, this old fucker.'

Zondi took the old man under his arms. The Zulu writhed and twisted. Zondi gave him a short-arm jab to the abdomen that quietened him down. Dell lifted his feet and they carried him out into the dark, dumping him on the sand by the car wrecks, where he had no view of the room. They went back for the hunchback, who was as light as a child. Left him lying a few feet from his father.

Zondi crossed to the Ford and opened the passenger door,

said something that Dell couldn't hear, and the woman slid out. Zondi led her into the hut, a canvas bag with pouches and zippers slung over his shoulder.

Dell stood in the doorway, saw the doctor crouch beside the trauma bag, unzip it and remove a pair of white surgical gloves and roll them onto her hands. Find a penlight, click on the beam and reach across to Inja. She said something to Sunday in halting Zulu, and the girl moved away, staring at the blonde woman.

The doctor pulled the blanket aside, and lifted the T-shirt off Inja's abdomen. Played the penlight over the unconscious man's flesh. Intestine bulged pink and wet from the mouth of the wound.

'With what did she stab him?' the woman asked in her accented English.

'A knife,' Zondi said.

'Be more specific.'

Zondi questioned the girl in Zulu, and she whispered her replies. 'She says it was a kitchen knife.'

The doctor felt for Inja's pulse, prodded his abdomen, moved the beam up to his face and lifted his eyelids, examining his pupils. She opened his mouth, inserted her fingers. To free blockages to his airways, Dell knew. Remembering his medic's training. A lifetime ago.

'How long was the blade? Was it smooth?' the doctor asked.

Zondi spoke to the girl again. She held her index fingers a few inches apart. Then drew a squiggle in the air.

'A steak knife, then.' The doctor's gloved fingers back on the wound. Index finger disappearing inside Inja's body, probing. Her face impassive.

'What do you think?' asked Zondi.

'I think he needs to be in an operating room.' She slipped her finger out of the wound and wiped her hands on a square of paper towel. 'Tell the girl to boil water.'

Zondi spoke to Sunday, who crossed to the paraffin stove. Removed a blackened pot from it, caked with offal. Took the pot and a plastic bucket of water and went out the door. Dell heard the splash of water as she washed the pot.

The doctor reached into the bag and found a stethoscope, the chrome diaphragm beaming an ellipse of light onto the scuffed wall as she brought the tubes to her ears. She placed the bell on Inja's chest. Listening. A strand of her blonde hair falling across her face. She was beautiful, Dell realized. Wondered where Zondi had found her.

The girl returned and lit the Primus stove. Placed the pot of water on the purple flame. Retreated into shadow, watching.

The doctor lifted a silver space blanket out of the bag, kept it folded in a rectangle and placed it beside Inja in the light of the paraffin lamp. Removed a series of items from the bag and arranged them on the blanket. Pressure bandages. A scalpel. A plasma drip. Scissors. Tweezers. A bulb syringe. Surgical tape and gauze.

'I'm going to need one person to assist me,' the doctor said. 'Not the girl, because I don't have enough Zulu.'

When Zondi stayed mute, Dell stepped forward. 'I was a medic. In the army. Years ago.'

She looked up at him, as if she'd noticed him for the first time. Dell suddenly felt very aware of his bare chest, the skin of his face and arms still smeared with boot polish.

'What is your name?'

'Rob.'

'Rob.' *Rib*. 'Wash your hands, and put on a pair of gloves.' Spoke to Zondi and the girl. 'You two are to go outside, please.'

Zondi motioned to the girl and they went out the door. Dell washed his hands in the plastic bucket. Dried them on a paper towel from the bag and pulled on a pair of gloves. Crouched down next to Inja, across from the doctor.

She lifted one of the saline drips. 'You have ever set up an IV line?'

'Long ago.'

She threw the drip bag and the needle across to him. 'Find a vein.'

Dell lifted Inja's arm. He was in luck. The man's veins were close to the surface, running like ropes up his skinny arms. Dell stripped the heavy needle from its plastic sheath. Took a breath. Shoved the needle into Inja's arm. Felt the man jerk. Hooked up the IV, held the bag aloft. Watched as the doctor swabbed Inja's abdomen, blood and plasma welling from the jagged wound.

'What do you want me to do now?' Dell asked.

'Pray.' Not looking up at him, hair masking her face. Maybe she was serious.

chapter 72

SUNDAY SQUATTED IN THE SHADOWS, A RESPECTFUL DISTANCE AWAY FROM the man, who sat with his back against the cinderblock wall. Keeping herself invisible, an art the girl children in this valley learned before they could walk.

But the man watched her. 'Come here.' She went across to him, hovering in a kind of a bow, not looking him in the eye. 'Sit, please.' She sat. 'Your name is Sonto?'

Nodding. 'But my mother called me Sunday.' Darting a look up at him.

'I knew your mother, Sunday.' She watched him. Alert. 'When I was young, your age, I lived here. And we were friends, your mother and me.' The girl said nothing, but she knew now it was his number in the book. The Pretoria number. 'Have you ever been away from here?'

'I have been to Dundee,' she said. Thinking, *I nearly went to Durban.* Saw Sipho bleeding in front of her. Dying. Saw her mother and her father and her cousin. Dying.

The man was speaking again, 'I want you to come to Johannesburg with me.'

'Johannesburg?'

'Yes. I need you to tell people about the man inside. Inja.'

'Tell them what?'

He shrugged. 'What you know of him.'

'I know he killed my mother.' Found the courage to speak the words she had never in her life spoken before.

He stared at her. 'What are you saying, girl?'

And she told him. About the night Inja and his men came. Told him about the shooting and the fire. And the police breaking the limbs of her family like they were tree branches, to get them into the truck. Telling him about Inja shooting Sipho.

The man watched her without speaking. But there was a look on his face like something was stabbing at his flesh.

'Why won't you let him die?' she asked.

'He may yet die.' He shrugged. 'There is another man who is as bad as he is. Worse, maybe, who will go free if Inja Mazibuko doesn't speak. So, I'm trying to keep him alive and I will try to get him to speak. But I know that I may fail in both. You understand?'

She nodded. She understood that this is what men did. Fought each other. Even when they didn't know why they did it.

'So you'll come with me? Tell what you know?' he asked.

Staring at him, not used to being offered choices. Nodding. 'Yes. I will do it.'

The man looked at her, a softness in his face, in the moonlight. As if he wanted to say something more. Then the door opened beside them and the white woman with the light hair stood framed in the doorway.

ZONDI ROSE AND WALKED ACROSS to the doctor. 'Well?'

'I have closed the wound. Maybe he will live if you get him to a hospital.'

She snapped off her bloody gloves and threw them back into the room, next to where Inja lay covered by the space blanket. Dell stood over him, holding a drip bag that fed into his arm.

The doctor stepped out of the doorway, taking her Gitanes from her jeans pocket. Slipped a cigarette into her mouth. When she struck the match and took it to the cigarette, Zondi saw a smudge of blood on the front of her white shirt. She saw it too, rubbed at it, distracted.

'What's with that shirt?' he asked.

Smoked, shrugging. 'It's my lucky charm.'

'Where did you get it?'

'From another doctor. An Ethiopian. When I was with MSF.' Saw his questioning look. 'Médecins Sans Frontières. Doctors Without Borders.'

'Where is he now? The Ethiopian?'

'Dead.'

'I thought you said it was lucky?'

'For me, yes. For him, not so much.' He heard something in her voice. A need as deep as a well. She tried a laugh that didn't take, dropped the cigarette to the dirt and killed it with her shoe. 'I think now, Disaster Zondi, that I would like to go back to my room.'

THE HUNCHBACK HAD VERY NEARLY FREED HIS HANDS, SAWING THE PLASTIC rope against a spur of jagged metal on a rusted fender. He'd cut into his palms as he hacked, felt the blood warm on his hands and wrists, but not long now and he would be loose.

He looked across at his father, the old man lying gagged and humiliated. He had never before seen his father treated this way. Not by a black man, at least. Not by family. There had been a Boer once, a farmer, who had taken a bullwhip to his father back in the days when white men felt it was their right to do this. Whipped his father in front of his wife and children.

His father had said nothing while the hunchback's mother bathed his back, cuts like deep furrows cross-hatching his skin. And he'd carried on working for the Boer, his back mending, thick scar tissue growing over the whip wounds. Acting subservient. Calling the white man *boss*.

Then one night the boy had seen his father leave the hut, carrying a hammer. A pig-killing instrument. He came back an hour later without the hammer, and the boy heard him snoring within seconds of laying his body down on his mat beside his wife.

The next day police were called to the farmhouse, walked into a bedroom filled with blood and brains and flies. They questioned the Zulu workers. Were met with blank stares. Shakes of the head.

Yes, such a man was his father. And now, for this rubbish who was ashamed of his people and his skin, to come here and do this…

The hunchback sawed away. Heard feet on the sand and stopped. Hid his hands. His cousin appeared. Squatted in front of him, wearing shoes that could have bought two horses.

'Where's my car?' he asked.

The hunchback knew where it was. In Durban. Sold for a handsome profit. But he shook his head. 'When we awoke this morning it was gone.'

Zondi laughed as he stood. 'Doesn't matter, it was a piece of shit, anyway. I've got my eye on the new Audi.' He walked away.

The hunchback heard distant voices, the double smack of car doors, and the churning of the Ford engine, the suspension complaining as the car bumped out of the yard. He attacked the ropes. He could still hear the rumble of the truck, drifting off into the blue pre-dawn, when he felt his wrists separate.

He grabbed a length of toothed metal and hacked through the rope at his ankles. Went across to his father, pulling free the cotton waste from his mouth. The old man spat, and gasped for air. The hunchback started sawing away at the ropes holding his father's hands.

'Waste no time on me, boy. Go now! Run like the wind!'

The hunchback sprang up, leaving his father trussed like an animal, and raced toward the room, flinging his one shoulder before him as he ran. Knowing what he must do. He tracked through the blood on the floor. Searched the clothes piled next to his mat until he found his cell phone, and ran out, toward the hill.

He climbed, jumping nimbly from rock to rock, moving with surprising speed. He kept his finger on the menu button of the phone as he went ever higher, watching the illuminated face for any sign of a signal. Nothing. Could still hear the faint vibration of the Ford's exhaust echoing through the valley. Climbed on, his breath coming in gasps, ill-matched legs pumping.

Then, as he neared the top of the hill, he saw a few bars appear on the face of the phone, like stones stacking them-selves. A signal. The hunchback turned toward the first light of morning, facing the direction of his fleeing bastard cousin, and dialed the number.

chapter 74

ZONDI DROVE THE FORD THROUGH THE RETREATING DARKNESS, THE DOCTOR and the girl squeezed in beside him. Dell and the wounded man in the rear. He slowed the truck at an intersection in the middle of nowhere. People piling into a minibus. As the Ford stopped, the blonde doctor was skewered by the taxi's headlamps, and a kid ran across, begging hands held out before him.

Zondi accelerated away. The Belgian sat smoking, staring out at the road twisting and dwindling into the squalor of Bhambatha's Rock. She was as remote as the star of one of those subtitled European movies. He wondered what penance had brought her here.

They arrived at the hospital, the metal cross above the chapel black against the dawn sky. Zondi left the Ford idling and stepped out. He scanned the street. Taxis. Goats. Traders laying out their sad wares in the dirt.

The doctor slung the trauma bag over her shoulder and headed toward the hospital entrance. He walked after her. 'Martine.'

She turned, and it took a moment for her eyes to focus on him. As if he were a stranger. 'Yes?'

'Thank you.'

She shrugged. Lighting another cigarette. 'You're not coming back here, are you, Disaster Zondi?'

'No.'

'Good.' She walked away, disappearing into the cold fluorescence of the lobby, a blue smudge of cigarette smoke left behind.

Zondi got back into the truck. The girl glanced his way, then stared straight ahead, silent. He observed her for a moment, trying to find anything of himself in her. He couldn't.

Zondi steered the Ford out onto the road and hit the gas. Time to catch that chopper in Dundee. Get back to Jo'burg, where hungry blondes, crack whores – and even the possibility of parenthood – didn't seem that much of a threat, after these last days out here on the torn edge of the world.

THEY DROVE FOR MAYBE twenty minutes, the Ford laboring up the hills, then they escaped the valley and hit the plateau. Grass and trees appeared when the sun ran yellow as egg yolk over the low hills. Dell could see cows grazing. Distant huts almost picturesque against the green ridges.

He sat in the rear of the Ford, his back to the cab, wearing one of Zondi's shirts. The kind of thing he wouldn't have been seen dead in, in his old life. An honest-to-God Lacoste, powder blue, the little green alligator looking like it wanted to take a bite out of his left nipple.

The crisp shirt jarred with the rest of him. Matted hair, face and arms still streaked with boot polish, white skin peering through in leprous patches. His dead man's khakis a Jackson Pollock of blood. His father's blood. Sheep's blood. The blood of the man who lay unconscious in the bed of the truck, naked beneath the silver space blanket. His wound taped closed and bandaged.

A drip bag, suspended from the Ford's roll bar, fed into Inja's arm. He cried out, and his eyelids guttered like blown fluorescents. Then he lay still, eyes closed. The girl turned and looked back. Framed in the rear window of the Ford, in her tribal clothes, like a snapshot from another time.

They came to a town, bigger than Bhambatha's Rock, but still tiny. Not Dundee. A few stores and a taxi rank. A phone container. Traditional healers' iron shacks. The Ford rattled into a gas station. Three pumps. No convenience store.

A pair of minibuses were attached to two of the pumps, their passengers milling around the forecourt. Members of an African Christian sect, men and women wearing long white robes with green trim. Headgear emblazoned with stars and crescent moons. Dell had glimpsed people like these since his childhood, praying under trees at the roadside, or singing hymns within circles of rock in the veld.

Zondi stopped the Ford at the empty pump, behind one of the taxis. A pump jockey in a soiled overall crossed to the driver's window. Zondi spoke to the man in Zulu, and the attendant nodded and clanked the nozzle of the pump into the side of the Ford, shooting a glance at Inja lying under the blanket. Looked at Dell. Quickly lowered his gaze to the nozzle.

Dell caught a chemical hit of the gasoline, and his eyes burned. He felt for Inja's pulse. Faint. Irregular. But the man's heart was still beating.

Dell jumped off the truck, wandered across to where the church people were buying corn on the cob from an old woman. Cooked on an open fire in an empty lot next to the pumps. He ignored the curious glances and the muttered Zulu comments. Looked up to see Zondi walking over to him.

'Go back to the truck,' Zondi said. 'You look like hell.'

Dell didn't move. 'How far to Dundee?'

'A half-hour or so.'

'Then why're you filling up?'

'In case the chopper aborts. It's unlikely, but...' Letting it hang.

'And this chopper? Who's laying it on, exactly?'

'A faction that wants change.'

Dell found a smile. 'A force of good?'

'Good has nothing to do with it.' Zondi shrugged. 'They want to take the minister down. For that to happen, Inja needs to talk.'

'And if he doesn't?'

'Don't worry. He'll talk.' Zondi impassive.

'What happens to me, when we get to Jo'burg? I broke out of jail. Killed a man.'

'A hit man. A low life.'

'Still.'

'It'll be spun, Dell. Like a top. That's what these people do.'

Like you're spinning me, Dell thought. 'So you're telling me there's a future?'

Zondi shook his head. 'No. I'm telling you there's tomorrow. And the day after. That'll have to do until the future gets here.' Zondi's eyes moved back toward the truck, where the girl sat still as carved wood in the front seat.

THE CHURCH AUNTIES IN THE TAXI in front of the Ford sang a hymn, their voices high and haunting, spiraling out into the early morning. It was a hymn that Sunday's mother used to sing when she carried her around on her back, and for a moment her mother's warmth and scent enveloped her like a blanket.

Sunday wondered about her mother and the tall man. She sneaked a look back to where he stood with the white one. Quickly turned her head away, not wanting him to see her staring. Thinking about going to Johannesburg with him. Excited and frightened at the same time. Thinking that all this had come about because of the wounded dog who lay in the bed of the truck behind her. She couldn't suppress a feeling of joy, a sense of wonder that something good had come out of something so bad.

She sat watching the aunties rocking the parked taxi as they swayed side to side, clapping their hands. A few men came over carrying fire-cooked corn, and they joined in the harmony, their voices low and deep. For a moment Sunday let the music take her far away.

Then she was aware of something at the very edge of her hearing. A low throb. Somehow familiar. She saw a windshield flaring, and the sheen of blue paint. A car coming toward her, along the main road. A blue car. A pink blur behind the windshield, something swaying, moving slow as reeds in water. Pink dice.

Sunday wanted to scream a warning. Reached for the door handle. Heard the smack of gunshots and glass shattering.

chapter 75

ZONDI SPRINTED FOR THE TRUCK, PISTOL IN HAND. MEN SHOOTING FROM the blue car. The singing in the taxi cut like a blade sliced across a throat. Then screams.

He saw a man running from the street, in a low crouch, firing bursts from an AK-47. Some of the bush Christians went down, red splashes on their white robes. The gunman reached the back of the Ford and aimed down at Inja. The rifle bucked, spitting spent cartridges. Zondi fired as he ran. Missed. Fired again. The gunman brought the snout of the rifle toward him, then pitched forward onto the oil-streaked concrete.

As Zondi reached the Ford the face of the pump exploded, raining glass over him. He dived behind the wheel. Turned the key, hearing rounds smacking into the door of the truck. The engine caught and he threw the Ford into reverse. Another man coming from the road. Firing.

DELL TUGGED THE PISTOL from his belt, fumbling for the safety catch. Saw the truck reversing away from the pump, the nozzle springing free and rising like a snake, spraying gasoline into the air. A black man in a yellow Kangol hat blasting at the Ford with an automatic rifle.

Dell heard his father's voice: *Just point your finger.* Did. Squeezed the trigger and the man dropped. Dell sprinted and caught up with the Ford just as Zondi found first gear. Dell dived for the truck, landing hard in the flatbed beside Inja, who was bleeding from the face and the chest.

The truck bucked its way over the rocky sidewalk, and Dell grabbed hold of the roll bar to keep himself aboard. The right fender of the Ford caught the side of the blue car. The impact threw open the tailgate of the truck, and as Zondi floored the Ford, leaving rubber and smoke, Inja flew from the rear. The space blanket floated to the earth and the naked man landed in the spreading pool beside the pump.

The arcing nozzle threw a jet of green-blue gasoline onto the old woman's cooking fire. The fuel ignited in a trail of flame that ran low to the ground, zigzagging like an animal. Hunting Inja. Dell, clutching the roll bar, watched as the naked man disappeared in an explosion of black and orange flame.

SUNDAY LOOKED BACK as they sped away. Saw the dog burning. There was a heat in her head, like she could feel the flames that ate Inja. She touched her fingers to her temple, brought her hand away red with blood.

She heard a torrent of voices, as if all the radios in the world were playing at once. Then Sunday heard only her mother's voice, sweet and true. Welcoming her home.

ZONDI SPED INTO A CURVE, fighting the oversteer, nearly losing the Ford. He took the truck off the road onto gravel, scattering traders and chickens and goats as he barreled between shacks of tin and wood. Hearing screams and curses.

Found another road, a track that disappeared toward a clutter of huts, huddled around a low hill. Looked back. No blue car in pursuit. Just Dell, bouncing, gripping the roll bar. Zondi looked across at the girl. She lay slumped against the door.

The Ford drifted to a stop beside a fence of rusted barbed wire. Hundreds of brightly colored plastic bags caught in the twisted spikes, buzzing in the breeze. Zondi took his hands from the wheel and reached across to the girl.

Dell jumped down from the truck and went to the passenger door, the girl's face pressed like putty against the starred and bloody glass. He opened the door slowly and felt her weight as she sagged against it. Her hand dangling down, limp fingers dripping blood onto the sand.

chapter 76

ZONDI DROVE BACK DOWN TOWARD BHAMBATHA'S ROCK, FEELING AS IF THE flesh-colored earth was swallowing him. The girl sat with her head resting on the back of the seat, like she was asleep. He was startled by his cell phone, chirping and vibrating in his pocket.

Zondi saw the name of the caller: M. K. Moloi. The signal evaporated before Zondi could answer, and he dropped the phone onto the seat. He passed the hospital and fought the temptation to drive in and fetch the Belgian doctor. Beg for some miracle. Pointless. The girl was dead. The mystery of her parentage gone with her. Zondi was nobody's father.

DELL'S EYES CLOSED. He felt the thrum of the tires on the road as the Ford sank down toward the town. He was in a place beyond exhaustion, but he didn't want to sleep. Because sleep meant waking, having to fight panic and grief and tell himself some lie about life going on.

Dell opened his eyes. Saw men in overalls erecting a yellow and white striped marquee on the open ground between the hospital and the first cinderblock buildings in the main street. Workers unloaded chairs from the rear of a truck, the white plastic kicking the fierce sun back at Dell.

The Ford slowed and stopped, waiting for a rig that rattled toward the tent with a hiss of air brakes. An old woman standing beside the road, dressed in a blanket, a water container balanced on her head, saw the dead girl in the front of the truck. She crossed herself, and brought her fingertips to her furrowed mouth and kissed them.

The Ford rattled on and turned into the alley beside a funeral parlor. Stopped outside the rear entrance, beside a black SUV, the mortician's name painted on the door in ornate gold script. Zondi left the truck and walked into the mortician's. Didn't look back.

An outlet pipe in the wall of the building burped, and spewed gray liquid onto the sand. Dell got a lungful of embalming fluid, bringing with it memories he couldn't handle right now. He swung himself off the back of the truck, wanting to escape.

Then he stopped, looking in at the girl slumped in the front seat. Felt he shouldn't leave her here alone. *Wherever she's going, she's already there*, he told himself, and walked up to the mouth of the alley.

ZONDI FOLLOWED THE FAT MAN out into the yard. Giraffe paused a moment, staring at the dead girl in the truck. Zondi could hear the undertaker's breath, like the roar of a distant waterfall. 'Can you take care of this for me?' Zondi asked.

'Of course.'

'I can't be bothering with death certificates and so on.'

Giraffe shook his head. 'This is Bhambatha's Rock, Zondi. Bits of paper have a way of blowing away in the wind.'

Two men in overalls stepped out of the doorway, wheeling a gurney toward the Ford. Zondi didn't want to see this. 'Only the best, please, Giraffe.'

'Of course, Zondi. Of course.'

Zondi turned and walked up the alley to where Dell stood like a scarecrow who had lost his field.

DELL, IN THE SHADOW OF A POSTER of the minister of justice, watched as two men strung a cloth banner up against the side of a building. The banner was in Zulu and Dell saw the minister's name, the rest incomprehensible to him.

He heard feet on gravel and turned as Zondi joined him. 'You okay?' Dell asked.

'Yes,' Zondi said, staring off toward the hills.

'So, what are you going to do now?'

'Bury her. And then get the hell out of here.'

They stood a while in silence, then Dell said, 'She was your daughter, wasn't she?'

Zondi looked at him. Face impassive. Shrugged. 'To be honest, I'm not sure.'

Dell heard the workmen shouting instructions to one another in Zulu. 'What's all this about?' Pointing at the banner, the minister's face revealed as the banner was unfurled.

'Don't you know?'

'Know what?'

'He's addressing a rally here tonight.'

'Jesus. You're kidding?'

'No.'

'At the marquee across from the hospital?'

'Yes.'

Dell nodded, scraped a hand across his beard. Looked up at the minister. The tight mouth like a gash in the fleshy face. Dell had once admired this man, when he'd been a freedom fighter. Long ago.

'Can I take the Ford?' Dell asked.

Zondi looked at him, impassive, reading his mind. 'It'll be suicide.'

'Assisted suicide, maybe.' Dell laughed, thinking of his father.

Zondi shrugged, fished the truck keys out of his Diesels and dropped them into Dell's dirty hand. Then he turned and walked away down the main road.

Dell went back to the truck, breathing through his mouth to avoid the smell of embalming fluid. Didn't help, he ended up tasting it. He opened the passenger door and tried to wind down the bloody, bullet-starred window. The winder was stuck. Dell picked up a rock and smashed the window, the broken glass falling onto the red sand.

A black man in overalls and white rubber knee boots appeared in the doorway of the mortician's, watched Dell for a moment, then went back inside.

Dell dropped the rock and crossed to a hosepipe that was coupled to a faucet at the rear of the building. He turned on the water, a slow, stuttering trickle, and dragged the pipe toward the Ford. He hosed the girl's blood from the front seat and floor of the truck, disturbing the meat flies. Rinsed his hands and closed the faucet.

Dell started the Ford, the clutch and gas pedal as soft as wet newspaper. He bumped down the alley and turned into the main road, driving toward the marquee, the minister watching him from every fence and pole.

chapter 77

ZONDI WALKED ALONG THE SIDEWALK, DODGING VENDORS AND BEGGARS. As he passed the liquor store he saw a familiar yellow Nissan truck parked outside. The big man with the dent in his skull leaned against the fender, smoking a cigarette. Two of Inja's soldiers emerged from the liquor store, lugging crates of beer. They dumped the booze in the rear of the Nissan, bottles singing like wind chimes. The big man said something Zondi couldn't catch, and all three laughed as they climbed into the front of the truck. The driver gunned the engine and the Nissan took off toward the hills. Word of Inja Mazibuko's death had reached Bhambatha's Rock.

Zondi walked on, past the eating house, until he found the clearing. It looked exactly as it had twenty years ago. A rusted steel and Formica kitchen chair stood in the sparse shade of a thorn tree. A transistor radio balanced on a rock, blaring out Zulu choral music. Five old men were hunkered down in the dirt, playing *marabaraba* with bottle caps on a wrinkled square of cardboard.

As Zondi approached, the most ancient of the men burst into a toothless cackle, and swept money from the board with a horny hand. He looked up at Zondi. 'A haircut, my son?'

'Yes, grandfather.'

The old man poured the coins into his pocket, and levered himself upright, old bones complaining like night crickets. He wore a dirty blue shirt, khakis and tire sandals, long yellow toenails curling almost to the dust. His white hair was a little sparser, and his face more furrowed, but otherwise he was exactly as Zondi remembered him from his youth.

The barber pointed to the chair. 'Sit.' Zondi sat. The old man shook out a sheet, frayed and torn, and draped it over Zondi's shoulders. 'You are from Durban?'

'*Egoli*, grandfather.' *Egoli*. City of gold. Johannesburg. 'But I was born here.'

'And who is your father?'

'He was Solomon Zondi.'

'Ah, yes. Yes. I used to cut his hair, many years ago.'

'I remember, grandfather.'

The barber rubbed a hand over Zondi's neat hair. 'What do you need, boy?'

'A *cheesekop*.' Cheese head. Shaved.

'You are bereaved, my son?'

'Yes. I am bereaved.'

The old barber rested his palm on Zondi's shoulder for a moment, then he lifted the hand-powered clippers and started thinning Zondi's hair. Zondi listened to the radio. Sweet voices singing about God. Beneath the choir, he caught snatches of the conversation of the old gamblers. They were talking about Inja. One of them saying, 'He burns still, that one. Where he has gone.'

Amen to that, Zondi thought.

The old man laid the clippers on the rock beside the radio and brought a jar of paste and a brush up to Zondi's head. Zondi felt the coolness of the shaving cream on his skull. The barber stropped a straight razor on a length of leather tied to a low branch of the thorn tree. He stood over Zondi and took away a stripe of shaving cream and hair in one smooth motion, Zondi's skull gleaming.

Zondi wasn't sure why he was doing this. He didn't need a haircut. And if he was doing it in the name of ritual, he wasn't observing the correct timeline. Africans in mourning shaved their heads, true, but only the day after the burial. Believing that life is concentrated in the hair. Shaving it symbolizes death, and its growth symbolizes a new cycle of life.

What the hell, he'd go with that. Even if he was a day early. He needed a new beginning.

chapter 78

IT WAS THE MORNING OF DELL'S BIRTHDAY AND HE LAY ALONE IN BED, THE sheets still warm from his wife's body. He sat up and looked out at the sun, last traces of a nightmare about his father dispersing like smoke.

The sound of his children laughing in the kitchen lifted Dell from the bed. He pulled a shirt over his bony shoulders and stepped into a pair of Levi's. Barefoot, toes curling up against the stone floor that still held traces of night chill, he left the room.

Dell walked down the corridor, past Rosie's studio. One of her huge abstracts leaned against the wall. Unfinished. Abandoned a year ago. He entered the kitchen, the table piled with birthday gifts wrapped in bright paper and ribbon. The twins burst through from the sitting room and ambushed him, climbing Dell's tall frame like he was a jungle gym. He spun them around and they laughed.

Rosie stood in the doorway, wearing one of Dell's old T-shirts over sweat-pants. Her eyes making a lie of her smile. He lowered the twins and they stood beside his wife and the three of them sang 'Happy Birthday' to him, and he had to fight back the tears. They were just so bloody beautiful, his family.

Dell hugged the twins and kissed them. Tommy broke loose and ran out into the cramped backyard. Mary clung to Dell. When her small fingers finally released him, he set her down gently. She smiled at him for a moment then she went out after her brother.

Rosie put her hands on Dell's shoulders, looking up at him, dark hair falling over her eye. 'Happy birthday, Robbie.' She kissed him on the lips, then she wrapped her arms around him and hugged him. Hard. He returned the embrace, smelled her skin. Like almonds.

Dell lifted his wife's face and kissed her again. 'I love you, Rosie.'

'I love you too.' Her eyes deep and dark and troubled.

The scream of a buzzard brought Dell back to where he sat on a boulder on a hillock, staring down at the striped marquee wavering in the heat haze. The bird circled lazily above him, then flew off, its shadow grazing the red earth. Dell felt a pain in his heart. As if the grief and the longing would stop it beating. Then he took himself into a place beyond pain. Into nothingness.

Shadows chased themselves across the sand, and the sun sagged toward the horizon. A burst of music blared out from the public address system in the tent. Choked off abruptly. A man's tinny voice said, 'One, two. Testing. Testing. One, two.'

Dell drank bottled water. It was warm and he spat most of it back onto the dirt. He took the container of Cobra boot polish from his pocket. The black and red tin, with the rearing serpent. Dipping his fingers into the melted polish, he smeared it onto his face, using the inside of the silver lid as a mirror, covering the areas where his white skin shone through. Blackened his arms and hands. Then he watched as night strangled the valley.

He heard the low rumble of a generator kick in and the marquee glowed with yellow light. Minibus taxis arrived in swarms, spilling the rural poor out into the area around the tent, where bonfires burned. A buzz of excited chatter hung on the night air.

BMWs, Mercedes-Benzes and SUVs with up-country plates bumped to a halt at the rear of the tent. Dell watched through the cheap binoculars as the dignitaries took their places on the plastic chairs facing the platform and the microphone. Armani and Gucci rubbed shoulders with tribal gear. Beemer keys and cell phones dangling from the waistbands of animal-skin kilts.

Dell heard sirens, and a convoy of vehicles, blue lights flashing, slid in from the night. Flashbulbs strobed as the minister, resplendent in hyena tails and leopard skin, led his number-one wife, a hefty woman in a giant white Maidenform bra and towering headgear, into the tent. The sound of cheers and ululating rolled across the plain.

Dell checked the pistol. He'd fired it twice at the gas station. Six rounds left. Enough for what he had to do.

chapter 79

DELL APPROACHED THE MARQUEE, HANGING BACK OUT OF RANGE OF THE lights and the fires. The minister's deep voice, an amplified bellow, thundered Zulu out into the night, whipping up the crowd, who were dancing and chanting, fists raised. Taking Dell back to the illegal political rallies he had attended back in his twenties, both as a reporter and as a participant. The lines between his job and his convictions blurring in those days, when a newsman could get arrested as easily as a black kid hurling a rock.

Dell found a spot in the shadows. He could see past the raised fists, onto the speaker's platform. The minister in his traditional garb, belly swelling over his loincloth, raised his clenched fist. Loud music blared from the speakers. A Zulu war chant, set to a street beat. The crowd picked up the words, and the minister joined in, stamping his feet, *toyi-toying*, fist raised.

He left the platform and stepped down into the audience, swallowed whole by the adoring crowd. Dell caught glimpses of the minister's bodyguards, men in dark suits, fighting their way through the mob, following their master's sweating bald head, gleaming like a beach ball in the sea of admirers.

Dell followed, too, moving along the side of the tent, skirting guy ropes. The crowd spat the minister out near one of the raised tent flaps, and the big man stepped into the dark alone, the bodyguards trapped by the mob. The minister gripped one of the tent poles, chest heaving, battling to catch his breath.

Dell moved fast. Drew the pistol, rushed the sweating man. He put the barrel to the minister's head, and felt his body tense. 'Move,' Dell said.

'Who are you?' the Zulu asked.

'Just move.'

Dell pushed the bald man beyond a generator truck, away from the bonfires. He heard the voices of the bodyguards, shouting out into the night. '*Nkosi! Nkosi!*'

It would have to be now. 'On your knees.'

The minister looked at him, the moon catching his glasses, enough light to see his mouth was a twisted slit. Not a man used to obeying orders. Dell still wore the dead farmer's heavy boots. Raised his foot and kicked the Zulu in the kneecap, heard him suck air. The minister sank down onto one knee. Dell kicked him again and had him kneeling. Heard the shouts of the searching men.

'Tell me who you are,' the minister said.

'My name is Robert Dell. Your dog killed my family.'

The Zulu's head jerked in recognition, seeing beyond the boot polish. 'Whatever Moses Mazibuko did, it was without my blessing.'

'Shut the fuck up,' Dell said. Cocking the gun. Pushed the barrel against the bald head.

'Please. I don't deserve this.' Something high and weak cracking the baritone.

No, you deserve something much slower, you fucker. Dell felt the trigger beneath his finger. Ready to squeeze. But he couldn't do it. His finger refused to obey. Heard his father: *You just flat don't have the goddam balls, do you, boy?*

The gun drooped away from the minister's head and the man said something but Dell was in the morgue with what remained of his family, his nostrils thick with the stink of charred flesh, and when he heard the shot he thought he was being fired upon. Then he felt the recoil still flowing up his arms and understood what he had done.

Panicked shouts rose above the noise from the marquee and

the minister sagged until his chest and chin touched the ground, fingers crawling like a spider across the sand, breath coming in wet rasps. Dell shot him again and he was quiet.

Dell heard the men's voices coming closer, and he turned and walked off into the night. When he left the tent behind he slowed, looked back as flashlight beams sliced the darkness, Zulu shouts echoing across the plain.

Dell slid the magazine from the pistol and threw it far into the night. Dropped the gun into a deep crease in the earth. Made his way back to where the Ford was hidden on the sand above the main road.

As he started the truck, exhaustion flattened him . He killed the engine and slumped onto his side, folding in on himself, bringing his knees to his chest like he was a child. Letting the moans of the sirens lull him to sleep.

chapter 80

ZONDI SAT BESIDE THE OPEN CASKET. THREE WHITE CANDLES DRIPPED WAX
onto the grass mat, the flickering light creating the illusion
of life as it played across the girl's face. She looked older in death.
Even more like her mother.

The coffin was the most expensive Giraffe had to offer. He'd
displayed it proudly, fat fingers caressing the polished oak, the
gleaming bronze handles and the plush velvet interior that
reminded Zondi somehow of a bordello.

He knew it was absurd. Empty symbolism. The girl could just
as well be buried in a pine pauper's coffin, but he'd handed over
his credit card, no match for the voices of tradition that were
still hardwired into him. Sitting now, in a sort of vigil, in the
small room Giraffe had set aside for him at the funeral parlor,
the smell of death and embalming fluid creeping in under the
door.

Zondi remembered these funeral vigils from when he was
a kid. All the mirrors in the hut covered by cloth. He couldn't
remember why. The coffin was brought into the hut and set down
on a mat. The three candles were lit. So the ancestors could see
the dead and guide him on his journey, he seemed to recall. The
elders would sit beside the coffin, receiving visitors who brought
condolences and gifts.

He'd come down from Jo'burg on the day of his mother's
funeral, too late for the vigil. Intentionally. Not wanting to be
trapped in the cramped hut, stifled by superstition. But here he
sat. Alone. No visitors to receive. Paying lip-service to something
he'd scorned. He rubbed a hand over his shaved head, and stared
at the candles, dust motes circling the flames.

Then he heard sirens. Too many for anything other than a calamity. Fucking Dell. Heard the clatter of helicopter blades coming in low, the high whine of the engine powering back. Within minutes the chopper lifted off, rattled the tin roof, and took its noise away into the night. Zondi wondered what else it took with it.

He didn't sleep, but subsided into a kind of stupor. Didn't notice the sunlight seeping into the room from the one high window. Took a while to hear the knocking at the door. 'Yes?' he said, standing. His body stiff from the hard floor.

Giraffe entered, in a charcoal suit with a dove-gray vest and matching necktie. The rings on his fingers shining like embers against his black skin. 'Have you heard, Zondi? The minister is shot?'

'Dead?' Zondi asked.

Giraffe nodded. 'Yes.' He adjusted the hang of his coat, smoothing the lapels. 'I would have offered my services, naturally, but they flew him down to Durban.' His rubbery face wearing a look of disappointment.

'I heard the helicopter,' Zondi said. 'Have they got the gunman?'

Giraffe shook his head, still far away in a world of missed opportunities. 'No, no. He made his escape.' Flashing a professional smile. 'So, you're ready to leave for the graveside?'

'Yes, I'm ready,' Zondi said.

He watched as Giraffe tugged up his trousers, leaking breath as he kneeled beside the casket. The fat man lowered the lid and the girl was gone.

Zondi felt a sudden panic and hurried from the room, down the corridor and out the back door, his silhouette disintegrating in the fierce sunlight.

chapter 81

DELL AWOKE TO DARK FACES PEERING IN AT HIM THROUGH THE SMASHED SIDE window of the Ford. As he sat up, waiting for the bullets, three skinny kids yelled and fled, darting wild-eyed looks over their shoulders, legs pumping beneath their torn shorts as they disappeared into the eroded earth like moles.

Dell opened the car door, hinges screaming for oil, and stood up. While he took a piss, he looked down at the marquee, which was under siege by the fancy cars and SUVs the media favored. A helicopter circled low, blades kicking up dust, a news cameraman sitting in the open doorway, feet braced on the skids. The lens caught the sun and winked at Dell as he shook himself dry.

Police and military vehicles circled the marquee and Dell could see roadblocks at both bridges that allowed access to the town. Somehow he had been overlooked. What did they say about hiding in plain sight?

He went back to the Ford. Sat a while, door open. *And now what?* he asked. When nobody answered he slammed the door twice before it caught, turned the key in the ignition and listened to the engine cough like an old dog. Jammed the gearshift into first and took off across the rutted sand, avoiding the media scrum outside the tent. His colleagues in another lifetime.

As Dell reached the main road a police vehicle sped past him, siren blaring, disappearing into the jumble of breezeblock buildings. He drove to the mortician's and parked at the rear door. Went inside to find Zondi.

The man in overalls and rubber boots was on his hands and knees, scrubbing blood from the concrete floor with a grass brush and a bucket of foamy liquid. Dell asked him where Zondi was. The man mimed that the funeral party had gone. Gesturing toward the hills.

Dell saw a small gray chunk of Sunlight soap lying on the floor beside the bucket. He pointed at the soap, then at himself. The man nodded and Dell took the soap and went back outside.

He turned on the faucet, and dragged the hose, hissing and spitting, over to a thorn tree. Dell slung the hose over a branch, just high enough to dribble water down onto him. Pulled the Lacoste over his head and hung it from the branch. Stood under water that was hot from the sun, and washed himself. He scrubbed at his skin, but the black boot polish still clogged the grooves in his arms and hands, and he knew that he would have the face of a coal miner for days to come. He shrugged the shirt on over his wet body, and killed the hose.

Dell got the Ford started and as he headed out he glimpsed his reflection in the windshield. The hair dye had faded, revealing his salt and pepper streaks. His face was covered in gray stubble. He looked almost like his old self.

On the road Dell had to stop and wait for a military convoy to rumble by. A cow stood in a mess of garbage at the roadside, rooting for food. A herdsman, thin and bent, whipped the cow and the animal moaned and shambled forward, udders swinging lazily. The cow's hooves scuffed through the trash and Dell saw the minister smiling from a poster that had come free of its pole.

A vehicle slid up beside Dell. Silver SUV. The driver stared down at Dell. A white guy, around his age. A senior reporter on Durban's largest daily paper. He and Dell had often argued politics during the endless junkets they had covered. They'd never liked one another. Dell saw the shock of recognition in the man's eyes.

Dell looked away. The convoy passed and Dell took off,

checking over his shoulder to see whether he was being followed. The SUV was on his tail. Dell swung the Ford onto the track that traced a path toward the graveyard. He glanced back through his dust. No SUV.

chapter 82

THE PREACHER MUTTERED AWAY IN ZULU, MOST OF HIS WORDS LOST in a beard that grew like steel wool from his chin. Zondi wasn't listening anyway, knew it was some mongrelized blend of Christianity and traditional beliefs. Giraffe had dug the bush Christian out of a hole somewhere, with his threadbare cloak and bare toes curling through the cracks in his shoes.

Even if Zondi had wanted to listen, the sermon would have been drowned out by the woman with the withered leg, who wailed like a skinned cat. She'd been putting on a show ever since the taxi had dropped her at the bottom of the hill, barely letting her set foot on the dirt before it spun in a U-turn and took off back toward Bhambatha's Rock.

Zondi, standing at the graveside, had watched her struggle up the slope, dragging her leg behind her. At last she arrived on the ridge with its growth of uneven white crosses.

The woman looked at Zondi, looked at Giraffe, took in the preacher mumbling away to his makeshift god, then her eyes were drawn to the coffin, shiny as a Cadillac on the lip of the grave. She let out a wail that would have scared bats from a cave, and threw herself at the casket. Sobbing, beating her fists against the wood. 'Open this box! Let me see her! Let me see the child of my sister!'

The preacher stuttered to a halt. Giraffe stepped forward and seized the woman beneath her armpits and lifted her to her feet as if she were a glove puppet.

'Please, ma. This is not the time.'

'Why was I not allowed to sit vigil? For my own flesh? My own blood?'

'Ma. Please.'

'After all that I have sacrificed?'

And there it was. The opening gambit. This was all about money. Zondi dug his wallet out of his pocket and removed a wad of cash. Walked across to the woman, who had sunk to the ground again, her cheek pressed to the wood of the casket.

Zondi held the money out to her. 'Take it.'

She sniffed, calculating the value of the bills in his hand. Found it wanting. 'I have done so very much for this child.'

Zondi crouched next to her, shoved the money into her hand. 'Take it and shut up, or I'll throw you down the hill.'

She stopped wailing, fixed him with a bloodshot eye. Saw he was serious. The money had disappeared beneath her black blanket, and she'd stood, confining herself to a low keening. Still loud enough to drown the mutters of the preacher, but not the misfiring engine. Zondi turned and saw the Ford approaching, trailing dust.

DELL STOPPED THE FORD next to a black pickup truck, identical to the one that had sent his family to their deaths. But this one carried the mortician's gold logo on the door. He left the Ford and climbed the hill, up to where he'd gunpointed Zondi two days before. Walked through the crosses toward the small group gathered around the coffin.

A bald Zondi stood beside the undertaker, impassive, hands clasped in front of him, eyes hidden by his shades. Dell took his place at the graveside, staring down into the earth. Realized he was waiting for some voice to speak to him. To make sense of the last few days of his life. He heard nothing but the mumbles of the preacher and the wails of the skinny woman in the blanket.

The preacher raised his arms wide, and lifted his face toward the sky. Stood frozen for a minute, eyes closed. Then he lowered his arms, opened his eyes and nodded at the undertaker. The fat man beckoned four gravediggers who squatted in the sand, waving away flies. They rose and approached, reaching down for the ropes that snaked beneath the coffin. The men pulled the casket toward the hole, and grunted as they lowered it, sweat flowing from their faces onto their torn and dusty clothes.

Zondi stepped forward and took a fistful of sand and threw it onto the coffin. It made a sound like hard rain on the wood. He turned and walked away from the grave and started down the hill. Dell fell in beside him.

'So, it's over?' Zondi said.

'Yes.'

Dell stopped on the footpath, watching a convoy of white police vehicles boiling up out of the dust on the road below. 'I think that's my ride,' he said. Zondi looked at him. 'I was recognized in town. One of the media people.'

'Are you ready for this?' Zondi asked.

Dell said, 'Yes, I'm ready.' Handed the Ford keys to Zondi and went down the hill.

The vehicles stopped, uniformed men spilling out, taking up shooting positions. A loud chatter from above as the news helicopter circled like a vulture.

Dell was near the bottom of the footpath when he heard a voice made hard and metallic by a loudhailer. 'Robert Dell, get down on the ground.'

Dell kept on walking, ignoring the shouted warnings.

The first round was like a punch to his right shoulder and Dell stumbled but held his course. More cops opened fire and their bullets spun and danced him and then he was on the sand, face down, arms flung wide like he was about to be crucified.

As the men approached with weapons growing from their fists, shadows black as paint on the sand when they encircled him, the helicopter swooped low, blades stirring up the dust that settled on Dell like a shroud.